W9-AWN-703

DATE DUE

DISCARD

Couple Gunned
Down—News at Ten

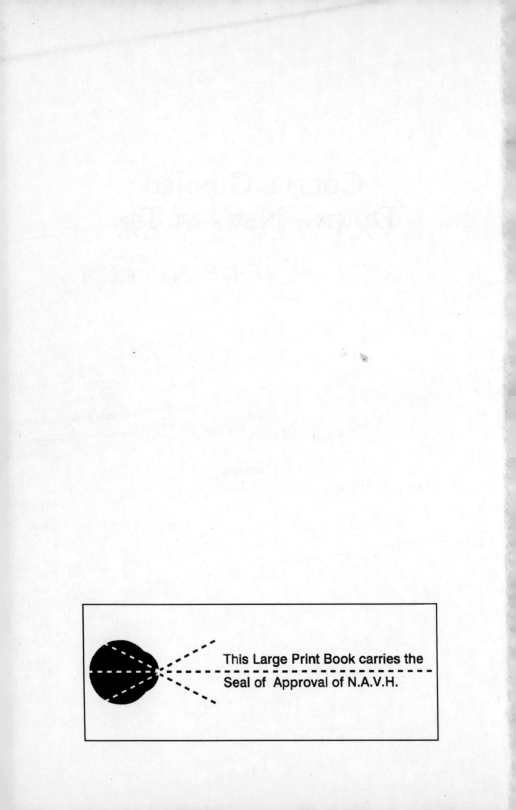

This Large Print Book carries the
Seal of Approval of N.A.V.H.

COUPLE GUNNED DOWN—NEWS AT TEN

LAURIE MOORE

THORNDIKE PRESS
A part of Gale, Cengage Learning

Detroit • New York • San Francisco • New Haven, Conn • Waterville, Maine • London

GALE
CENGAGE Learning

Copyright © 2011 by Laurie Moore.
Thorndike Press, a part of Gale, Cengage Learning.

ALL RIGHTS RESERVED
This novel is a work of fiction. Names, characters, places, and incidents are either the product of the author's imagination, or, if real, used fictitiously.
The publisher bears no responsibility for the quality of information provided through author or third-party websites and does not have any control over, nor assume any responsibility for, information contained in these sites. Providing these sites should not be construed as an endorsement or approval by the publisher of these organizations or of the positions they may take on various issues.
Thorndike Press® Large Print Core.
The text of this Large Print edition is unabridged.
Other aspects of the book may vary from the original edition.
Set in 16 pt. Plantin.

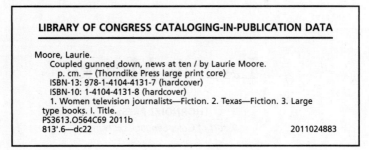

LIBRARY OF CONGRESS CATALOGING-IN-PUBLICATION DATA

Moore, Laurie.
    Coupled gunned down, news at ten / by Laurie Moore.
        p. cm. — (Thorndike Press large print core)
    ISBN-13: 978-1-4104-4131-7 (hardcover)
    ISBN-10: 1-4104-4131-8 (hardcover)
    1. Women television journalists—Fiction. 2. Texas—Fiction. 3. Large
type books. I. Title.
PS3613.O564C69 2011b
813'.6—dc22   2011024883

Published in 2011 by arrangement with Tekno Books.

Printed in the United States of America
1 2 3 4 5 6 7 15 14 13 12 11

To Laura

ACKNOWLEDGMENTS

Many thanks to editors Tiffany Schofield and Mary Smith at Five Star for their continued confidence in me, to Roz Greenberg at Tekno Books, to Diane Pieron-Gelman and Tracey Matthews; and a special thank you to Daryle McGinnis and Tom Unterberger, who assisted with technical information; and always to my lovely daughter Laura for being such an inspiration to me.

CHAPTER ONE

The last thing WBFD-TV Channel 18's newest anchor expected in the early-morning hours before her debut broadcast was to end up on the wrong side of the law. Cold steel from the inmate bench penetrated the threadbare fabric of Tarrant County's jail khakis, chilling Aspen Wicklow's thighs. She shivered, not so much from the atmosphere of cold indifference as from fear. WBFD-TV's ironclad policy distilled into three parts: *Never become part of the story; get everything preapproved; don't end up in a body-cavity search.*

WBFD, the formerly worst-ranked television station in the Dallas–Fort Worth Metroplex had recently moved into third place thanks to twenty-three-year-old Aspen's fresh face, hard work, and a compassion that had endeared her to a viewing audience of millions: upon reporting tragedies, she unabashedly wept.

It also didn't hurt that she'd lucked into meeting Spike Granger, the Johnson County sheriff, a colorful man whose beef with the Texas penitentiary system about prison overcrowding led to video footage during sweeps month that got her nominated for several broadcast excellence awards. But the unlikely liaison that evolved into an off-camera romance between herself and Granger couldn't help at the moment. She'd been dispossessed of her personal belongings and couldn't use her cell phone to call for help.

And the shame of it all . . .

Her mind went into free fall.

What if another news station catches wind of this?

I'll be the laughingstock of the broadcast industry.

What if I can't find anybody to bail me out?

Wonder how bad my booking photo looks?

Not only had the darling of WBFD-TV managed to get arrested, the authorities also photographed her. And even though this wasn't like college sorority photos where they gave you a set of proofs to take home, she could imagine what her mug shot looked like: silk kimono, wild red hair that made her look like she'd survived electrocution, gemstone-green eyes against an alabaster complexion — now corpse-like, without a touch of tawny blush and the slight line of eye pencil and mascara to give her coppery lashes a bit of definition.

"Aspen Wicklow." The booking sergeant belted out her name.

Leg irons clanked as she stood. With manacled hands belly-chained at her waist, Aspen took geisha-steps to the counter.

"When do I get my phone call?" Her voice trembled with the effort of speech. It'd taken all the courage she could muster not to cry, but holding in the shame and embarrassment had swelled her chest until her lungs burned from the pressure. Her chin corrugated. She bit her bottom lip to still the quiver. The tear teetering on the rim of her right eye spilled over onto her cheek.

"Says here you're charged with deadly conduct. A felony." The sergeant, full of bluster, held the paperwork at arm's length. Stooped with age, he peered over the top of his half-glasses, eyes drifting over the page. "Third degree."

"There's been a mistake." Her words rushed out. "You must have me confused with somebody else." She lifted her hands enough to point to the booking sheet. "That can't be mine."

He sliced a look in her direction. "You

Aspen Wicklow or not?" The heads of a few uniformed deputies, previously bent in concentration, popped up at the sound of her name. They turned in her direction in one collective shift.

Aspen lowered her voice to a whisper. "I violated a city ordinance. The policeman called it a Class C misdemeanor. He was supposed to write me a ticket."

But he hadn't.

Unluckily for Aspen, Gretchen Pendleton, the neighborhood harpy with a nose off a Picasso portrait and legs that were trellises of varicose veins, had burst out her front door emitting an operatic melodrama akin to the chorus of the Hebrew slaves from the third act of Verdi's *Nabucco*. While Aspen spoke to the patrolman, his field training officer — an imposing figure with a nasty scar near his forehead — conducted an interview with "Old Lady" Pendleton. Next thing she knew, Aspen found herself riding downtown in the caged back area of a Fort Worth patrol car with the ominous words of the scar-faced FTO echoing in her ears: "You can beat the rap, but you can't beat the ride."

It'd make a soundtrack-worthy moment.

The man had seemed familiar; still, she couldn't place him. Then realization dawned. She knew him, all right. He was one of the officers who'd gotten suspended after WBFD aired her *Asleep at the Wheel* piece during sweeps month. Only this time, he wasn't hiding at the rear of a building, snoozing behind the wheel of a patrol car on company time, with drool leaking from one corner of his mouth.

The wind kept whipping at the flap of her festive silk kimono as she stood near the black-and-white with the "Molly the Cow" decal affixed to each side of the patrol car. To add to the humiliation, they hadn't even given her an opportunity to dress properly. She'd made the trip downtown wrapped in the same getup. Kind of like those "come-as-you-are" parties her parents let her throw for her friends back in junior high, where you show up at a friend's house, unannounced, and take them back to your house the way you found them, even if they were in the middle of washing their hair. Clad only in a Victoria's Secret peekaboo bra and panties beneath the sheer robe, wearing scuffy lavender house slippers on her feet, she'd glanced out the rear windows at the blur of DWIs and *real* criminals on the sickening ride down to the police station.

"Well, it may have started out as a Class C misdemeanor," drawled the old sergeant, sounding like a derelict at a detox center, "but it looks like somebody bumped the charge up to a third-degree felony."

His observation spawned the ultimate Whiskey-Tango-Foxtrot moment. For a second, the room went out of focus.

"But that's just wrong."

"Not for me to say." He flicked his hand in a dismissive wave, floating the scent of stale cigarettes embedded in his clothing up her nostrils. "You'll be transported to Mansfield where you'll be taken before the magistrate."

"When will that be?" The air around her thinned.

"Dunno. I don't make out the judge's schedule."

With the counter separating them, she inclined her head as close as she could without standing on tiptoes. "You don't understand — today's my first day as the new television anchor for WBFD-TV. If I'm not there to go on camera, I'll be fired."

"Yeah? Well . . . not my problem."

"Please." She fought the quiver in her voice. Getting her point across was like trying to grasp smoke. If she went to jail, she'd end up giving swine-flu reports from Mexico City. "I can't be here." Her gaze swept the room. She lowered her voice to a whisper.

"I can't be in . . . *this place*."

"Betcha can. Next." Steely eyes flickered past her shoulder. "Tyrone LaMont Washington. Izzat you?" His jutting chin gesture encouraged Tyrone to belly up to the counter.

"Wait," Aspen shrilled. "My phone call. What if I can post bail?"

What was she saying? The question was born out of desperation. Of course she couldn't post bail. She had no checkbook or credit card with her. She needed that phone call. Spike would bail her out if they'd only let her use the flipping telephone.

Just when she'd started to think the booking officer couldn't crack the code, he turned his attention her way. "Phone's on that wall. It's collect. Give the operator the number. Next."

Behind her, a jailer outfitting inmates in prisoner garb shouted a pejorative that singled out an "old school" convict. "Hey, school — what size shoe you take?"

"Eight and a half."

"Yeah? Well, we don't have half sizes." He turned to the property control officer. "Give him a nine."

Aspen shuffled to the wall phone with her restraints clanking. Still manacled at the

15

waist hands-to-waist, she rose on tiptoes, pulled the wire cable, and dislodged the receiver. It hit the wall with a *crack!* Sensing critical stares from those behind her, she wrangled it enough to tuck it between her shoulder and cheek. Momentarily, the operator came on the line.

She recited Spike's number and breathed a sigh of relief.

When his cell phone routed itself to voice mail, the operator intervened. "There's no one to accept the charges."

"Wait, let me try another number." The operator could connect her to the Johnson County Sheriff's Office. Maybe Spike had been called in on an emergency. That happened from time to time. Since the SO was staffed 24-7, there ought to be someone who could route her to Granger. But when Aspen couldn't furnish the actual number, the operator summarily turned down the phone request.

Now what?

No way could she call her parents. Her father, Wexford Wicklow, and her mother, Jillian, were divorced but living in the same nursing home and rehab center; him with Alzheimer's and her with a closed-head injury.

She recited the only other local number

she knew by heart — the one for WBFD-TV.

Rochelle LeDuc, office manager, secretary, and personal assistant to station manager J. Gordon Pfeiffer, answered the call with crisp efficiency. Thank goodness. Rochelle normally headed home in the early evening, but, once again, she'd stayed as late as it took to complete Mr. Pfeiffer's monthly reports by deadline. Before Aspen could blurt anything out, the operator intervened.

"I have a collect call from the Fort Worth Police Department." After what seemed an eternity, the operator said, "One moment; I'll find out." To Aspen, she said, "What's your name, caller?"

Oh, dear Lord.

Trying to keep a secret from Gordon's middle-aged assistant was like trying to corner a spider monkey. After all, it was Rochelle who pinkie-swore not to breathe a word about Gordon's wife having an affair with one of the intern's boyfriends. And when the intern, Dainty Prescott — a spoiled, indulged debutante on loan that semester from the broadcast journalism department at Texas Christian University — wondered why Rochelle spilled her guts, the woman insisted the boss knew Green

17

Beret tactics and that she'd been tortured.

"Rochelle? It's Aspen."

"She can't hear you," said the operator. "Your full name, please?"

"Aspen Wicklow."

Another dead pause, and the operator came back on the line. "She wants to know if you're calling from jail."

"Don't answer that. Tell her it's an emergency and that I'll pay her back if she'll accept the charges."

The woman muted Rochelle's response, then came back on the line snuffling with laughter. "Go ahead, caller."

"Rochelle?"

"This better be good. I just sat down to a glass of fresh-squeezed orange juice and I have to get rid of the evidence before the fruit Nazis storm in and arrest me."

Everyone at the station had heard the story. The fruit Nazis worked for the United States Department of Agriculture. After Rochelle had practically instigated the verbal equivalent of a running gun battle with a pair of the USDA's Dallas agents over a couple of citrus trees she bought on eBay that'd been illegally trucked in from a quarantine state, she'd convinced her colleagues that inspectors had her under visual surveillance, not to mention a couple of

18

directional mikes they'd aimed at her house.

Aspen closed her eyes, relieved by the sound of a familiar voice. "I need to speak to Dainty Prescott." The request came from sheer desperation. She doubted Dainty'd be at the station in the wee hours of the morning, but maybe Aspen could charm a contact number out of Rochelle. Then again, the blue-eyed blonde intern with the bee-stung lips might be keeping vampire hours. Rumor control around the office suggested Dainty was doing a bit of part-time sleuthing for the station manager on the side. Dainty could come up with bail money. Probably had that much in her checking account. She drove a silver Porsche and dressed like she'd just stepped off the cover of *Marie Claire* magazine — hardly the poster child for poverty. "It's an emergency."

"What sort of emergency?"

"Can't talk."

"Okay, bye," said the woman regarded around the station as devil spawn.

"No, no, no — don't hang up." Her heart fluttered, and not in a good way. "I didn't mean I couldn't talk —"

"That's what you said."

"I meant I'm unable to talk *here* . . ." Her voice dropped to a whisper. ". . . in this place."

"Are you in jail?"

"Of course not," Aspen scoffed, but she was thinking, *Not yet.* The erratic pulse in her neck quickened.

"You sure about that?"

"Everything's fine . . . fine and dandy." Which everyone standing around knew meant not so fine. "Just please put Dainty on the phone."

"Sorry to have to tell you, but Gidget's not here."

Rochelle called all the interns Gidget. That way, she didn't have to learn their names.

"Not there?"

"Nope. You're out of luck, dear. Is there someone else you'd like to speak to?"

The news stretched Aspen's frayed nerves tighter than banjo strings. "Do you have the number to Dainty's cell phone?"

"I'm sorry," Rochelle said with a put-on professional air, "but I'm not allowed to give out employees' phone numbers."

Well, I never!

"Then let me talk to Reggie."

Reggie, Aspen's favorite of the two photographers, would help her. Not Max, though. Max wouldn't lift a finger to help his own mother.

"You want to talk to Reggie?" Rochelle

repeated with a trace of danger in her voice. "No can do."

"Why not?"

"He's on assignment."

"Then put Max on the phone."

"Sorry. Not here."

Gordon's assistant was messing with her. Getting into a protracted conversation with the woman was like the old Chinese torture, death by a thousand cuts, applied to her eardrums.

"Who's left?"

"Gordon."

For no good reason, she felt the spirit of her dead grandfather channel right through her: *Are you outta your damned mind?*

No way could she tell the station manager she was on her way to the slammer.

"No. Not Gordon. Put Misty on the phone. And don't tell me she's not there."

"Okay."

Misty Knight, WBFD's curvaceous, honey-haired meteorologist, was slightly more intelligent than a bucket of rocks. But given the choice, talking to Misty was preferable to talking to Gordon. If Gordon learned she was cooling her hocks in jail, he'd skin her alive and wear her around like last year's Bally loafers.

Then realization dawned. Rochelle hadn't

transferred the call. Aspen could hear breathing at the other end of the line.

"What's going on, Rochelle?"

"Not a thing. I'm merely following instructions. You said not to tell you Misty's not here. So I didn't." Said cheerily.

For the love of God, were they all bipolar? With her frayed nerves sparking, Aspen did the last thing she intended to do — asked for Gordon Pfeiffer.

"I'm sorry to have to tell you, but Gordon isn't in."

The excessive, if not cloyingly sweet, tone frayed her last raw nerve. "Mr. Pfeiffer's always in. Connect me."

"No can do."

"You said he was in. What — are you screening his calls?"

"You're in jail, aren't you?" Rochelle emitted a diabolical chuckle that sounded like an assault rifle with a silencer. Then her muffled voice sang out beyond a mouthpiece muted by hand, *"Houston — we have a problem."*

"I'm not in jail."

But she knew she and Rochelle shared a simultaneous thought: *Look at the jam the new anchor got herself into.*

The booking sergeant kept sliding her dirty looks. She gave him a tight smile.

"Yeah, you are. What'd you do, kill somebody?"

"Please let me speak to Mr. Pfeiffer."

This wasn't working out the way she'd thought it would. Now everyone in the room seemed to be looking at her. Her heart banged against her ribcage, as if trying to escape. She wasn't embarrassed and her cheeks weren't flaming. These people just needed to dim the lights and lower the thermostat.

Rochelle forced her hand. "I'm not transferring your call to Gordon. Not until you tell me what happened. Out with it."

She visualized Gordon's assistant seated at her desk in a smartly tailored suit, with her dark hair strained back from her pale, flawless face in a chignon, her thinly plucked brows arched, and scary gray eyes that were as hard and translucent as ice cubes. No wonder the staff at WBFD suspected Rochelle might be a member of Black Ops. Rochelle, who directed a vast network of spies, should've become an intelligence agent interrogating prisoners of war.

Aspen spilled her guts.

A call came in while she rattled on about her predicament in mind-numbing detail, and Rochelle clicked over to the other line. Anyone having to deal with the menopausal woman knew the drill. Since hiring on with WBFD as an investigative reporter two months before, Aspen had been subjected to these shenanigans with painful regularity — a theme she was getting pretty tired of.

The line clicked over and Rochelle returned, all crisp and efficient. "Now, where were we? Ah, yes — you went on a rampage and brandished a gun."

Aspen's sigh of resignation shuddered up to the acoustical ceiling tiles.

"I always knew you had it in you," Rochelle added with pride. "People around here think you're Miss Goody Two Shoes, but I know different." Followed by the battle cry of confidence, "You go girl."

Whatever.

"So you'll help me?" Said weakly . . . hopefully. Tears blistering behind Aspen's eyeballs abruptly turned into a sniffle of relief.

"Oh, *gawd* no. I have my reputation to think about, so I couldn't possibly get involved."

Aspen found Rochelle's chipper lilt a cruelty to the ear. While thoughts of Rochelle giddily disseminating gossip misfired in her head, she picked up with her story at the point Gordon's assistant had summarily cut her off. After finishing her narrative, she ended with, "Please don't spread this around."

"Don't worry, hon, your secret's safe with me. But let's err on the side of caution, shall we? So, I probably ought to take you off speaker phone . . ."

CHAPTER TWO

An hour later, shackled to two robust female prisoners, Aspen thought she'd entered a Rada wormhole when the ride to jail continued in the Fort Worth PD's paddy wagon — a windowless van used to transport prisoners from their holding tank to the Mansfield Law Enforcement Center for their magistrate's warning.

She didn't care to make conversation with anyone who had the capacity to snap her like a pretzel, not even idle chitchat. Spike's advice for surviving incarceration was identical to his remedy for withstanding Mexico vacations: saunter up to the first man you meet in any town and kick him in the testicles; then, in order to maximize your chances of avoiding sexual assault or being physically accosted, hunch your shoulders to make yourself look tough and dangerous. Sizing up these eastside toughs convinced her she shouldn't even make eye contact.

Seriously, these females could fold your clothes with you in them.

One of the women introduced herself as Absidy. "Spelled A-b-c-d-e." Said with pride, as though she'd just revealed her true identity as Anastasia.

Aspen gaped.

"And this —" Abcde pointed at the other female "— is LaDasha."

"Spelled La-a. The dash don't be silent."

Aspen felt like the sitting duck in a carnival shooting gallery.

A scrawny, rangy-smelling woman who wasn't on intimate terms with good grooming sat on the bench opposite them. After a moment of silence, she cackled over something Aspen wasn't privy to, and carried on a conversation with someone invisible to everyone else in the transport van. Clearly, this "unseen other" wasn't there because the inmate focused on some distant point in space while carrying on. Not that it mattered, Aspen thought. At this rate she was starting to see things herself.

Abcde and La-a exchanged awkward glances of the *Is she crazy?* variety.

Aspen developed a splitting headache. Then she remembered Part Two of Spike's theory on how to survive incarceration — the three Bs: brute strength, bribes, or big brass balls. Since she didn't possess either the former or the latter, she resorted to bribes.

Short-circuiting the trip switch to her common sense, she yelled out in frustration. "For the love of God, lady, if you'll shut up for five minutes, I'll find a way to put you on television."

A swift journey to clarity told her she'd just made a huge mistake. But if anyone else noticed they didn't let on. They probably saw she'd gone white in the face, and were too busy taking bets on whether she'd successfully fight off that panic attack.

Then La–a said, "Girl, how you gonna put us on TV? You got connections?"

Her chest swelled with importance; she couldn't help it. And when she announced, "I'm the new TV anchor for WBFD-TV," her tone suggested great pride in accomplishing what amounted to an unlikely feat.

"You don't say? Well, you know how you're a news anchor?" Abcde dripped sarcasm. "And you know how I'm a famous movie star?"

Raucous laughter broke out among the other inmates.

Aspen got the feeling she was starring in her own B-flick, low-budget, straight-to-video feature. Only she'd been demoted from her minor supporting role to that of an extra.

"Forget I said that. I don't know anyone on TV," she backtracked, immediately relegating herself to an unpaid extra with a nonspeaking part.

"I get messages from the TV," said the woman who'd been talking to the entity that Aspen suspected might be an invisible CIA operative. "They gives me my assignment on account of I work for the gummit."

Aspen decided she meant government.

Sharing a bumpy ride in a van filled with recidivists made last night's Mexican combo roil in her gut, especially when someone's stomach started making the same noises as her cappuccino maker. She closed her eyes and willed herself not to gag. The air in the transport van smelled as bad as the Mexico side of the Rio Grande.

As they traveled to the Mansfield unit, a correctional facility on the outskirts of Fort Worth, the drama queens on either side of her talked about the advantages of having a pimp versus working solo. She went in and out of the conversation as they moved on to questionable birth-control methods and finally to lingerie.

"At least that embarrassing thing with yo' thong won't happen again," said Abcde.

"One time. It was an isolated incident," Aspen said before realizing they weren't talking to her. By the time the van pulled into the sally port, she itched with imaginary cooties.

A ripping noise that sounded like torn fabric turned out to be the van's emergency brake being yanked up. The two marshals bailed out, and she sat ramrod straight waiting for them to unlock the back of the transport van. The door of the paddy wagon opened to a prolonged squeak, the kind used in horror films just before the villain jumps out and cuts everyone in half with a chainsaw. They stepped out into the crisp morning air. As Aspen drew in a deep inhale, a full moon — known around these parts as a *coyote* moon — shone like a lustrous pearl. She let out a bitter chuckle at the irony.

When the marshals marched the chain gang through the corridor to the holding tank, she glimpsed her own haunted emerald eyes reflected in a glassed-in wall directory where peg-letters spelled out names and locations of employees. Baggy, unflattering jail khakis washed out her alabaster skin; her tousled red hair hung to the shoulders in ringlets.

Comets flashed behind her lids. Her throat

tightened; scalded eyeballs burned with tears. She needed another shot at the phone.

Where's Spike?

Why didn't he answer his phone?

I can't do time, I'll die.

Beyond Aspen's vision, a heavy metal door banged open. The crash of steel against cinder blocks reverberated off the walls. One by one, the transport officer called out names written on a prisoner list clamped to his aluminum clipboard, while his partner unhooked each inmate and funneled them into a holding cell. The air was stale, and the room smelled like Cambodia after the release of tracers and Agent Orange. The steel commode reeked with the odor of Calcutta in August.

Aspen clutched her stomach.

"Stay with me, girl," La–a said, "don't be startin' no vomit wave, 'cause if you pitch, I pitch."

Gotta get outta here.

What am I saying? I'm turning into a flight risk.

Ohmygod, they'll shoot me in the back.

Waiting for the magistrate to appear only heightened Aspen's anxiety. Then a bailiff called out her name. So far, she'd hit the trifecta of trouble: local cops, a couple of hardcore hoochies that made her look like the soft, creamy filling in the middle of an Oreo, and a court bailiff with shoulders like a water buffalo. She rose from the bench and inched forward; the sound of chains on her feet preceded her. As she shuffled across the concrete floor, jingling louder than the Jolly Green Giant's pocket change, the rest of the court personnel waited inside the courtroom while a jailer removed her handcuffs, belly chain and leg irons.

Dizzy with the promise of hope, the prospect of fresh tears evaporated as quickly as raindrops on hot asphalt.

The bailiff jutted his chin toward the courtroom and addressed her in a corrosive tone. "I don't chase people. Just so you know."

Means he'll shoot if I make a break for it.

Not that it matters.

Knees are jelly. Pretty sure I'm having a stroke.

Massaging blood back into her hands and fingers, she realized she actually could feel her extremities; the arresting officer had clamped the handcuffs on too tight. Now, two angry reddish-purple bruises ringed her wrists. No need to go to makeup and wardrobe to get concealer applied — for this kind of damage, she'd have to locate a couple of wide bracelets in the costume jewelry bin.

The bailiff sliced her a feral smile. "Don't even think about pulling any shit out there. Understand?"

Her head shook like a bobble-head Chihuahua on the back dash of a *barrio* low rider. As he motioned her to move past him, vanity kicked in.

I look a mess.

Need lipstick. A little color in my cheeks.

What am I thinking.

Scratch that. Maybe this way, no one will recognize me.

When she fluffed her hair and pushed it behind her ears, her fingers shook. This sucked.

The courtroom wall clock read two-fifty-five as the bailiff finally paraded her inside. A mere three hours had passed since she'd walked, unwittingly, out her back door. Any other morning, her alarm would've gone off in another five minutes, and within the hour, she would've showered and primped and headed off to WBFD before the morning's drive-time broadcast aired.

Events that led up to this moment had been a carnival of thrills compared to what happened next.

Energized by the possibility of release, Aspen's heart kicked into high gear. Even the air in the courtroom smelled different.

I might actually get out of here in time for the broadcast.

Can make it to work without anyone knowing.

Have to bribe Rochelle to keep quiet, though.

I know — I'll give her Mom's double-strand pearls.

The whole experience had been out-of-body. While she positioned herself in front of an empty podium and contemplated her own freedom, the judge swept into the room, wearing a pinpoint Oxford beneath a robe that had enough starch in it to double as body armor and crackled when he moved.

The cheese stands alone. Just like the song.

The pasty-faced jurist resembled a funeral director with a vitamin-D deficiency. He flipped open a manila folder, and his eyes darted over the contents. Then his gaze dipped past the bench and settled on her. "Aspen Wicklow," he announced to the room at large. "Are you Ms. Wicklow?"

"Yes, Your Honor."

With cold, dispassionate intonation, he ran down the charge pending against her with frightening accuracy. "Ms. Wicklow, you're charged with deadly conduct, a third-degree felony punishable by two to ten years in the penitentiary —"

In a fractured voice, she interrupted him. "Can I please call my mom?" Not that Jillian Wicklow with her closed-head injury could help her out of this mess, but the clench in Aspen's chest was starting to feel like the time she sought out a trainer at the fitness center — the guy was supposed to whip her into shape, not induce a coronary. She needed her mother's calming influence.

His brow furrowed. "Do you understand the charges?"

Hello, I didn't do anything.

The air thickened. Poise deserted her. "All I did was —"

He held up a hand as pale as a latex surgical glove. "I don't want to hear the facts of the case, Ms. Wicklow —"

"— try to protect Stir Fry."

"— I just need to get your plea: guilty, not guilty or no contest."

Tears welled. One large bead teetered along the rim of an eye before spilling over and tracking her cheek. She loved that dog.

"Stir Fry is my dog. *Was* my dog. I took an armful of boxes out to the recycle bin. That's when I saw him."

The judge gave a slow eye blink. "You named your dog Stir Fry?"

Snickers erupted behind her, from a spot

35

where she'd last noticed a congregation of uniformed officers.

"I didn't name him. My boyfriend found him behind a Vietnamese buffet. He came to me that way. Stir Fry was a gift from Spike."

"You have a boyfriend named Spike?"

"Samuel's his Christian name. People call him Spike. I don't know why." Realization dawned. She frowned. "Brought on by a prickly disposition, I suppose."

"The only Spike I know of is that crazy sheriff down in Johnson County."

You either loved Spike Granger, or you loathed him.

Aspen swallowed hard. Even she had to admit the crusty lawdog had been an unlikely suitor. Not to mention the age difference. She was a bit young for Granger. Friends and colleagues had remarked on it — mainly the part about how he was getting around Megan's Law.

The tension in her muscles had short-circuited the signals coming from her brain and she stood, petrified, instead of seizing the opportunity to tell the judge how she'd inadvertently stumbled upon a coyote stalking Stir Fry while the dog was outside doing his business. The judge must know that the mechanic who'd murdered her sorority sister and at least one other young lady was still on the lam — it'd been front page news for a week. And for that reason, Spike had loaned her a pistol and told her to shoot first and explain later if the killer showed up on her doorstep. Only that's not what happened. When the coyote launched his attack on Stir Fry, she dropped the boxes and grabbed the revolver. Before she'd even had time to fire off a couple of rounds, Stir Fry's heartbreaking pug screams filled the air as the coyote carried him away.

Too bad one of the shells exploded Mrs. Pendleton's plate-glass window. When the bullet pierced the window, the sole sound was a hollow crack, followed by a ten-to-fifteen-second delay before the crash of shattered glass raining down.

So much for explaining what happened to the court.

Suddenly, this unfortunate matter had become all about Spike Granger, and — judging by His Honor's facial expression — not in a good way.

Outside the courtroom, the slip-slap of heavy footfalls echoed down the corridor. The unexplainable weight of impending doom settled onto her already sagging shoulders as the door sucked open behind her. She didn't dare turn around. With her wits fully sharpened, she breathed in air like a marathon runner until her lungs burned.

Without warning, the bailiff crossed the room. He stepped up to the bench, behind the podium, and held a hand to his face to prevent any chance of lipreading while he whispered in the judge's ear.

"You don't say." The judge focused on something beyond her shoulder, and the hardened contours of his face relaxed. Then he cast Aspen a sidelong glance. "Wait a minute. Are you — ? Well, what do you know?" he announced to the room at large. "We've got a celebrity in the house."

Aspen inwardly winced. Her future here in this hellhole could go either way.

"You're the TV girl."

She fumbled around, searched her enormous vocabulary, and came up with "Guilty."

"And is that also your plea?"

A growling baritone interrupted the proceedings. "Don't say a damned word, Aspen." To the judge, the man said, "She pleads 'not guilty' and she's represented by counsel."

Cold pinpricks rippled up the nape of Aspen's neck. She instantly regretted the phone call to Rochelle. Oh, and one other thing . . . she was starting to feel like

38

discharging a firearm inside the city limits hadn't been such a hot idea, either.

The magistrate's tough expression returned. Flinty eyes beneath thick brown eyebrows grew dark and forbidding. "And you are?" He smiled an unpleasant smile.

"The name's J. Gordon Pfeiffer. I'm here to post this *desperada*'s bond."

CHAPTER THREE

With thinning gray-brown hair raked back by a meaty hand, J. Gordon Pfeiffer stood in the law-enforcement building's corridor next to a snack machine and considered Aspen through thick, heavy wire rims. No wonder he'd arrived frothing at the mouth. Rumpled slacks that rode below a slight overhang of belly hung in gentle folds at the ankles, telegraphing that he'd slept in his clothes at the office again. He seemed to be on the verge of a coronary, with perspiration dotting his forehead and his shirtsleeves ringed in crescents of sweat. Even his jaw had started to twitch beneath his plastered-on smile. Which was about what she'd expect from a man who'd just put up five thousand dollars cash to spring her.

By the time he ended his harangue, she'd heard, "You did this wrong, you didn't do this right, and by the way, you could use a Tic Tac."

"I'm so sorry, Mr. Pfeiffer. I swear I'll pay you back." She couldn't say it enough.

"Button it. We'll talk in the car. Here . . ." He thrust a stack of clothes at her: slim-cut blue jeans, cashmere pullover sweater and a tailored leather jacket. "Rochelle said you got arrested on a morals charge."

Her head snapped back in surprise. She addressed this accusation in an upwardly corkscrewing voice. "Rochelle concluded I'd been arrested for indecency because I told her the police took me downtown in my robe? Is that woman familiar with the concept of slander? Is she insane?" But as she wound down to a normal tone, she already knew the answer to that one: You can't prosecute crazy.

"Actually, she said you were busted for running a side business out of your house."

Green eyes narrowed. "What kind of side business?"

"She said you had a dominatrix thing going on, and that things got out of hand."

"Well, that's better," she deadpanned. "At least part of it's true." *Not true.* "Rochelle's twisted. You know that, right?"

"Rochelle's a valuable employee."

She rather doubted it.

Rochelle had probably stockpiled a treasure trove of salacious blackmail material

41

on him for him to bestow compliments on such a mercurial employee as Rochelle. But that was fine because Aspen had dirt on Rochelle LeDuc that Rochelle didn't want to leak out — WBFD-TV had a nepotism rule, and Stinger Baldwin, the other investigative reporter, was Rochelle's son.

Gordon said, "I tried to imagine you in a black bustier and fishnet stockings held up by a garter belt, but I couldn't make it work."

Now that was a stretch.

God love him, in his own fumbling way, the portly, hard-drinking station manager was trying to take the edge off what amounted to the most humiliating experience of her life.

She moved toward him, speechless with gratitude, and studied the set of designer wear that looked too nice to have come from WBFD's wardrobe department.

Gordon apparently read her thoughts. "These belong to my soon-to-be ex-wife. Feel free to toss them out later if you don't like them. She'll never miss them."

Leaving him in the hallway to contemplate the nutritional value of vending-machine snacks, Aspen darted into the nearest bathroom with the hand-me-downs. She'd exchanged the jail khakis for the flimsy silk robe and lingerie she'd been arrested in, but she hardly wanted to exit the building looking like she was auditioning for *The Best Little Whorehouse in Texas.*

She located the station manager outside in the parking lot, standing by the driver's door of a company car with accusation written all over his face. Her heart started doing the rapid beat thing again. He'd been a good sport, all things considered, but there was still that pesky little *Don't get arrested* violation straight out of WBFD's employee handbook.

"Are you going to fire me?" She pulled in a deep breath and held it.

"Never gave it a thought."

They both knew that wasn't true.

"I really will pay you back."

"Damned right you will. I own you."

"Mr. Pfeiffer —"

"Gordon." Beneath the silvery glow of the streetlamp, he peeled back the wrapper on a twin-pack of peanut-butter cups and offered her one. He stuffed the other into his mouth like he was cramming paper into the shredder.

Chocolate. She barely restrained a sigh of pleasure at the taste.

With candy mortared between his teeth, Gordon opened the passenger door on the

43

five-year-old Lincoln he'd bought used at auction, then strolled around to the driver's side, climbed in and fired up the engine. The big black luxury car slumped heavily out of the parking lot and onto the street. Moments later, they cruised down the highway and headed toward the station with Aspen neatly folding the fluted brown candy paper into quarters.

She dropped it into a molded cup holder before twisting in her seat to face him. Blurred scenery rolled by in shades of gray, with the occasional neon sign of a fast-food joint popping into view. "I really am sorry about all this."

"You won't be delivering the news today, Wicklow. I'm pulling you off the air. I have something else in mind."

"What?" She said this on a whoosh of air. That ripped it. Rumors about Mr. Pfeiffer's tanking marriage to an insatiable wife must be true. Well, just because he posted her bail didn't mean he could talk her into doing something stupid. She drew the line at sex in the workplace.

"It's too late for you to do the drive-time show . . . too early for the evening news. So I'm putting you back on assignment."

The tires droning against the pavement

whispered, "Demotion, demotion, demotion."

"Please don't do that."

"Fine. Make your choice: You can either do your debut broadcast in a half hour, or you can check out a tip that came in. And by the way, if you choose to do the broadcast, you should know you're going on just the way you are now, and you look like seven shades of shit."

The turncoat behavior startled her. His ultimatum hit full force. For several seconds, she pretty much stared.

"I'm confused, Gordon. First, you promote me to anchor the news; then you demote me back to investigative reporter. I don't know what you expect me to do."

"I expect you to do your job."

"Am I no longer the anchor for the evening news?"

"You're still the anchor. But you know good and well WBFD's an independent station. I don't have the budget of these national affiliates. If I did, we'd have more talent —"

He meant better people with star quality and they both knew it.

"— and you *blow-dries* wouldn't have to double up from time to time and do things you don't want."

He'd picked up that pejorative from Rochelle. She used that particular hair salon terminology to refer to all of the on-air talent.

"When's the last time somebody had to do something they weren't hired to do?" Aspen challenged him.

Gordon didn't miss a beat. "Yesterday afternoon."

"And what was that?"

"Dainty Prescott delivered the *Live at Five* broadcast. Did a damned fine job, too, considering she went on-air half naked —"

"I'm sure that'll boost ratings," Aspen ventured, with an uncharitable sniff.

"— and managed to report the news while everything around her went to hell in a handbasket."

Aspen had seen the broadcast so she knew about the red pashmina Dainty'd wrapped around herself. The oversized scarf was held in place with an impromptu belt that, two seconds before, had functioned as an extension cord plugged into the wall socket. Never mind the mispronounced Thai name of a visiting diplomat or the video footage that got mysteriously switched and didn't correspond to the top story . . . which probably *wasn't* a mistake, because working with backstabbers and cutthroats in an every-man-for-himself industry tended to do that to a person . . .

"You need to be a team player in the WBFD family, Wicklow."

She bristled at the notion. *WBFD mafia, more like.*

Which was starting to take on the hallmarks of a crime family, thanks to this unfortunate brush with the law. Not that at least half of their SMU interns hadn't been arrested for DWI. But they weren't permanent employees. At least Gordon got plastered at home, or in his office, and bunked over when the employees played "hide the car keys." Then there was Rochelle, who'd spent three hours in front of the grand jury the previous week for an outrageous display of vigilantism when she evened the score with a man who'd beaten and raped her best friend's daughter and left her for dead in a ditch.

Gordon punctured her reverie. "I have a project I'm putting you on 'til this whole *cranking-off-shots* hoopla dies down. File's on my desk — I'm turning it over to you." He glanced in her direction. "You familiar with Kirk House?"

She'd heard just enough about Kirk House to know that the short answer should be *No,* she was not familiar with it; the

47

longer version being *Hell no;* and that an explanation accompanied the longest version — that she didn't wish to become an authority on a haunted house where two wealthy sons of a prominent food purveyor one county over had been murdered.

"I want you to go out there. Nose around."

"You really hate me, don't you?"

"I'm counting on you to come up with a fascinating piece for sweeps month. It's just around the corner. You remember — sweeps. See if you can put some interesting footage together like that segment you did on that psycho sheriff down in Johnson County."

She reminded him that she and that psycho sheriff were dating exclusively. And she reminded him that he'd promoted her to the anchor position vacated by Bill Wallace, who'd taken early retirement for medical reasons — invasive cancer that had metastasized and spread to his kidneys.

"Go home. Get some shut-eye. Come back tonight after the ten-o'clock news and grab one of the photographers."

Good idea. She hadn't had any rest since the ordeal began. Anyway, sleep deprivation made her sound like a drunk reading the news. It was bad enough having a criminal record. The last thing she needed was a reputation as a boozer.

"What's the assignment?"

"Go out to Kirk House and find out if the scuttlebutt's true."

She knew better than to think the warnings of high schoolers about midnight screams coming from Kirk House were real. The buzz would, in all likelihood, turn out to be obvious lies spread by small-town cops to cut down on the number of parkers trespassing on private property. Salacious rumors were the things urban legends were made of, like the pet alligators flushed down the toilets in Houston, now full grown and living in the sewers.

Note to self: If ever in Houston, turn on the bathroom light before sitting down on the toilet seat.

Gordon said, "Let's see what Dainty Prescott's made of. Take her with you. She can be your sidekick."

"Psychic? I don't believe in that stuff."

He looked at her, laser-eyed, until she realized the swishing traffic had dulled her ability to hear.

"Oh." She experienced a polar shift.

Despite Dainty's blonde hair, the TCU coed was actually quite smart. Still, the last thing Aspen wanted was to be paired with a gorgeous petite blonde, teach the intern the investigative ropes, and have her steal the anchor position out from under Aspen's nose.

Besides, even though Aspen had that fear-of-the-dark problem she'd just as soon keep under wraps, there was also the pesky little difficulty of the fugitive mechanic lurking around out there, possibly orbiting her universe and waiting for the opportunity to do her in.

"So tell me what happened tonight," Gordon said.

She took a bracing breath before launching into a blow-by-blow description of events leading up to the present moment.

"I tried to tell the judge what happened, and I swear I could see the moment his medication stopped working."

But Gordon had fixated on something totally different. "So the cop from your *Asleep at the Wheel* exposé made the decision to haul you downtown?"

" 'Fraid so."

"Screw with my people . . . you screw with me," he announced to the air in their shared space.

She'd gotten so caught up in her story that she'd lost track of where they were. But when Gordon's car bumped over the railroad tracks, she knew he'd overshot the station and was driving her home.

There was still enough time to dress and deliver the noon update. "Are you sure you want me to do this? I could be back in time to do the twelve o'clock broadcast."

"You have to go to Kirk House. We're shorthanded. Get some rest while I head back to the station. I've got work to do."

But Aspen knew what he really had in mind was to lock his office door and bob for olives. The latest rumor circulating the station was that Gordon's wife, Paislee — a statuesque brunette with a lovely face, a laugh like musical chimes, and a body that caused car wrecks — wanted a divorce and had hired Dolly Hastings, a nut-cutting family lawyer over in Dallas, to represent her.

"I don't understand. Why not put Tig on it?"

Tig Welder, one of WBFD's two investigative reporters, had once been her idol — back when he'd been a guest speaker at one of her broadcast journalism classes at the University of North Texas. He was about the most delicious man Aspen had ever laid eyes on. On the day Gordon hired her and Rochelle introduced her to the on-air talent, her face must've betrayed her when they arrived at Tig's office because Rochelle said, "Try to resist the urge to slingshot your panties at him." It only took working with him a few days to realize he was nothing like his public persona. He wasn't all that helpful; he didn't want to mentor anyone; and he aspired to have his own talk show in the national market — a goal for which he'd been willing to steamroll anyone who even looked like they might get in the way. And he had a cruel streak. At their first meeting, he'd nicknamed her "Investigative Reporter Barbie."

She took another stab at it. "Let Tig cover it. He eats that up. He probably went out to Kirk House and made those spooky noises himself so there'd be a story to report. I wouldn't put it past him. He's an evil genius, in case you don't know."

Behind the wheel, Gordon sat, glaze-eyed, staring at a distant point in space. He seemed to be suffering from sensory over-load. It was if he hadn't heard her.

She tried again. "Why can't you send Tig?"

"That veneer-toothed, fake-tanned, ego-maniacal putz?" Gordon drew in a sharp breath. "Because I'm fixing to fire him."

"Fire him?" Okay, this was crazy talk. If Gordon wanted ratings, Tig put the "sin" in sensational. True, the man was a backstab-bing cutthroat, but he was probably the station's best investigative reporter. "Why on Earth would you fire him?"

He skewered her with a look. Then he flashed a genuine smile — a sight rarer than a Laotian rock rat. "The SOB's screwing my wife."

CHAPTER FOUR

Thirty miles southwest of Fort Worth, Sheriff Samuel "Spike" Granger trudged into the Johnson County Sheriff's Office with a load on his mind. His former friend from high school, Neil Lindstrom, had called a press conference the month before, to announce his candidacy for sheriff. And last night, Lindstrom held another press conference calling for jail reform. Another of Granger's longtime friends clear back to grade school, Buster Root, had been locked up in the county jail for the last few days on a Disorderly Conduct charge. And while a misdemeanor didn't spell the end of the world for Buster, it sure as heck might for Granger.

Buster fancied himself an escape artist. And the last thing in the world Granger needed was for Buster Root to bust out of his jail.

" 'Morning, Lucinda." As he passed his

secretary's desk, Granger gave the brim of his white ten-X beaver cowboy a respectful touch. He kept on walking, mindful of the weight of the double-rig — two gun belts — strapped on his hips, with holsters that held identical Colt .45 Lightweight Commanders sporting ivory grips inlaid with gold longhorns.

When he reached his office, he let himself inside with a key, removed the hat and hung it on the peg of a mirrored antique hall tree near his desk. Then he caught his reflection in the old mirror that needed resilvering, and ran his hand across the top of his head to smooth down his hat hair. For a few seconds, he scrutinized the bald spot that had started a year or so before. It reminded him of the sinkhole that opened up down in Daisetta, in Liberty County, that'd grown the size of three football fields in a matter of weeks. It'd devoured buildings, telephone poles and roads at an alarming rate. And just like the sinking feeling he got watching the news down at the café this morning as the Daisetta sinkhole gobbled up a tractor, he knew the clump of hair that came out in his hand when he showered earlier was only the beginning.

He'd no sooner unhooked the double-rig and dropped it over the hall tree when the jail captain framed himself in the doorway.

Granger said, "Whatcha got, Fred?"

"It's Buster Root. Word around the cell block has it that he's gonna bust out today."

Granger snorted in disgust. "I'll tell you how to keep him from escaping . . ."

"I don't think we can neuter him, Sheriff."

"Tire him out."

"It's against the law to make him bust rocks. It's in the Geneva Convention or something, right? Cruel and unusual punishment?"

Granger shook his head. "I'm not talking about hard labor. Put him in a trusty uniform and let him out with the work crew. Or stick him in the laundry room and make him do laundry. That'll keep him so busy he won't have time to plot."

"Why're we making him a trusty?"

"So he'll be wearing stripes in case he does escape."

"I'm on it," said Fred, who left as abruptly as he'd appeared.

Granger shut the door, seated himself in the big leather wingback behind his desk and mulled over his options. Buster wouldn't resort to violence in order to break out. He'd rely on rural cunning. After all, the Johnson County Houdini wanted to spend the rest of his life as a celebrity, not rotting away in a maximum-security prison.

Too bad prison reform made it so Texas didn't have correctional facilities on the order of Angola and Alcatraz. Or the extreme example of a supermax prison such as ADX Florence up in Colorado, where the worst of the worst got to spend the rest of their natural lives locked up in solitary confinement. By the time Buster figured out how to tunnel through the vent ducts, he'd be so old guards would hear bones creaking as he tried to make his way out.

For the next few hours, Granger intermittently thought of ways to curb Buster's desire to escape the Johnson County jail, and rejected them just as quickly. If Granger made his stay too nice, the rest of the inmates would be hollering discrimination. If he made things too unpleasant, the jailhouse Houdini'd be long gone before anyone figured it out.

In many ways, Buster had a genetic predisposition for escape. His grandpa Root had been one of a handful of men who'd successfully escaped from Colditz Castle, the Nazis' most impregnable prison, back in the forties.

What he really needed was to have a little sit-to with Buster. Maybe drive him into town and feed him lunch at the café instead of letting him eat a dry baloney sandwich and drink a carton of warm milk like the others. Maybe let the guy know what an embarrassment it'd be if he lost the election because of a jailbreak. Buster'd understand, wouldn't he? Because once upon a time they'd been pretty good friends, hadn't they? Until Buster turned fifteen and stole his first car to celebrate the occasion.

Granger took a deep breath and slowly let it out. He got up and strode over to the credenza to brew a pot of coffee. He'd just finished measuring enough grounds to make eight cups when the phone rang. As soon as he said, "Granger," he recognized the caller's voice, and the weight on his shoulders marginally lifted.

"Peggy Sue, how do you do?" He settled back into his chair with the scent of Columbian roast lingering in the air.

"I just called to say the sweets are ready to be picked up, Spike. But you have to keep them refrigerated so you won't want to get them 'til you're ready to head for home."

She was talking about the special dessert he'd asked her to make for tonight. He'd invited Aspen Wicklow for supper, and he hoped she'd stay until dawn — in his bed. Not like last time when she stayed the night in the guest room because of the burglary at her house. And since there was the possibility that she'd spend the night in his bed, he'd orchestrated every romantic detail he could think of, right down to the hand-poured Belgian chocolates he planned to put on her pillow.

Peg had offered to concoct a dessert at her bakery, Peggy's True Confections, while her sister Ida Lou, down at the flower shop, had promised to save a bag of fresh rose petals — which she suggested he should sprinkle over the bedspread. For two old ladies, friends of his late mother's who were more like old maiden aunts, they still believed in fairy-tale romance. And they'd helped him plan this dinner with Aspen to a "T."

Granger cracked a smile.

The first time with Aspen should be perfect. And memorable.

He was taking down Peg's instructions when the jail lieutenant, out of breath and beet-faced, burst through the doorway. The man spoke in such a hyperventilating rush that Granger didn't hear any of it. He just sat there, eyeing him up, wondering what new atrocities the man had on tap for him today.

"I may have to call you back," the sheriff mumbled into the mouthpiece. Unless the building was on fire or someone released a container of sarin gas, nothing in the world could compete with Peg's coaching at this precise moment. "What?" he growled, muffling the receiver with a meaty hand.

"Buster escaped."

Say what?

Granger's eyeballs bulged. His thoughts turned to Neil Lindstrom. If they didn't find Buster before word got out, Neil would be all over this disappearing act like skin on a skeleton.

He held up a sausage finger long enough for the lieutenant to quiet his rant, unhanded the telephone mouthpiece and, in the most cordial of voices, told Peg he'd be over in a bit. Running this place was like watching satire. It was as if he'd just done an impression of himself remaining calm.

He slammed down the phone. "How'd it happen?"

"Don't look at me." The lieutenant, clearly expecting a good dressing down, shifted the blame from his shoulders squarely onto Granger's. "You're the one wanted to make him a trusty."

Granger pounded a fist on the blotter. "I made him a trusty so he wouldn't escape. I hoped it might discourage him from pulling any shit if he could get outside once in a while and get some fresh air." Buster'd always been an outdoorsy, rawboned kind of fellow. Granger's eyes thinned into slits. He wrangled his tackle-box-shaped frame from the chair, reached for his double-rig and started buckling up. "What'd he do — walk off the work crew?"

Granger rather hoped he had. He'd be easy enough to spot wearing stripes and an orange Day-Glo safety vest. Then the phone would start ringing, calls from concerned citizens.

"You know better'n that," said the lieutenant. "If he'd walked off the work crew, I'd be here telling you we shot him."

Granger did some quick ciphering in his head. "He's three days into a fourteen-day sentence. Dumb SOB's earning three-to-one as a trusty . . . that's nine days credit. Why the hell would that idiot escape when he's only got a day and a half left to serve?" he wondered aloud.

Yet he knew. Buster bored easily.

Prisoner escapes were no laughing matter to Granger. On a good day, there was enough anarchy going on around here to cost him the election. But losing to Neil Lindstrom would be unbearable, given their history.

He pulled his sidearms one at a time,

checking the cylinders for bullets. Nobody had monkeyed with his six-shooters, of course — they'd been right here next to him the whole time — but old habits died hard and he'd been double-checking his weapons for almost twenty-five years. "So how'd he get away?"

"We had him on laundry duty."

Granger's heart sank.

"We found his stripes in a pile on the floor next to one of the dryers. I think it's safe to say he traded them in for a set of khakis."

"You're telling me nobody saw him walk out?"

"Well, that's the thing, Sheriff," the commander hedged. "He didn't walk out."

Granger brightened, relieved. The only other way out of that room was if Buster managed to get to the roof. Stupid bastard probably locked himself out and was trying to figure out how to get down without breaking his neck.

He chuckled. "So he's stuck on the roof?" He moved toward the door with the lieutenant in tow.

"I wouldn't say stuck."

Granger whipped around. "What's that supposed to mean?"

"He swiped a couple of sheets and took the handles off a couple of brooms. Looks

like he strung them together and used them
to hang glide off."

CHAPTER FIVE

When Buster Root got a book on magic and a set of lock picks for his fifth birthday, he spent the afternoon picking the cheap lock on his parents' bedroom door. By the time he was ten, he routinely performed amateur magic shows at school assemblies. When the Texas Department of Public Safety turned him down for a hardship license on his fifteenth birthday, he hot-wired a pickup from the local dealership and led police on a high-speed chase. It took a rolling roadblock and a couple of spike strips to finally stop him, but he only spent three days in the juvenile lockup for his crime. At the time, Judge Pace planned to give him time served and put him on probation.

Rather than take the plea deal, Buster escaped.

By the time he was recaptured and his jail sentence — increased for his escape attempt — finally ended, he came home to find his parents had locked him out of the house.

That's when he learned to make a bump key.

While his folks were at church, Buster let himself inside and stole everything of value — which he promptly pawned — including his dead grandpa's leather bomber jacket and World War II medals.

Granger had become privy to this background information because he and Buster had gone all the way through public school together. They'd visited at each other's houses and played sports. And even though Granger expected Buster to follow the law like every other Johnson County resident, the irony of Buster's genetic predisposition to escape always made him crack a smile.

But Granger didn't trade on old friendships.

This time, when Buster pulled his jailbreak, Granger called in the bloodhounds. This noble and dignified breed could detect the scent of a human over a hundred hours old on a trail that lasted a hundred miles. Fortunately, it only took one hour and a couple of miles for Buck and Molly to track the escaped inmate. Baying with excitement, they promptly treed him.

Within minutes, Buster shimmied down the big oak onto *terra firma,* where deputies slapped leg irons on him and handcuffed him around the waist to a belly chain. The inmate didn't look so tough now. The sheet and broomsticks he'd used to hang glide off the roof didn't do much to break his fall. Misguided daredevil — small wonder he didn't break his neck. He only had a couple of scratches on his face — though judging by the raw skin visible through the frayed fabric of his jail khakis, his knees and elbows were scuffed to a fare-thee-well. Still, Buster's delft-blue eyes twinkled with mischief, the cowlick in his dark-brown hair remained unruffled, and his grin stretched from ear to ear.

After Granger calmed down, he gave the soon-to-be-indicted felon a ride back to jail in the front seat of his unmarked patrol car. As they rode down Main Street, Granger slid his prisoner a sideways glance.

"We need to have a little sit-to." He gave a slow head shake. "Of all the people you'd fuck over, I never thought it'd be me."

"I didn't set out to do any such thing," Buster said with a touch of defensiveness.

"Well, you did. In case you don't read the papers or keep up with what's going on in this town, Neil Lindstrom threw his hat in the ring for my job. You remember Neil, don't you?" Whether Buster could place him or not, Granger went on with his rant. "You're making me look bad."

Buster brightened. "Isn't he the guy who used to stand up during pep rallies and yell, 'Eat a dick' when everybody else was yelling, 'Go, Yellow Jackets'?" Buster head-bobbed at the memory.

Granger remembered as though it were yesterday.

Neil had been tall for his age, almost Lincolnesque, with long arms and gangly legs, and tended to tower over everyone. It wasn't that his peers disliked him, he just wasn't all that popular. Always a bit out on the fringe, and constantly seeking attention.

Certainly not athletic. The son of the local bank president, with too much money and not enough sense.

Granger had never considered Neil a close friend, but they weren't mortal enemies, either. Not until that damned high-school prank went bad.

Back then most schools had a silent yell. Before a big game, students gathered in the auditorium for pep rallies. The way it worked, at the close of each event, the head cheerleader would announce the silent yell, leaning forward and shouting in a cadence, "Are the Yellow Jackets going to win tonight?"

The students would silently count to ten. Then everyone would rise up as a body and shout, "Hell, yes," at the end of the ten count.

Except for Neil. While others went along with the cheer, Neil had started shouting, "Eat a dick."

At first, Neil's deviation was only audible to the people standing around him, done for the benefit of those in close proximity. After all, the idea was to do it and get away with it. But as football season wore on and he grew more brazen, a lot of students heard it. Pretty soon, everyone except the teachers knew what Neil was shouting. The handful of teachers who actually made out the words hadn't been able to identify the voice or pinpoint where in the stands it had come from.

It'd been Buster Root who notified Granger and the rest of their circle of friends of a movement afoot to play a prank on Neil at the Homecoming pep rally. No one identified the architect of the plan; they just knew that it sounded like great fun, and people quickly got on board with the idea. Word of the prank spread throughout the high school. This time, during the silent yell, the student body would remain mute and seated at the end of the ten count.

And that's exactly what happened.

Nobody actually expected to collectively pull it off, or was naive enough to think nobody would spill the beans and tip off Neil. But as the student body waited, breathless with anticipation, through the countdown, *one-two-three;* casting sideways glances, *four-five-six;* leaning in to search the faces of the people on the other side of the friends sitting beside them, *seven-eight-nine;* they reached ten. Neil came flying out of his seat, his long arms rising, and flailing overhead. "Eat a dick!"

The command reverberated in the absolute silence of the auditorium.

Instead of laughter, everyone sat in stunned silence. It was like watching the drivers of two cars playing chicken: You know you shouldn't watch, but there's a certain fascination, so you do.

Then the administration reacted. Teachers stationed at different parts of the auditorium converged, moving toward the bleachers at a rapid pace.

The exits had been blocked off. Neil had nowhere to run.

As teachers closed in and apprehended him, he was led off to the principal's office. Nobody saw him at school again for ten full days.

"I remember the guy," Buster said. Laugh lines bracketed his mouth "He got suspended."

"Yeah? Well, he thought it was me who set him up."

Buster stared through innocent eyes. "You mean you didn't?"

"No. But somebody told Neil I did it." Granger fixed Buster with a gunslinger gaze. He'd never forgotten what Neil said just before the teachers hauled him off.

"Granger, you SOB, you'll rue the day you did this to me."

"Wait a minute, Spike —" Buster lifted his shackled hands and pointed to his chest. "You think it was me who told him?"

"All I know is he's been gunning for me ever since."

"Why, that's just crazy," Buster said with an innocence that seemed contrived. "That'd be like me holding a grudge against you for riding shotgun with your highway patrolman daddy the night I stole that car."

"What's that supposed to mean?" But Granger saw where this was headed and didn't like it one bit.

"Everybody knows that's how you got your nickname. On account of Trooper Granger told you to roll out the spike strip that stopped me from getting away."

70

Silence stretched between them.

"Only I didn't blame you, Spike. Nosirree. You were just doing what you were told." But Buster's shrewd eyes telegraphed otherwise. "So Neil's running against you," he said dismissively. "Means nothing. Anybody can run for office. Maybe he really wants the job."

Granger shook his head. "He's out to settle an old score."

"It was high school."

"This isn't the first time he's burned me," Granger said warily, still studying the escape artist with the intensity of a cobra.

"What? Did he whip into the parking spot at the front door of the Grab-'n-Go before you did?" Buster laughed, hamming it up even more. "Did he toilet paper your house? Steal the pink flamingos from your lawn?"

"I don't have pink flamingos."

"Not anymore, you don't," Buster joked, as if they were back in junior high and this was all just a barrel of laughs.

It was high time to bring Buster back down to Earth. "It's a helluva lot more serious than that. He's the slimy sidewinder who ran off with my wife."

Hand to chin and suddenly sobered, Buster mulled this over. He spoke under the weight of Granger's nickel-plated gaze.

"I think I know a way to turn this thing around for you."

"I'd give my front seat in hell to see that."

CHAPTER SIX

After Gordon let her out at the house, Aspen took a long, hot shower and primped to perfection. Consumed with the need to be proactive in her legal defense, and realizing she still had too much adrenaline coursing through her veins for her to be able to sleep, she climbed into her ten-year-old Honda and headed down to rural Johnson County. She didn't relish the thought of telling Spike about Stir Fry's demise, but she could use a bit of country wisdom, and that's where Spike came in.

Even though Gordon was convinced the criminal charges against her were born out of the *Asleep at the Wheel* exposé, and even though the boss promised that the company lawyer would defend her on the deadly conduct charge, she didn't want to lose sleep fretting over what might happen at subsequent court appearances.

Nobody could come up with a battle plan

like Spike. After all, hadn't he taught the Texas Department of Criminal Justice not to mess with him during the state's prison-overcrowding fiasco?

Damned right he had.

And hadn't he turned into an overnight legend, the envy of the sheriffs of the other 253 Texas counties?

You bet.

He could help her out of this scrape, too.

So why wasn't he answering his cell phone? He always had it with him. Left it on the bedside table when he slept. Had he stuck it in the charger? Lost it? Inadvertently turned it off? Or worse, had something bad happened to him? Then her gut really sank. What if he was out on a date and turned off his phone? It could happen; they weren't exactly in an exclusive relationship.

After this dreadful morning, she needed Spike Granger. With any luck, he'd take her home with him, and they'd spend a few hours lolling away the afternoon in his bed.

The morning's events had her so rattled that she didn't pay much attention to the Jaguar ten car lengths behind her. But when she turned off the expressway at the Burleson exit, and the Jag popped up in her rearview mirror, she suspected she'd picked up a tail.

Panic gripped her throat. The mechanic? The idea didn't seem so farfetched after considering the sadistic killer had access to any number of vehicles waiting to be worked on out at his last place of employment — Pop's Auto Salvage and Repair.

She couldn't make out the driver through the heavily tinted windows, but she knew this stretch of road from her trips down to see Spike. Whoever did the engineering study on Highway 174 should be horsewhipped. None of the twenty-some-odd traffic signals were synchronized, and despite her attempts to strand the Jaguar's driver by running the amber lights, her efforts failed miserably due to the high number of school zones. She hadn't been able to jot down the license plate number, either.

Hatching a new plan, she scanned the highway in hopes of spotting an American flag waving high atop a flagpole. All government buildings in small Texas towns flew them — meaning the chances of her finding a fire station or police department were exceptional. The last place the mechanic would want to follow her to was a PD.

But when she reached the little town of Joshua, the luxury car suddenly changed lanes and shot past like the Stars' winning hockey puck.

False alarm.

She let out a punctured-tire sigh, promising herself to be more cautious next time. When the red light cycled to green, she adjusted the rearview mirror, glancing furtively to ensure no one else had tailed her. This was no irrational fear, she told herself. Any man brazen enough to defeat her door's deadbolts, enter her home — *her sanctuary* — and lie in wait, would have no hesitation abducting her on some country back road, or from a public place in a one-horse town.

The passage of time had not diminished the level of posttraumatic stress she'd suffered.

She could recall the minutest details of her almost-demise at the mechanic's hands, as if he'd struck yesterday: the way he smelled, his breath, the shape of his teeth, the dead eyes — and the reality that she and Rochelle had almost become part of the body count. If not for Rochelle, she probably would've died. Would've been locked away in his torture chamber like the other two girls and made to suffer unspeakable atrocities until she begged for the sweet release of death. But together, she and Rochelle had drawn strength from each other and somehow managed to avoid their own grisly murders.

At the time, she'd had no idea he'd come after her. But it made sense in a weird sort of way — after all, as WBFD's newest investigative reporter, she broke the story on him, and he held her personally responsible for his undoing.

Spike had been so certain the mechanic would return to finish what he'd started that he wanted to hire a round-the-clock bodyguard for her. But it didn't seem right to expect someone she'd only known a short time to furnish that kind of security, much less finance it out of his own pocket, and Gordon pleaded poverty on behalf of the station. So when Spike showed up on her doorstep with a made-up story about how he'd rescued Stir Fry from the back of a Vietnamese restaurant that had a failing report card from the health department, and how the animal shelter planned to gas the dog if nobody adopted it within a few days, she took in the pug to provide another set of ears.

And it didn't hurt that the stray provided an extra heartbeat around the house, which turned out to be a nice benefit for a lady living alone.

She groped her purse for her cell phone and hit the speed-dial button for Spike. The call routed directly to voice mail. So far she'd called him four times, and that's where she drew the line. Any more than that, and he'd suspect she had stalker tendencies.

She decided to drive by Kirk House on a reconnaissance mission before stopping by the SO. Maybe kill time scoping out the place before she and Dainty Prescott returned after dark. At least she'd become familiar with the layout. Not like waiting until eleven-fifty-nine at night to discover hobos and squatters were the reason behind the ruckus.

Or bogeymen.

Which everybody knew there was no such thing.

Lulled by the droning of tires against the pavement, Aspen took Highway 377 south past a new residential area that'd sprung up within the past several years, modeled after one of those seaside villages carved out of an Italian cliff side. Million-dollar houses topped with terra-cotta tiles popped up as far as the eye could see, with the occasional slate-roofed, modern brick home that stuck out like a sore thumb. The land value of such a lovely development would increase with age, provided the nonnative trees that'd been trucked in took root and flourished beneath the hot Texas sun.

She wondered how to break the news to Granger, that overnight a pack of hungry coyotes had Stir Fry for dinner while at the same time she'd been branded a criminal. And she wondered whether anything in the cop code would prevent him from hanging out with the likes of her. She certainly hoped not. Granger was, hands down, the most interesting person she'd ever met.

Only now, maybe he wouldn't want to sleep with her. And marry her.

It'd taken so long for them to get comfortable with one another — well, mostly it was her getting comfortable with him, not the other way around. But getting publicly dumped in Dallas at the five-star restaurant on the top floor of the Timmons Building by Roger, her then-boyfriend of two years, had made her gun-shy of starting a new relationship.

Upon meeting Granger, she'd pegged him for a mental case. How arrogant did a man have to be to take on the Texas prison system? The sheriffs of all the other Texas counties had already decided that nothing could be done about the overcrowded prisons. Oh, sure, they'd groused about it, but none of them except Granger had bothered to single-handedly take on the

Texas Department of Criminal Justice and bitch slap it into submission.

She caught herself smiling and almost missed the huge, penis-shaped silo jutting up from the ground in the distance.

Kirk House.

She slowed her speed, and eased over onto the shoulder to let the car behind her pass. The road had narrowed to two lanes a mile back, making the possibility of vehicles roaring up behind her doubly hazardous.

A smattering of live-oak trees thinned out enough for her to see the huge, wrought-iron gate that sealed off a gravel road leading back to the tree line. Each gate half was supported by a tall pillar constructed of granite blocks that were mortared and stacked. She lowered her speed to twenty miles per hour, bumped off the highway, and pulled up to the entrance. In the distance stood the shell of what had once been a pink-granite, two-story mansion. Sawtooth apexes now jutted above the treetops like the jagged fangs of an animal.

She shut off the engine and took in her surroundings from the sanctuary of the Honda.

The massive iron gate had a thick chain pulled through the two halves where the edges met to keep it closed. A huge padlock, imposing and impenetrable, dangled from one section of chain.

This was a fantastic discovery.

She got out of her car. With gravel crunching beneath her feet, she stepped cautiously toward the gate. She didn't see any *No Trespassing* signs, but what if the house and land were part of Kirk corporate holdings? It wasn't Gordon's nature to invite a lawsuit. If the gates were locked, then someone in authority who had a connection to the derelict estate — a caretaker, perhaps — would need to grant WBFD access. Despite the property's reputation as a lovers' lane for high-school teens, Gordon would hardly expect his reporters to trespass.

Assuming she and Dainty Prescott couldn't get past the gate, they wouldn't even have to make the trip. If she played her cards right, she'd wait until the last minute to tell Gordon, and with no way to gain access short of cutting the padlock with bolt cutters, he'd make an executive decision and scuttle the plan.

Besides, the place had a creepy feel with the house barely visible from the roadway.

There had to be a logical explanation for the renewed folderol surrounding Kirk House. The murdered brothers, Bill and Joe, had been killed before she was born.

Something about a robbery gone bad. Smatterings of conversations between her parents popped into mind, dating back to occasional trips over to Bluff Dale, a flyspeck town on the map whose only claim to fame happened to be a killer German restaurant, now defunct. As she played with her Barbie dolls in the backseat of the family Chevrolet, dressing them in appropriate attire for the ball or the beach, her parents' talks, which they thought were private, were actually being stored in the recesses of Aspen's mind.

And one had just flashed across her memory.

"We should make an offer. They'd probably sell it cheap. Nobody'd want to live in a murder house."

"Wex! Hold your voice down. She's right behind us. Besides, I'm one of those people who doesn't want to . . . you know . . . live in a house where people were . . . executed."

Silence stretched between them.

"They didn't have to shoot them. The Kirks had more money than they could spend in a lifetime. They would've given those thugs the rare-coin collection." Jillian Wicklow had made the sign of the cross. *"God rest their souls."*

"They came loaded for bear, hon. Probably heard about the arsenal of collector guns the

old man owned. Maybe figured if those boys got the chance, they'd open fire on them."

"Can we please not talk about it anymore? It's depressing. Can't we just for once shut out the rest of the world and take a pleasant family drive, for God's sake?"

And then the car slowed to a crawl, and her father lowered his voice.

"We should go in, Jilly, just me and you. Leave the kid in the car for a few minutes. We can watch her from a window opening."

"I already told you, I don't want anything to do with that place."

"Not to buy it, Jilly. To . . . get a little."

Sex pervert that he was, and still is, Aspen thought as she shook off the reverie. Anyway, she didn't believe in ghosts.

The bogeyman — now that was different.

So what if these alleged cries came from squatters illegally living on the Kirks' property in an attempt to keep others from discovering their hideaway? Or high schoolers playing pranks on each other? Or maybe it'd turn out to be the call of someone's escaped parrot. Parrots could mimic any sound. She once knew a girl whose parrot could imitate sounds the kitchen appliances made when in use.

Whatever the explanation, "paranormal" had nothing to do with it. The reality was

— like the old Negro spiritual sung about John Brown's body — the Kirk brothers were moldering in their graves; and if one believed in heaven and hell, which she did, their souls were most likely soaring above the clouds; and the rest of the story, in the tradition of the late, great Paul Harvey, was most likely the result of human drama brought on by over-imaginative, high-strung people.

Or nut cases.

Still, the sound of rustling leaves in the breeze only added to the mysteriousness of Kirk House. She could almost hear the soft echo created by each gust of wind whispering: *Go away, go away, go away.*

She'd seen all she needed to see, and hurried back to the Accord. Safely seat belted inside, her eyes flickered to the rearview mirror. The reflected image of a dark-blue BMW rolled by.

Her heart stalled.

Creeping along the highway, the car slowed to a snail's pace.

Her heart jump-started itself with primal fear. She'd made a huge mistake. Hadn't Granger verbally hammered it into her a hundred times — how, if she was out in her car, not to get boxed into a situation she couldn't get out of? Didn't he tell her to always park with the snout of her vehicle pointed in the direction that would provide her an easy escape?

Her heart shifted into high gear. Gabrielle Foster, one of the mechanic's murder victims, had driven a BMW. And during her disappearance — before she showed up dead in a culvert — the Beemer had vanished as well.

Panting for air, Aspen fired up the Accord. The driver of the BMW made a sharp U-turn in the middle of the highway.

Aspen stomped the accelerator, churning up pebbles, and backed out into the roadway. The luxury auto had stopped on the shoulder of the highway opposite her. Heart drumming, she sped away, watching the Beemer recede in her rearview mirror, wondering what to do if he followed her. Or worse, ran her down, clipped her rear bumper and forced her into the ditch.

Nothing stood between her and civilization except for a smattering of distant farmhouses and rolling acres dotted with hay bales and livestock. Realizing this, she pulled her own mid-highway U-turn and headed back toward the road that led to Cleburne, the Johnson County seat, and to Granger himself.

She had every intention of taking down

the license plate of the BMW; the hunter had become the hunted. But when she returned to the mouth of Kirk House, the BMW had moved on.

She gave the pink-granite bulk of Kirk House one last look before flooring the Honda's accelerator. The next time she drove out to nose around this God-forsaken place she'd back the car into the mouth of the driveway the way law-enforcement officers did. Easy getaway and all that.

She took the highway to Cleburne. In less than half an hour, she'd be at the SO, wrapped in the protective embrace of Granger's strong arms.

Granger would advise her what to do.

Granger knew everything.

CHAPTER SEVEN

"What do you mean, we should put on an inmate magic show? That's the craziest thing I ever heard."

"Not really, Spike. Think about it. You can get a couple of sponsors to help set up the staging area, and then get your girlfriend to cover the event. She's hot, by the way." Without changing his expression, Granger balled up a fist. Seeing this, Buster hurried on. "It's a win-win situation, my friend. I get the TV coverage I need for people to consider me the best magician in the world, and —"

"And what?" Granger dripped sarcasm. "You get to announce to reporters after the show's over that your previous escape attempts were a publicity stunt to get people to come to the show?"

"Exactly," Buster said, only the expression on his face said different. "You have to do it!"

"I only *have* to do two things: pay my taxes and stay white. That's it. So if you're thinking that'll save your skin from a felony conviction, you don't know this new DA we've got." But what Granger really thought was that maybe while Buster was getting sawed in half by another inmate, Granger'd be getting his dick sawed off at the polls.

"We should set the magic show up a week before election day," said the jailbird. "That'll give me time to teach a couple of guys on the cell block these new card tricks —"

"Not crooks," Granger said, vetoing the idea. He didn't want other inmates learning anything that might improve their con-man skills. "You can teach my deputies those card tricks, but you're not holding a class for inmates because I'm not up to having a jailbreak." Granger stopped speaking. He'd just heard himself talking like the magic show was a go. Had he taken leave of his senses? This was crazy. "Forget it," he snapped. "No magic show. I'm charging you with felony escape for the dumb stunt you pulled, and you're doing your time like any other inmate — behind bars. No more Mister Nice Guy. And when you're done doing your time, you're walking out the front door like the rest of the convicts."

But Buster wasn't finished. "No, no, no. Just listen." Desperation resonated in his tone. "We go back a long way, Spike. I wouldn't jerk you around."

"Already have, dimwit."

"Nah, I was just foolin' with you. Just messing around to see if I could do it. I was on my way down to the courthouse square to get a real meal at one of the cafés; I've had it up to here with green baloney" — he measured a hand up to his hairline — "and I planned to come back, soon as I was done eating."

"Sure you did." Granger slid him another sideways glance. "That's lame."

Buster switched tactics. He laid out a plan, one-two-three. "You've been having a problem with the prison system. I know, because I read about it."

Granger snorted in disgust. "Fancy that. You can read."

"You don't have to get nasty about it, Spike. I read lots of books on lots of subjects. If you don't believe me, just ask the librarian. She sends over the books I order if we don't have what I need here at the jail. I'm trying to help you. This could be a plum for your career."

"Wonder why I keep envisioning this so-called plum turning into a big, fat watermelon crammed down my throat?"

"Would you listen? Just hear me out." Buster paused. "You're having problems with the warden not taking your people at the penitentiary."

"Not my people. They're convicts. If you shuck right down to the tamale, they're *your* people."

With a concessionary head bob and a dull "Whatever," Buster launched back into his plan. "What you do is sell tickets, see? Even if we only bring in a hundred bucks, that's fifty bucks more than you have in the county budget to feed us, right?"

"Whoa. If you think you're taking a fifty-percent cut, you're crazy."

Buster's face fell. "Why not? It was my idea. I deserve part of the take. I'm the one doing all the work."

"I have a better idea. Let's call the whole thing off, and you can cool your hocks in the cell all day. Let's see . . ." He calculated Buster's punishment on his fingers. "That's your original forty-five days — because you just lost your three-to-one — see, Buster, you don't get to keep your 'good time' if you screw up." He twisted his head à la *The Exorcist* and cast the evil eye on his prisoner. "So counting your original forty-five days plus the maximum for escape . . . that comes out to —"

"No, no, no. Stop. Let's not get nuts. You don't have to go all psycho on me. Fine. You'll keep all the money for the inmate food fund. If we sell ten tickets at ten dollars each, you'll have a hundred dollars. That'd be word of mouth, counting a handful of employees who might want to come and bring their kids. But if you could get the newspaper to run you a free ad, you'd get more people interested in coming to see the show. And if you could get your girlfriend —"

"She's not my girlfriend," Granger said, but he felt himself smiling and knew his protest had lost effect. "And I'm not trading on my relationship with her to get your mug on TV."

But Buster had other ideas. "How 'bout we let her decide?"

"Fair enough. I'll mention it next time I see her." *Not.*

Buster looked down at his foot. "By the way, I think I broke my ankle when I hang glided off the roof."

"Bullshit."

"It's true, Spike. If I'm lyin' I'm dyin'."

"Lemme see." Granger's eyes squinted in calculation. "Pull up your pants leg."

"Can't. You put me in a belly chain."

"You're a contortion artist — so contort."

Buster stretched out his fingers and gathered a handful of fabric at the knee. He grimaced and recoiled. In a voice fractured by urgency, he said, "Come on, Spike, drive me to the hospital. I'm in pain. I need medical attention."

"Didn't act like you were in pain five minutes ago."

"I usually have a pretty high threshold for pain," Buster said, "but it finally got to me."

But Granger was thinking he'd have to be crazier than a baboon on crack cocaine to buy into Buster's crap. *High threshold for pain, my ass,* he thought. "Deal with it."

"Probably just a hairline fracture, but we'll never know 'til it's x-rayed."

Buster's whining made Granger grind his molars. But an ugly visual of the inmate hiring an ambulance chaser to sue the county kept popping into mind until Granger could almost feel the sting of a process server slapping a trumped-up lawsuit into his hand.

Fit to be tied, he did a mid-block U-turn and headed for Memorial Hospital. En route, he radioed for a couple of deputies to meet him at the ER. He needed to return to the office. Buster wasn't the only brush fire he had to put out today.

Meanwhile, he'd assign a bruiser or two

to guard Buster while doctors x-rayed his banged-up foot. One could never be too careful.

Especially with Buster.

CHAPTER EIGHT

Back at the Johnson County Sheriff's Office, Spike Granger was sitting comfortably in the big leather chair at his desk, waiting for the deputies guarding Buster to report in from the ER. He'd just ambled in after stopping to do a bit of politicking at his favorite café on the courthouse square, shrugged out of his leather frontier vest, loosened the turquoise-and-silver bolo tie, and planned to settle into the rest of his morning routine until Buster returned from the hospital. If Buster felt up to it, Granger would transport him over to the high-school gymnasium to check out the place and get an idea of what all needed to be done to host a fund-raiser. Now that he'd had a chance to mull it over, putting on a magic show seemed like a fairly decent idea. Which meant Granger needed Buster.

Trouble was, word had already gotten around the yard that Buster was planning another escape in order to shore up his escapology reputation. So far, Granger had managed to contain the *Buster-up-a-tree* incident. But another breakout would torpedo his reputation as a real "Git-R-Dun" sheriff, and cost him a slew of votes in the upcoming election.

The lesser of the evils meant cultivating these half-baked ideas and letting the modern-day Houdini design and craft the items he'd need with the help of a couple of trusties. By giving him a tour of the new gymnasium, specifically the stage, Buster could factor in the amount of space he'd have available to build props and put on his magic show.

After starting a pot of coffee, Granger shook out the front section of the *Cleburne Times Review* looking for political news. His eyes drifted over the page.

The photo he'd dreaded seeing jumped out at him. He stared at the grinning face of Neil Lindstrom. His jaw tightened. His chest constricted.

Lindstrom, a recently defeated mayoral candidate, had no law-enforcement experience. He'd only managed to become a licensed peace officer because one of Granger's biggest detractors, a "wheel" in the Texas prison system, had commissioned

Lindstrom in the scant hope he'd put Granger out of office.

But it wasn't Lindstrom's cheesy mug that torqued Granger's jaws as much as it was the woman standing next to him in the photo.

A painful knot twisted his stomach.

Lindstrom had no business running for sheriff. He was only doing it because his twisted narcissistic, heart-stomping bitch of a wife put him up to it.

It'd been, what? Over a year? And still, each time Granger heard the mention of Lindstrom's wife, or glimpsed her photo in the newspaper's society section, the same old clench in his stomach caused bile to bubble up into his throat. With pleasure, he had quit attending social functions so he wouldn't have to run into her. It was more than a custom; he'd made it a rule. But now that Lindstrom had thrown his hat into the sheriff's race, they'd be bumping elbows all the time.

The coffee pot on the credenza sputtered, shearing his thoughts. He set the newspaper aside, wrangled out of his chair, and helped himself to a cup of Columbian grind. What he really needed was a cold beer and to bed Aspen Wicklow — not necessarily in that order. With any luck, it'd happen tonight after dinner. He'd looked forward to the pretty redhead's return after her interview with CNN. Now that she'd arrived back home, he couldn't wait for their reunion.

And the idea of steamy sex.

Lord Almighty. The anticipation of hot sex with Aspen was almost more exciting than he imagined the actual experience would be.

Aspen Wicklow was a keeper. That's why tonight needed to be done up right. He intended to take things slowly, savoring each moment.

Not like animal sex with Carliss down at the post office, where you had two lost souls, each going through a divorce, each rejected by their spouses, and both seeking comfort in each other's arms. He was glad he and Carliss stayed friends after the ink had dried on their respective divorce papers. Nobody else in the world knew exactly what kind of hell they were going through at the time. Two messed up people experiencing a world of hurt, walking around with fake smiles plastered on their faces, jaw-jacking, backslapping and glad-handing the towns-folk. Making inane conversation like, "Nice day, isn't it?" Or, "How you been, Joe?" Or, "I declare, Saralee, have you always been this pretty or is it just my imagination you grew up right before my eyes?"

Stuff like that, while their guts were hanging out.

And all the time he and Carliss were carrying on like a couple of stoics, pretending their hearts hadn't been ripped out of their chests by the divorce gorilla and shoved, still pulsing, inches from their faces . . . and while all their friends pretended not to notice they'd become mere husks of people . . . and the rest of the idiots who hadn't figured out they were dying inside, well . . . eventually, there came a point when it really didn't matter.

In the end, his and Carliss's little mercy fling ended, but they remained friends, the way people bonded by tragedy often do. They didn't marry each other the way their exes had done.

Thing is, Aspen knew how it felt to be cheated on. They unfortunately had that in common. So he rested assured that if their relationship progressed to the point where he ever felt comfortable asking her to marry him, she'd be faithful. Like the gray wolf that mates for life.

One wolf, one wolfette. And someday, maybe a den full of wolf pups.

Not like his ex-wife, a narcissistic, histrionic woman who waited until after they were married to tell him she didn't want kids because she didn't want to ruin her figure; when the real truth was that she was so damned selfish, she wouldn't have gotten up off her ass to feed or nurture anything but herself.

Bitch.

For no good reason, his mind replayed the haunting imagery of that awful night when he caught the woman who'd vowed to love him no matter what in an eyeball-searing sexual position she'd steadfastly refused to engage in with him during the course of their marriage, but had assumed right in front of him with Neil Lindstrom.

He shook off the ugly visual — the past should stay in the past — and replaced it with a vision of Aspen wearing the silk teddy he'd bought her from Victoria's Secret.

Since Aspen appeared to be about the same size as his secretary, he'd talked Lucinda into going to Fort Worth and picking out something elegant. He'd also given her extra cash to buy a bottle of expensive champagne, which sat chilling in the little refrigerator in his office, waiting to be taken home and transferred into a bucket of ice.

He returned to his comfy chair and sipped from his coffee mug.

In the quiet of his office, with nothing but

the soft sound of rushing air pouring from the AC vents, he imagined how this magical night with Aspen would unfold. After all, anticipation was the next best thing to being there. Ask any guy. If they said they didn't think about it, they were liars.

He punctuated the notion with a nod, and his thoughts returned to Aspen.

They'd have a quiet dinner at his house; not because he couldn't afford to take her to the finest restaurant, but because he didn't particularly want to run into anyone who might recognize him and ask how the campaign was going. He'd grill filet mignons on the barbeque pit, toss a crisp lettuce salad with avocado slices arranged on top and serve the special dessert from Peggy's True Confections. He'd ply Aspen with champagne and let her tell him about her trip. Didn't matter that he couldn't share her enthusiasm for the Broadway play she took in, or the little mints in pastel colors the hotel placed on her pillow each night —

Doggone it, he should've remembered to get mints, too. Oh well, no time now.

Anyway, it wouldn't matter that she'd want to gush over her trip or that she'd want him to share in her excitement. Because just hearing the sound of her voice and knowing she was within arms' reach was enough to make it hard to walk.

It wouldn't matter if they got all smoky from the steaks — matter of fact, a little smoke might work to his advantage — that way, they could start with a warm shower and he'd see her naked for the first time.

Would the circle of skin around her nipples be pink or brown?

He imagined various shades of both. And whether her breasts were big or small. Not that it mattered, but one never knew until the bra came off and you learned it was either one of those padded push-up numbers, or not.

Note to Spike: Don't forget to pick up the rose petals from Ida Lou after work.

He downed the rest of his coffee, stood up, unhooked his double-rig, and draped the guns over the antique hall tree next to his desk. He didn't mind removing them while tending to his administrative duties. After all, he carried a backup pistol in the sleeve of one boot and a serrated survival knife stuck down inside the other.

By now, Buster ought to be about done over at the ER.

He rummaged through his top drawer for a peppermint, removed the cellophane wrapper and popped it into his mouth. Then he traded the front page of the newspaper for the sports section. As the minty taste cleared his head, he checked the football scores, and hoped for an uneventful morning.

Without warning, a known terrorist slipped past the front desk and burst into Granger's office carrying weapons of mass distraction.

CHAPTER NINE

It took a skidding heartbeat and a couple of eye blinks for Granger's brain to process what had just happened.

Dallas Ostrander.

This was no run-of-the-mill Middle Eastern terrorist slipping past homeland security with a Stinger missile, nor the offspring of a transplanted cell, brought here to wreak havoc on everything and everyone. This was devil spawn, unexplainably hatched into one of the nicest families in Cleburne. Over the years, this vixen and her stage mother, Alice, nearly drove her father, Herb, into the poorhouse. Consider the rampant spending from entering all those beauty pageants — Dallas still couldn't accept the fact that pageant judges didn't crown her Miss Texas, but instead gave the title to a wholesome young lady from Sweetwater. And that little stint in reform school for unauthorized use of a vehicle when she was still a juvenile —

depending on who you talked to, Dallas either "borrowed" the car or stole it. Not to mention money wasted on lessons: piano, guitar, voice, modeling, acting, dance — with all the sparkly costumes and high-dollar clothes that went with them. Talk about pouring money down an empty hole . . .

Forty-one years later, Herb Ostrander still had no idea that the night Dallas was conceived it was Beelzebub who'd materialized and impregnated his wife. If any justice in the world truly existed, Dallas Ostrander would've been kidnapped at birth and delivered to the gates of hell in a gift basket.

Okay, that might be a bit harsh.

Once upon a time, he hadn't felt this way.

It seemed like an eternity with no words exchanged as they watched each other in quiet assessment. In reality the wall clock proved that less than thirty seconds had elapsed.

As Granger sat stricken with his mouth agape, the intercom buzzed.

Dallas made it to the desk in two strides and hit the disconnect button. "Hello, Samuel." She used his Christian name, speaking in the same sultry voice that once sent lightning bolts to his groin.

Granger took in her presence through narrowed eyes: thoroughbred legs that went on for miles and a short leather skirt to showcase them; low-cut cashmere sweater stretched so tight that it looked embedded in her skin; platinum mane that fell down her back like a palomino's tail; a luscious mouth glossed with her signature pink lipstick; and yellow contact lenses that accentuated her huge brown irises and gave her the appearance of a jungle animal on the prowl. To further ensure her eyes were so shockingly captivating that they practically jumped out of her head, she'd added false eyelashes and swiped on mascara so thick and black that they looked like whisk brooms tarred in pitch.

He lowered the sports section enough to eyeball her shoes.

Dutch ancestry had given her the height of a runway model. Dallas never wore a shoe higher than a two-inch pump unless she wanted something. This particular morning, she'd put on a pair of black strappy sandals with stiletto heels that could pluck out a man's eye faster than a pissed-off ostrich.

He gave a derisive grunt. "What're you doing here? Trolling for new victims?" Said nastily. He placed the sports page on top of the blotter and fixed her with a hard stare.

"Don't be mean." She addressed him through pouty lips, exuding lust, as if she had every right to be here. "I was on my way to the post office —"

"Which is in the other direction." He thumbed at the window.

"— and thought I'd drop in to see if Lucinda had a safety pin. Silly me," she said with coltish enthusiasm, showing him what amounted to a spaghetti strap of cloth that had broken free of the swatch of fabric meant to hold her voluptuous breasts in check. "Only Lucinda wasn't at her desk and the guy relieving her said she was feeling kind of queasy and ran to the restroom."

She stepped into the sunlight slanting through the window, smiled, and struck a pose that took his breath away. She'd framed herself so that he had a bird's-eye view of her derriere beneath the little square of cowhide that made up her skirt. He tried not to look, but he couldn't help himself.

She hadn't worn panties.

His throat constricted, making it nearly impossible to speak. Nor could he pretend to be a paraplegic from the waist down. "There's someone else at Lucinda's desk?"

"Uh-huh, and he's cute, too," Dallas said airily, her gaze flitting over the room, "if you happen to like younger men, which I don't. Then again, I often wonder how it'd feel to be a cougar."

Granger wondered if a new hire let Dallas get past him. Lucinda knew to warn him if she ever showed up at the office. Since Dallas and the secretary were friends, he'd gone so far as to threaten to fire her if she let the little sneak in without giving him a heads-up. He had every confidence that Dallas would eventually trade on the friendship and try to talk her way past the front desk; he just didn't know when.

And the idea of someone else manning Lucinda's desk was no excuse.

Because the SO was a governmental office and a public place, he couldn't very well exclude Dallas from the building, so he did the next best thing. He'd had the graphics store down at the square print a ream of color copies with Dallas Ostrander's picture on it, to place in each new-hire packet so employees would recognize her on sight and warn him if she showed up.

New hire be damned, he made a mental note to fire the guy.

"By the way . . ." She scrutinized the top of his head from her place near the door. ". . . something's different. More hair, maybe?"

Yep, she wanted something bad, all right.

107

Bad enough to place herself in the trajectory of his wrath.

"That must be it," she went on, smoothing the front of her sweater as if to draw his attention to her magnificent breasts, especially the flap of cloth that had shifted enough for him to see her nipple protrude and the edge of areola peeking out. "I believe your hair's actually starting to come back." Without invitation, she tossed her designer handbag over the arm of the nearest guest chair. "You're not using one of those hair-growth products, are you?"

She pulled a maneuver straight out of *Flashdance,* slid her bra out through her sleeve, and tossed it onto the chair.

Granger stifled a gasp.

His eyelids fell to half-mast. He caught himself being sucked into her invisible force field and gave a dedicated eye blink to break the spell. Instead, chills snaked up his torso. He pulled the rip cord on a reserve chute in his memory.

Anger flared. "Once I stopped yanking my hair out five minutes after you kicked my ass out of your house, I've managed to regrow plenty of it. By the way, you're exposing yourself."

"Oops. Wouldn't want to do that." Her girlish giggle filled the room like musical chimes. She pulled the shoulder of her lopsided cashmere sweater back up and covered herself.

That's how she did it — made a man drive up the ass-end of an eighteen-wheeler in his brand-new pickup, or run a fingertip through a skill saw cutting wood, or put a knot on his head walking into a lamp post. And so on.

There ought to be a law that forced her to mist herself in an obnoxious scent, like the additive the utility department put in natural gas so you could smell it and get yourself the hell outta Dodge before you passed out or went up in flames. Or like those miners who carried canaries into the mine shafts, she should be forced to carry around a buzzard so that unsuspecting men with raging hard-ons would know she was the kind of woman who could pick your bones clean. In other words, make her carry a sign warning men to save themselves . . . or tattoo her breasts with a warning like the one the Surgeon General branded on packs of cigarettes: *Smoking Causes Lung Cancer, Heart Disease, Emphysema And May Complicate Pregnancy.* Only Dallas's would say: *Shallow, Do Not Dive In.*

Granger swallowed the taste of bile. "What do you really want, D?" He dropped his

109

gaze to her double-Ds. And she *did* want something.

She stepped beyond a shard of light slanting through the window, back-kicking the door hard enough to rattle the frame and send an echo down the hall as it slammed shut.

He didn't want his ex in his office with the door closed. But it wasn't as if he could throw her out. The Johnson County Sheriff's Office was a public place. Dallas was the public. So the vixen had a right to come down here anytime she saw fit. What she didn't have the right to do was invade his personal space.

Granger was about to get out of his chair, take her by the elbow and escort her from the premises when she shimmied around the desk and plopped herself down on his lap. Slim arms snaked around brawny shoulders. The fragrance of her perfume permeated his senses and unraveled his core. He half expected an anesthesiologist to materialize and order him to count backward from one hundred.

"What the — ?"

The rest of his protest was swallowed up by her fleshy, glossed lips. They sealed off his protests as her tongue sought out the

110

last of the peppermint dissolving in his mouth.

Or his tonsils.

Then it registered: She wanted his soul.

His groin involuntarily stirred. If he didn't get her off him right this second, he might as well stand in the restroom and use his pecker for a towel rod. Scratch that. At this point, he could stand in front of the hardware store with a five-gallon paint can hung on it and point the way inside to the home decorating section.

Dallas grabbed one of his hands, forced it under the cashmere, pressed it to her breast, and held it in place. He wrangled in the chair until he got enough leverage with the other hand to slip it around her jaw and un-suction her full, provocative lips from his mouth.

"It's not what *I* want, baby," she said practically panting. "It's what *you* want. Don't tell me you don't think about us —"

New memory. Pull rip cord on emergency chute. "I think about all the trouble you caused."

Should've shot her when I had the chance.

"— the way you used to love to —"

"Get off me." He gave her a violent shove, but she hung on tight. He grabbed her waist and tried to lift her, but he needed a fulcrum

111

to pull off that move. She sank her teeth into his neck and sucked so hard he realized she was trying to mark him. Chills traveled the length of his body. "Now wait just a damned minute."

Ought to put a gun to her head. Scare the living daylights out of her.

And yet . . . having Dallas's tongue snaking into his ear . . . and her hand — digging at his crotch in an effort to free him —

He let out an involuntary groan.

— having her untethered breasts close enough to . . .

. . . and the way she smelled . . . the fragile scent that belied the damage she should cause to a man's ego . . .

Granger felt his eyes roll back so far back in his head he could almost see the locked door with the good memories of Dallas Ostrander with the sign that read: *Danger — Do Not Enter.*

"Go home, Dallas." His voice sounded like a fifth-generation echo of itself.

"Give it up, Sammy. You may be able to take down bad guys, but you're no match for me." She used her husky, bedroom voice. Her kisses traveled the length of his jaw, settling on his lips, where she used her tongue as a probe.

He couldn't have gotten up and walked

over to the door to lock it if he'd wanted to. She had him completely under her spell, and now all he wanted was to get it over with. Like a beheading, he needed the quickness and finality of a guillotine.

"Stop it, Dallas." He called on his reserve brainpower. He'd never known anyone like her — so perfect, yet so flawed —

He reminded himself she was as close to a sociopath as the worst criminal he'd ever locked up. And yet —

— at this very moment, with time suspended, he wanted her —

No, I don't —

Yes, you do —

Do not —

Do, too —

His internal struggle continued until she unexpectedly unleashed him from his khakis, throbbing, and in pain; her, with slim cool fingers stroking his exposed flesh and him just wanting her to put an end to it.

She hiked her skirt up to her hips, and ground herself against him.

Not worth losing your job over —

Nobody'll know —

I'll know —

The door . . . lock the door.

She was going for the jugular again. She released his hand and caressed his face.

113

The last of his resolve slipped away. Instead of uncupping her breast, he skimmed her nipple with his fingertips.

Gut instinct warned him to stop. He must've developed a bad case of anal glaucoma, because he sure as hell couldn't see his ass doing that.

Heaven help me.

Her seduction was almost complete. Granger needed garlic and a cross. Or a wooden stake.

Steak.

His brain short-circuited. He thought of the filet mignons he'd be serving tonight.

That broke the spell.

"Get off me, you crazy bitch." His arm shot out toward the coat tree. He grappled for one of his Colts.

At first, his mind rejected the knuckle-rap coming from across the room, but when the door cracked open a sliver, a ghost of a shadow materialized. Denial turned to dread.

"Spike?"

The door swung fully open.

Then all hell broke loose.

CHAPTER TEN

"Aspen —" Granger gasped her name. "It's not what you think."

"Oh, good." Nice to know she'd read the situation completely wrong. Because she thought she'd just experienced the visual equivalent of a "Dear John" letter on steroids. "I'm so relieved. I thought you might be about to say something stupid." Said in a raw voice.

With a fresh shot of adrenaline, Granger wrenched himself out of the chair, effectively detaching the mouth of a shapely blonde from his neck and dumping her at his feet.

The smoldering vamp turned her lipstick-smeared face Aspen's way. Her light, bright hair, incandescent as the sun hit it, fell straight to her waist. She had spectacular eyes in an unexpected shade of honey that made them practically jump out of her head.

"Actually, sugar, it's exactly what you

think," the woman said from her place on the floor, eyeing what was left of the bulge in Granger's pants like it was gold from Fort Knox. She got traction against the carpet with the stilettos, steadied herself against the desk as she rose and readjusted her second-skin skirt. Her right breast had worked itself out into the open. Sending out whiffs of lavender, she tucked it, unabashedly, back into the sweater.

"Thanks, precious," the racehorse blonde said to Granger. "See you again soon." Tossing her palomino mane back over her shoulders, she snagged her bra with a manicured talon, grabbed her purse, and headed for the door. "He's all yours," she added with a wink.

As Aspen stood in stricken silence with the color draining from her cheeks, the blonde slinked out without so much as a backward glance, taking her flawless complexion and the predatory glint in her jasper-enhanced eyes with her.

For no good reason, Granger glanced down and noticed his unzipped pants. The zipper grated along its track as he zipped it back up. Punctured and deflated, he dropped back into his seat with the coordination of a stroke victim. "Aspen — swear to God — it's not what you think."

She spoke with dignity, in a voice icy enough to freeze salt water. "You have no idea what I think."

Actually, what she was thinking was that, until now, she had no evidence that Granger was this devious or even remotely capable of such cruelty. The reality was that she'd need scratch-and-sniff pictures to fully appreciate how much the leggy blonde reeked of his aftershave. And how Granger smelled like . . . well . . . like whatever that blonde had offered him.

She pivoted on one foot and flounced out the door with Granger hot on her heels. He'd grabbed a handheld police radio from a charger on his credenza on his way out, and was furiously adjusting the dials while trying to intercept her.

He caught up with her at the entrance to the building. "Aspen," he hissed, glancing around for spectators. "Come back inside. That was Dallas, my ex. I told you she was crazy."

"Ha!" The word exploded as if blasted from a cannon. A flock of blackbirds broke from the trees, kiting across the sky until they formed an inverted V-shaped pattern against the backdrop of clouds. She experienced an enormous temperature spike. "How stupid do you think I am?"

She gave him a narrow-eyed sheep-killing dog look, moving as far away from him as she could get without actually climbing over the hood of the car she'd been standing in front of.

The police radio crackled to life. A combination of background noise from the swishing of highway traffic and the excited screams of the transmitting deputy prevented a clear transmission, but she was able to make out two words clearly: *hospital* and *escape.*

Granger paled. "I have to go."

"Who's stopping you? Not me, that's for sure."

A couple of deputies burst through the front doors. Granger called out to them as they headed for the patrol cars parked on either side of the Honda. "Which direction did he go?"

"West toward the freeway," one yelled back.

Car doors slammed shut and dust churned beneath the tires. Aspen covered her nose with one hand and unlocked the Accord with the other.

"Darlin', come back to the office and wait for me. I'll explain everything."

"Do not ever contact me again." She snipped off her words like nail clippers.

She climbed into the Accord without so much as a backward glance. The door slammed shut with an authoritative clunk. As she sped away, she hazarded a glance in the rearview mirror in time to watch him mouth, "I love you."

Then he put his hand over his heart like a choreographed move straight out of a Britney Spears video.

Part of her thought, *Aww, poor thing.* Then her inner redhead flared. She gave him a backhanded salute with a stiff middle finger.

The last time she could remember feeling this kind of gut-empty void, she was sitting at the table in a five-star restaurant at the Timmons Building with her almost-fiancé, Roger, getting publicly dumped for an exotic dancer called Satin, whom Roger had met online.

She should've never let Granger suck her into this weird world of cops, where the good guys weren't always good and the bad guys weren't always bad.

Son. Of. A. Bitch.

Well, screw him and the horse he rode in on.

Thank goodness she didn't sleep with him.

She could almost hear him bragging down at the coffee shop. *"Yeah, fellows, the carpet matches the drapes."*

Haw, haw, haw.

Yuck it up while you can, Romeo, she wanted to say.

CHAPTER ELEVEN

Granger had no choice but to let Aspen go.

After dashing back into his office to put on his gear, he headed the snout of his unmarked patrol car toward Memorial Hospital, running hot with the emergency lights on and the siren yelping. He nearly cornered on two wheels at the entrance to the emergency room, barely clearing the five-mph speed-limit sign posted at the mouth of the drive. In the distance, deputies fanned out from their cruisers into the parking lot.

He turned off the lights and siren.

His heart raced. His breathing went shallow. Probably ought to see a doctor, long as he was here. Maybe get a prescription for blood-pressure meds.

He struck the steering wheel with the heel of his hand. Damn that Buster Root. If he did catch him, he'd find a really good reason to get the inmate admitted into the hospital for a lengthy stay — like pistol-whipping him bloody so his own mama wouldn't recognize him.

He did a cursory scan of the parking lot. No prisoner skulking around here.

He was all the way down one aisle and cruising up another when, up ahead and to the right, a manhole cover lifted a few inches off the pavement.

Granger slammed on the brakes. From his vantage point between two rows of parked cars, he watched. The open crescent turned into a gash. The top of a head poked up. He fished under the seat for a pair of binoculars and focused.

Buster.

The escapee peered out like an alligator looking over a log.

Granger unlocked his shotgun and quietly cracked open the door.

Buster's head came up out of the hole, then his hands, arms and torso.

Granger slipped out of the cruiser, into a crouched position. Hunkered over and weaving through cars, he made his way toward the prisoner.

Broken foot, my ass. I'll break his scrawny neck.

He couldn't afford to give away his position. The last thing he needed was for that rat fink to slide back down the manhole and disappear into the sewer system.

With the shotgun positioned at his waist, he waited beside a big black SUV.

Buster climbed the rest of the way out. He looked toward the highway and broke into a dead run just as Granger jumped out from behind the SUV.

"Freeze —" Granger racked a shell into the shotgun and let loose a string of profanity that not only called Buster's parentage into question, but cast aspersions on how he used his anatomically correct parts while nobody was looking.

Momentum carried Buster a few steps farther, but his hands flew skyward in the surrender position — or, as Granger liked to think — the *¡manos arriba!* position.

"Face down on the ground, down on the ground," he yelled. "Get your goat-smelling ass face down on the ground." He punctuated the command by opening fire near Buster's feet.

A chunk of pavement shot up into the air, making a believer out of Buster. The prisoner kissed the asphalt.

Granger trotted up with the shotgun in the ready position and stood over his childhood friend, menacing him with a boot heel placed strategically in the middle of his back.

"Take it easy, boss, I ain't goin' nowhere." And then, "Reckon we could go back to the ER? I think some of that shrapnel hit me in the leg."

"Deal with it," Granger growled, and applied a hundred foot-pounds of pressure.

Behind the sheriff and his prisoner, sirens pierced the calm. Tires screamed against the pavement and engines roared as the two hooples who were supposed to be guarding Buster Root bore down on him.

On the ride back to jail, Granger spent most of the time shouting profanity at Buster Root. "I'm filing a second escape on your ass and asking the court to stack your sentences so you don't see the light of day for the next five years." He punctuated each threat with every insult he could think of.

"Don't be mad. It's all part of the hype leading up to the magic show," Buster said with such calm that Granger felt inspired to drag him out of the cage and beat him into a pink stain.

"If you say one more thing about a magic show, I'm gonna whip out my magic wand and shove it right up your left nostril. You hear me?" For good measure, he tugged a tactical baton from its leather holder and shook it out in one violent snap. The collapsible metal baton telescoped out to its full length, about two and a half feet. He held the extended weapon up for Buster to see, making eye contact through the rearview mirror to make sure he had the inmate's full attention.

Buster stayed mute on the rest of the road trip back to jail, sitting with a distant stare that made him look zombiefied.

As Granger pulled into his reserved parking slot, Buster said, "So . . . did I get any TV coverage after hang gliding off the roof?"

"Hell, no. What do you think — that we're crazy? I'm weeks away from the election and I'm not about to call attention to your little jailbreak by alerting the media."

"But I need the publicity."

"For what? Being the world's greatest magician? Let me tell you something, bub, and you'd better listen and listen good. Your penny-ante bullshit's just not that interesting. It's not going to make national news and you're not the next Houdini. If you had half a brain, you'd be working at a real job and making a good living. Then a nice lady — not one of these skanks, but a nice lady — might want your sorry, no-good ass, and you could settle down with her like the rest of the decent, respectable citizens in this

125

town and have some kids."

"I'm not much of a family man, Spike. I might not make a good husband."

"Oh, don't get me wrong. I didn't say it'd last. I have no doubt that in a few years, she'll leave *you,* but you'll still have your kids. And since you'll only be getting older, if you pay child support like a good daddy, maybe the little bastards will take care of you someday so you don't end up in a nursing home." His thoughts flashed to Aspen, who'd stuck her parents in Tranquility Villas Care Center when she could no longer manage them.

A smile crept over Buster's face.

"What's so damned funny?"

"You might be able to keep the hang-gliding incident quiet, but you'll never keep the traps of those hospital people shut."

All afternoon, while Granger's secretary fielded calls from the press, the sheriff gave Buster's idea a good deal of thought. True, Buster'd planted a seed that had ripened into a kernel of doubt.

But if it worked . . .

Buster and the deputies could do a couple of card tricks. Maybe some mind-reading tricks using people in the audience. No handcuff lock-picking stunts, though. That might not set too well with the voters. And then after a one-hour show, he'd tell everybody to remember to vote for him on election day. He'd even take Buster down to the polls and let him vote, since he was thus far only a charged felon and not yet a convicted felon.

If it worked, he'd generate enough money to feed the inmates longer. Voters would conclude he was a fiscally responsible sheriff and reelect him.

So, if ten people paid ten dollars . . .

No, if a hundred people paid ten dollars . . .

Or a thousand people paid ten dollars . . .

Hot with excitement, he picked up the telephone and dialed.

Granger's first telephone call went to the editor of the local paper, who donated three days' worth of ad space. Now, he needed a place to host the magic show — someplace that already had a stage and seating because he didn't have disposable funds to build anything, even if his deputies pitched in and threw something together.

Once he confirmed the ad to run, he rang up the high-school principal. The principal, who knew Buster Root and thought Granger might be going temporarily insane, agreed to let him use the school's gymnasium —

for a small donation to the school's spirit squad. When Granger poor-mouthed him, he settled for the junior class to tour the jail. Juniors were still young enough to be in the juvenile justice system if they committed crimes, but were old enough to be influenced by the possibility of ending up in the adult justice system if they misbehaved.

In other words, they could end up like Buster Root.

CHAPTER TWELVE

After witnessing the seedy debacle with Granger and the individual whom Aspen had come to regard as *that hussy,* she returned home and crashed. She'd only intended to nap for a few hours, but when she finally roused from the much-needed slumber, she slitted her eyes open and looked at the clock's digital display. Then she picked up the remote control off the nightstand and switched on the TV. The *Live at Five* broadcast would be coming on any second, and she could listen from the bathroom while styling her hair.

She hadn't come fully awake, and lay propped up with pillows listening for WBFD's familiar musical intro to lead in the news. Instead, the jingle of a rival station built to a crescendo. While she dragged herself out of bed on a yawn, she looked down at the remote and poised her thumb to key in Channel 18.

"In tonight's top story," the anchor announced in a heady baritone, "a local newscaster was arrested for deadly conduct when she —"

Aspen sucked air.

Her stomach rolled over.

The rest of his words sounded tinny and distant. She stared at an exploded view of her mug shot in the top corner of the TV screen. After her eyes telescoped back into their sockets, she switched the channel to another competitor.

Different announcer, identical mug shot.

Each time she channel-surfed through competing local markets, the same police photo mocked her. Only now did she fully appreciate the picture that appeared on her driver's license. At least in that shot, she merely looked like a deranged meth addict. Not like a serial killer admitted to the asylum for the criminally insane; looking anxious and vaguely resentful, with Tasered hair and eyeballs that resembled partial eclipses.

Being the topic of tonight's lead-in story was a punch in the face.

Her brain's startle reflex kicked in.

She'd need to do a bang-up job for Gordon tonight. Because of her embarrassing arrest, and the negative attention it'd brought to WBFD, her future at the station depended on it. She tried to channel the spirit of her dead grandfather again. What'd he used to say? *"Your friends will believe you; your enemies won't. And after three days, nobody else cares."*

She hoped this was true.

After hiking up a pair of skinny jeans, she rifled through the sweaters in her closet until she came to a bright-green pullover that photographed well and complemented her flaming red waves. Then she pulled on a pair of hiking boots, grabbed a lightweight jacket and headed out the door.

Since she had no reason to see Granger on this trip down to Johnson County, she took a shortcut out to Kirk House, and traveled the oak-dotted countryside with her mind on autopilot. Completely in the zone, she ignored the architecturally significant houses as well as the antique stores and trading posts that cropped up along the way, and didn't stop until the big wooden penis-silo by Kirk House popped up in her line of sight.

She'd made the drive in less than twenty minutes.

The sun had dipped down below the horizon. Horizontal cirrus clouds in variegated shades of pink and purple striped the

131

sky. Now, the trees that surrounded the property, the ones she'd been certain had whispered a warning earlier, looked more like huge black hands.

Skeletonized hands that had clawed their way up to the surface from deep within the ground.

She shuddered at the image forming in her head. So far, the afternoon was turning into a real *Wuthering Heights* moment. Only this time, the gates were ajar. A small, ratty car had been parked up the road leading to the house. The opening wasn't large enough to drive the Honda through without getting out of the car and widening the gap, so she backed into the drive and parked at the mouth of the gate, effectively blocking the exit for whomever had shown up at Kirk House.

Seated behind the wheel with the engine running, like a gangster in a getaway car, she wasn't quite sure what to expect. Maybe whoever had shown up would let her in on the joke about the screams people claimed to hear. But just to be on the safe side, she telephoned WBFD to let someone know her location in the event she didn't return.

As usual, Rochelle answered.

"It's Aspen."

"How nice."

Not nice.

"Did you get a look at your latest glamour shot?" Rochelle needled.

"Please don't tell me WBFD ran that picture on *Live at Five.*"

"Not necessary. All the other stations ran it." Rochelle, whose body was a chemical and hormonal battleground, suddenly cackled. "Did you resist arrest? Because it looks like the cops stun-gunned your hair. And why's your face so white?"

Aspen inwardly cringed. Someone in Rochelle's covert operations network must've finagled a copy of her mug shot out of the PD files.

"Put Gordon on the phone."

"No can do. Hold, please."

"Don't put me on hold. I'm not one of your —" But Gordon's testy assistant had already sent her orbiting out in telephone no-man's land.

Momentarily, Rochelle came back on the line. "Now, where were we?" she asked with put-on sweetness. "Ah, yes. We were discussing your glamour shot. Really, Aspen, you should get a proper haircut. You're too old to wear it hanging down past your shoulders. What you need is a smart cut that shouts, 'I'm a professional, cosmopolitan woman.'"

"It was humid."

"It's always humid."

"When it's humid, it frizzes."

"This is beyond frizzy. It's clown hair."

"Where'd you get the picture?"

"I have connections."

Cementing the rumor that Rochelle's in charge of Black Ops.

"Who'd you show it to? I'll need a list."

"Well, now, that depends on you," Rochelle said with a trace of danger in her voice.

"Name your price."

"I dunno. Do you just want me to keep it in a frame at my house, or do you want to prevent me from ever showing it around the office, and at parties?"

"What'll it cost to make it disappear for good?"

"I'll mull it over. Hold on a second."

"Don't put me —"

The line clicked over and Rochelle was gone. Instead of waiting for her to return, Aspen hung up, and tried to think of names of people to call who actually gave a damn. She didn't see much use in calling a father with Alzheimer's, or a mother in rehab for short-term memory loss from a closed-head injury. And since Granger had effectively taken himself out of the picture, there simply wasn't anyone.

She concocted a contingency plan in case she didn't return — calling her home number to leave a message on the answering machine.

"Hello, Aspen? It's Aspen. In case I don't come home, you should know I'm at Kirk House, where those murders took place way back when. There's a little blue car here, and I'm about to check it out. Don't worry, though. It's probably nothing. And if it's not and I don't come back, the police will find this and check it out. *Hasta la vista, baby.*"

She clicked off and put the phone in her pocket, emotionally prepared to make the long trek up to Kirk House. And just in case things went sour, at least she'd positioned the car for a quick, easy getaway.

At first, the strange car appeared to have been abandoned. Even after scoping out this shell of a house from the tree line, she still didn't see anyone. But Aspen knew better than to barge in. She hung back, listening for movement behind the walls.

Seconds later, a human head rose in stages — first the dark hair, then eyes that had been painted like a clown's, then the nose, the mouth, and the chin. So far, nothing too sinister. More like an adolescent female

135

wearing mime-loud makeup. From the neck up, the girl's head became fully framed within one of the downstairs window openings. The glass panes were long gone; so were the casings. The night the Kirk boys were murdered, the house had burned.

"Hey, hello there," Aspen called out in singsong. The young female turned her head toward Aspen's voice. "Don't be afraid." Not like she'd been.

She stepped up onto the concrete foundation, past an opening that had originally framed a double front door, and came face to face with a teenager dressed all in black. Slight of build and with a gamine face, the girl looked maybe fourteen. Definitely not old enough to legally drive the car parked out front. She stood, frozen in place, looking frail and malnourished in her long, clingy dress that fell to the floor. Steel-toed boots added at least two inches to her height, making her stand approximately five-feet-four, at least three inches shorter than Aspen in pumps. Draped around her neck, silver chains in various lengths hung past her collarbone, stopping just above the scoop neckline of her clothing. She had big Texas hair in an unnatural shade of black that had been sprayed — correction: *shellacked* — to the point of immobility.

Huge blue eyes stared out from a pale white face that appeared to have been coated with liquid paper, and each darkly shadowed eye featured a diamond shape drawn around it. The uppermost tip of each diamond began slightly above mid-eyebrow; the lowest point stopped at the orbital bone. Each diamond had been blacked-in with eye pencil, and her full, fleshy lips had been accentuated and filled in with black lipstick. Gothic Lolita meets Alice Cooper. Or Kiss meets Morticia Addams. Björk meets Cirque du Soleil.

The Goth spoke in a soft, hypnotic voice, but she had eyes like the prongs on a stun gun. "Are you the new owner?"

"Who are you?"

"Nobody." And then, "Look, I saw them messing with the *For Sale* sign, so we knew it was only a matter of time before somebody bought it as a fixer-upper."

"Who's 'we'?"

"Nobody." She shifted in place. "Me and my friends. Look, we didn't tear up anything. It was like this when we started coming here."

"When was that?"

"Maybe a month ago. It was just a place to come and hang without a bunch of grownups hassling us."

"Why don't you let me be the judge of that?"

Panic settled in the Goth's face. "You're not gonna turn me in, are you? I'm almost off probation."

"For what?"

"Minor in possession."

It was a real *aha!* moment.

Now, this made perfect sense: local juvenile delinquents, a place to hang without supervision, maybe culminating in a rape or two. Probably accounted for those reports Gordon mentioned. With any luck, she'd have a report of her own that'd put an end to the hoopla. "You come out here to do drugs?"

"To drink. Some of them do a little X. Not me, though. Drugs are bad for you. I only drink. *José Cuervo.*"

"Oh, well," Aspen deadpanned, quickly making the connection between trouble and tequila, "as long as that's all you do."

"So . . . you gonna turn me in?"

"That depends."

The girl thrust out a hand. In her palm lay a silver cross with colorful stones embedded in it like the ones made by Native Americans on the reservation.

"I lost my mom's cross. I didn't steal it. I borrowed it from her jewelry box. I had to make the effort — my mom loves this cross. Would've bummed her out if I hadn't found it."

Aspen gave her a head nod of the *I see* variety. "So, what do you remember about the realtor sign?"

"It had a horseshoe on it." Her face went suddenly shrewd, adding ten years to her looks. "Hey, wait. If you bought the place, how come you don't already know?"

"If you don't want me to turn you over to the Johnson County sheriff, you'll answer my questions."

Aspen could see the moment when the girl's fear visibly evaporated. An unpleasant smile gashed her pale face.

"Yeah?" Blue eyes thinned into slits. "Well, I don't imagine there's a whole lot you can do about it."

"What makes you think that?"

"My old man's a cop."

CHAPTER THIRTEEN

When Aspen wheeled the Honda into the parking lot of WBFD around nine o'clock that same evening, she observed Dainty Prescott waiting inside the glassed-in foyer, dressed to the nines. The TCU intern had better clothes than any of the on-air talent.

She scoped out the area illuminated by the Honda's headlights and located an empty space next to Dainty's silver roadster. After slotting the sedan into the space, trunk-first, she scanned the lot for anyone who didn't belong.

Or who wanted to kill her.

Without knowing how long they'd be stuck at Kirk House, she figured the intern and their photographer, Reggie, would be thrilled that she'd packed a Styrofoam cooler with whole-grain bread, a variety pack of lunch meat, and a six-pack of fitness water. She'd dressed for warmth, in boots, dark skinny jeans, a forest-green pullover sweater and black peacoat, so was all bundled up when she heaved the ice chest out of the trunk and lugged it to the front door.

Dainty, on the other hand, opted for tailored wool slacks, a black cashmere sweater, and a hip-length vicuña coat that probably cost more than Aspen's entire monthly paycheck. Alligator boots added several inches to her height, as did a liberal application of volumizer to her pale, chin-length blonde hair. She was popping the tab on a Diet Dr Pepper when Aspen hobbled into the building with their provisions and greeted the resident debutante with a cheery hello and a sunny, "Where's Reggie?"

"Still out on assignment," Dainty said.

"Max?" Not that Aspen wanted Max to accompany them. After making a nice first impression on her when she hired on with WBFD, he'd turned out to be rather loutish; but now that she and Dainty had to investigate a reputed haunted house in the sticks, his considerable height and bulky frame made him infinitely more attractive.

"Same."

One of a dozen TV monitors that were anchored to the ceiling and situated in various locations around the station flashed "Breaking News" across the screen. The television had been volumed-down low enough to keep from annoying Rochelle and her minions, but was audible enough to make out the content if one concentrated. Aspen held up her hand in a *Hush* motion, and the intern immediately went quiet.

A thin strain of sound leaked out from the speakers.

A camera closed in on Steve Lennox, seated behind the anchor desk in his navy-blue sport coat and rep tie. Grim-faced, he announced, "Couple gunned down — news at ten." As abruptly as it had appeared, the image cut away and regular programming resumed.

This sensational gimmick, or teaser, was designed to encourage viewers to stick around for the ten-o'clock broadcast. Since Lennox didn't say where the victims were gunned down, or even how or why, for that matter, Aspen turned her attention back to Dainty. "Okay, I'll be in my office. Come get me when we have a photographer." She left the ice chest in the lobby near Rochelle's desk, and headed back to her office.

After booting up the computer, she entered the names of Joe and Bill Kirk and Johnson County into her preferred search engine. Seconds later, ten thousand possibilities popped up on the screen, but only fifty or so that covered the murders and subsequent trial.

The Kirk brothers had been popular kids. Separated in age by two years, they both played varsity football in high school, and later went on to play college ball for Texas A&M. As a rabid Aggie fan himself, their father, Delwin, had promised A&M his rare-coin collection. Detectives who worked the case surmised that the coin collection had sparked the impetus for the home invasion.

Hunkered over the keyboard with her face bathed in the glow of the screen, Aspen read on.

Twenty-five years before, while the boys were between semesters, Delwin and his wife Cynthia attended a series of holiday parties at the homes of other wealthy members of the Metroplex's social elite. The big topic of discussion among the guests was the number of robberies that had occurred while these globetrotters and jetsetters were on vacation — a coincidence not overlooked by Delwin Kirk. He and Cynthia had scheduled a trip to a Mexican resort over Christmas that year, so without mentioning it to the newspapers, Delwin donated the rare-coin collection the day before they left. Three days into their holiday, two men in ski masks pulled a home invasion at Kirk

House, shooting Joe Kirk through the window and forcing Bill Kirk, at gunpoint, to open the family's walk-in safe. When the coin collection couldn't be produced, the men shot Bill, execution style, and made off with Delwin's firearms collection. To cover their tracks, they set fire to the house. By the time firefighters arrived, the entire home was engulfed in flames, including the trees around it.

Cops caught the perpetrators several months later after a known fence contacted the sheriff when a number of Delwin Kirk's handguns were brought into his shop. Delwin and Cynthia never rebuilt the home. At trial, each testified that they'd been unable to go back since the murders, and had hired a caretaker to feed the livestock, since they still ran a herd of longhorns on the place. Over time, vines not only shrouded the granite pillars at the front gate, they wound their way into the house.

Prosecutors tried both of the masked men for Joe Kirk's murder. Each received the death penalty. A month after the last defendant's execution, Delwin Kirk committed suicide.

Aspen printed out a copy of the story and started a new file. On the surface, it had all the sensationalism for sweeps month. Too bad the midnight screams allegedly coming from the house were likely a hoax. After all, the Goth girl and her friends were probably responsible for a lot of the sounds that'd been reported. So they got a little rowdy . . .

But, hey — throw a sheet over Dainty and have her glide past the window openings a couple of times, and it might make an entertaining clip for the next edition of "Stupid Outtakes" that the staff could view at next year's Christmas party.

She picked up a remote, powered on a small television mounted just below the ceiling in the far corner of her office, and tuned to the ten-o'clock broadcast. Using an innovative approach, Gordon had decided to use each intern to deliver a broadcast segment, then score each performance and report the grades to their Radio-Television-Film professors. He made sure to keep it all very cloak-and-dagger, springing it on them at the last second so they didn't have time to work up a case of the jitters.

Either that or the boss was a sadist.

Tonight, one of the SMU interns sat behind the anchor desk looking like she'd been run through the wringer. At least she had perfect hair, though, long and dark, and huge blue doe eyes that appeared almost violet on-screen. But she'd forgotten to remove the simple gold cross that hung around her neck, and the guys would be making book on how long it'd take Gordon to bitch to high heaven about it.

Gordon hated jewelry. If a sponsor hadn't donated it, they weren't allowed to wear it. End of story.

A soft knuckle rap caught her attention. "Come in."

The door swung open, and Dainty, enveloped in cuteness, stood framed in the opening. "Are you busy?"

"Just looking up stuff on the computer."

Dainty noticed the television on and shifted her attention to the competition.

"She's cute," Aspen murmured.

"She's a bitch."

Aspen felt the corners of her mouth tip up.

"And she's mean," Dainty added, eyes focused, laser-like, on the broadcast. Her voice became soft, almost disembodied as she concentrated hard on her rival. "I can take bitchy and I can take mean. Hell, I was raised on it. What I find hard to deal with is bitchy *and* mean." She turned her head toward Aspen. "You know?"

Aspen volumed up the sound.

"In other news today, red tape holds up new construction at Cowboy Stadium," the coed announced. Her face went suddenly blank. She stared at the camera, doe-eyed. "Hmmm . . . don't think I'd want to go there if that's all that's holding it up."

Aspen barked out a laugh. A faint strain of contained chuckling filtered through the speakers. The cameramen, who could be unforgiving, were probably in stitches, having a rollicking good time at the poor intern's expense. Aspen looked at Dainty and knew they shared a simultaneous thought: This would make it onto the "Stupid Outtakes" Christmas video.

Aspen gave a slow head shake. "How do you suppose she got into SMU?"

Dainty pretended to meditate on the notion. "I think there might be a building on campus with her grandfather's name on it."

"I see." Aspen paused and considered her empty water bottle.

"Yeah, well, like my blue-haired, blue-blooded grandmother's always quick to remind me, this isn't rocket science. You don't have to think — you just have to be able to read from a script."

"Ouch." Aspen winced in acknowledgment. She, of all people, knew of the internal scars cutting words could leave.

"Well, I don't want to talk badly about other people. But you know how some

147

people drink from the fountain of knowledge? Well, that chick just gargled."

Aspen laughed. "We should beat her to death," she said, then winked to show she didn't mean it. The reality was, that was the kind of gaffe that endeared you to the viewers. She could only aspire to be that clever. Trouble was, she had an idea the SMU intern wasn't amusing at all — that the vacuous thoughts in her head were hotwired to her tongue.

"So, why are we checking out a vacant house?" Dainty dropped not very daintily onto the buttery leather loveseat beneath the television. She propped the heels of her alligator boots up on one of the sofa arms and shoved a down-filled decorator pillow beneath her neck.

"Because Gordon said so."

"Nice office."

"It belonged to Bill Wallace," Aspen confessed. "I only got it when Gordon gave me Bill's job."

"I don't get it," Dainty said, dazzled and uncomprehending. "You hadn't been working here all that long. How come he didn't promote Stinger Baldwin?"

"Because he fired Stinger the day he hired me."

"What about Tig?"

"I'm not sure." She wanted to finish reading the article, but Dainty had other ideas. In an hour and a half, it'd be midnight, and since neither photographer had returned from the field, the TCU intern wanted to take a company car to the location and get a feel for the place — maybe run a few lines — before Reggie showed up.

"Kirk House has a reputation. And there aren't any lights. You're not afraid?" Aspen challenged. As if.

Dainty flashed a beauty-pageant smile. "Hey, don't worry about me. I do some of my best work in the dark."

Aspen had a feeling they weren't talking about the same thing.

But the intern had a point. If they got out to Kirk House and walked around the place . . . maybe picked out a spot where Reggie could shoot the footage . . . came up with a few ideas . . . it'd give her a chance to rehearse, and they could cut their time in half.

And it wasn't as if they'd hear actual screams . . . right?

Maybe a coyote or two . . . like the kind that killed Stir Fry. Serial killers of the animal kingdom. That's probably what got this urban legend started in the first place.

"Fine. I'll leave him a voice mail with

directions. He can head out there when he finishes whatever he's doing. So . . . is that SMU intern really that mean?"

"She's still a couple of terrorists short of a jihad, but I'd watch her if I were you. Her daddy has money and she wants an anchor job bad enough to kill for it."

"And you?" Aspen parried.

Dainty expelled a wistful sigh. "I thought I did. But my priorities changed. Did you know I started a detective agency?"

By eleven o'clock, Aspen had the keys to a company car — a low-slung Ford Crown Victoria Gordon got a deal on at a fleet auction several months before — and she and Dainty were on the highway. Beyond the glow of the city lights, the countryside rolled by like bolts of navy-blue fabric unfurling. It took a while for the car's heater to warm their shared space, but talking girl-talk over the music of Evanescence that someone left in the CD player took a bit of the edge off the trip. Then the track with "My Immortal" leaked through the speakers. Raw with humiliation, thoughts of Granger that Aspen had managed to suppress floated to the surface.

She felt a sudden prickle in her nose. Her stomach gave a nasty flip. The unexpected

150

tears she wanted to cry turned into a splitting headache.

There had to be a better way of dealing with this unfortunate Granger thing than coming unglued in front of an intern, for God's sake. She slapped the on-off button and the strains of Evanescence that had presided over their conversation instantly evaporated.

She saw an advancing blur out of the corner of one wet eye as Dainty's hand shot out. "No," drawled the intern, "that's one of my favorite songs. Can't we listen to it?"

"No," Aspen snapped. "It'll make me cry." She shut off the music again; Dainty pushed herself further into the seat back.

Probably thinks I'm a head case.

What the heck? I am a head case.

Humiliation crept over her.

"What's going on, Aspen?"

She looked over and saw that Dainty had twisted in her seat until her back pressed against the door panel. Her infectious laughter and beauty-pageant smile dried up, leaving only a blank, scary expression on her face.

"I'm sorry. That song creeps me out," Aspen lied.

"That's not creepy-song stuff," Dainty declared in the face of Aspen's confession,

151

"that's broken-heart stuff."

For no good reason, the dam that held back her reservoir of tears burst.

"Aww, don't do that." Dainty patted her thigh. "Let's just have him killed. Who is he? I know people. Is he that sheriff? Cops suck. I ought to know. I'm in love with one. Did I ever tell you about the time he arrested me?"

Didn't take the intern long to connect the dots.

"You don't have to do this," Aspen said through a sniffle.

"Yeah, I do. You're the only one at WBFD who's been nice to me. People think because I'm blonde, I'm stupid. But I'm not stupid. I know stuff." The former debutante punctuated her comment with a head bob. She'd abandoned the fetal position and once again sat relaxed in the passenger seat. "What happened? Is this about the mug shot? Because you're not the only one having a bad hair day."

Actually, compared to her ashen face and those raccoon circles beneath her eyes, the hair seemed the least of the glamour shot worries. "So you saw my picture?"

"We all did."

Effing Rochelle and her multiple personality disorder. Gordon's crazy assistant had

152

forced her hand. Now, the only way to put an end to talk about the arrest would be to replace it with speculation as to which one Gordon would fire over the flagrant nepotism violation: Rochelle or Stinger.

"It's about the sheriff," Aspen said, trying to keep the thickening dismay out of her voice.

Dainty head-bobbed, *I thought so,* then treated Aspen's gaping emotional wound with the salve of a mournful "Bless your heart."

"I went to his office earlier today. I walked in on him and another woman."

By the time she finished telling the sad, sordid tale, Dainty — ever the fashion conscious — came up with a viable solution.

"I don't usually drink, but this calls for a double. I'm not much of a drinker, but if you want to hit a few bars after we're done at Kirk House, fine by me. Then we need to find that floozy and smack her so hard her clothes go out of style."

CHAPTER FOURTEEN

The gate to Kirk House was still open when Aspen pulled off the highway and into the drive. A sound like ripping-Velcro came from bumping over the gravel road. Pebbles crunched beneath the tires. By the time they reached the tree line, Aspen's heart had picked up its pace. Gordon's assignment sucked.

"Well, that ought to do it for me." She infused a chipper lilt into her voice that she definitely didn't feel. "I've seen enough. How about you?"

Dainty gaped. "Yikes. Pretty 'nice day for a white wedding' if you ask me."

"No kidding. Gordon thinks we might unearth a good story for sweeps." The man who signed her paycheck got to call the shots.

Dainty said, "Did you bring flashlights?" They exchanged blank stares.

Flashlights — now that would've been a

dandy idea. Aspen wanted to thunk her forehead against the steering wheel.

"Let me get this straight." Dainty sat in the seat with her back ramrod straight, her face toward the windshield and her eyes fixed on some distant point. Using her fingers, she ticked off her thoughts: one, two, three. "You're expecting us to get out of the car without flashlights . . . walk past this dense, dark thicket of trees . . . and stomp around this burned-out house?"

"Yeah." Aspen practically sighed the word.

"Not really." Maybe the intern would pitch a fit. Refuse to participate. Then maybe they could foist the assignment off on Tig or Stinger. "So, are you up for it? Think you can do it?"

"Sure. You got arrested yesterday. It's not like you set the bar real high." Dainty took a deep breath, popped open the electric door lock and stepped out of the car.

Aspen, who knew the way from her earlier reconnaissance mission, met Dainty in front of the hood and they fell into stride. When they'd walked twenty feet or so, the time delay went out on the headlight beams, leaving them in the dark.

"Wait — you didn't lock the car." Dainty grabbed the sleeve of Aspen's peacoat. "What if somebody's out here and they get

155

in it while we're knocking around the house?"

"Oh, great. Now that's all I'll be able to think about. Thanks a bunch." Exasperated, Aspen tugged out the keys and pressed the button on the keyless remote control. From their place near the tree line, she heard the locks engage with an audible click. Even though Dainty was starting to become a pain in the . . . neck, the simple act of locking the car would provide them both with newfound sense of security.

Or false sense of security.

Activating the remote to lock the doors had caused the lights to temporarily engage. As they stood in the pale yellow sweep of the Ford's headlights, Dainty must've been wondering the same thing, because she said, "What if somebody's already inside the car?"

"What're you doing?" But Aspen knew. The intern was scaring her.

"No, seriously. What if somebody got into the car while our backs were turned?"

"Don't you think we'd have heard the door open?"

"Maybe. Maybe not."

"Come on, let's walk," Aspen said, faking enthusiasm in a useless attempt to infuse bravery into her jelly-knees. "The sooner we get this over, the sooner we can leave."

"So you're not going to check to see if somebody's lying in wait for us back at the car?"

"Fine. Wait here."

Dainty gave a vehement head shake. "You're abandoning me? Are you nuts? What if there are little stick people hanging from the trees?"

For no reason other than instinct, Aspen shifted her attention to the stand of oaks. She had to admit Dainty was right. So far, this rapid descent into horror had all the makings of *The Blair Witch Project.* If she left Dainty standing by the tree line, she might well return to find her up in the house, standing with her nose in a corner.

"Damn it, Dainty, why'd you have to say that?"

"Fine by me. Don't check. Let's keep going. You're in charge. I'm just the intern."

This triggered an eye roll on Aspen's part. "Fine. I'll go back to the car to see if somebody snuck in while our backs were turned."

She pivoted on one heel and stormed back to the Ford in the vapors of fury, stopping several feet from the hood before activating the remote. A chirp came from the car as the locks clicked open. With her frayed nerves sparking, she yanked the door handle hard enough to dislocate a finger. For good measure, she shot the intern an over-the-shoulder glare. While Dainty stood on tiptoes, breathing down her neck, she double-checked the interior in the subtle glow of the dome light.

"No bogeyman. You happy now?"

"Yes. Overjoyed. Completely ecstatic."

Aspen slammed the car door and pushed the remote's lock feature. Headlights brightened long enough to illuminate the driveway in a gold wash of light that faded out at the tree line. She did a quick visual scan of the area, looking for telltale signs of wildlife that might send them stampeding back to the car: cracking sounds drifting out from the darkness . . . the rustling of dead leaves suffused with mold . . . beady eyes reflected in the headlights coming from the trees and beyond . . . humanoid stick figures woven with branches and suspended from the trees . . .

Before they reached the eerie mansion's concrete foundation, the headlights extinguished themselves again. The moon shone through thin, perforated clouds, making them look like huge gray doilies floating across the sweep of midnight-blue sky.

"I don't like this," Dainty whispered.

"What's not to like?" Aspen said, trying for bravado with a quivering voice. "Okay, so do you hear anything? Because I don't."

A cold breeze whispered past openings that had once been windows on the second floor. Wind gusts whistled through cavities that had previously supported vents for the attic.

Chills snaked up Aspen's spine. "So I've seen enough. How about you?"

"I'm good."

Then the reconnaissance mission went to hell.

A violent, visceral scream pierced the night. It erupted out of nowhere, followed by a shriek frightening enough to clot blood. The din reverberated throughout Kirk House, echoing off the walls like theater sensurround before reprocessing itself within the mansion's canyon-like acoustics.

The women supplied guts-out, bloodcurdling, murder-in-progress screams of their own. They fled the house through the enormous gap that had once held the Kirks' massive, double front doors. In the mad scramble to escape, they broad jumped the shallow steps, then ran full throttle, with the flaps of their coats whipping back and a veil of dust shimmering up from their footfalls.

"Give me the keys," Dainty shrieked.

The hell you say.

"Keys! Give me the damned keys."

Aspen's lungs burned. Pounding footfalls jarred her thoughts.

Automatic door openers.

Thinks I'll leave her.

"Now, damn it. Hurry," Dainty snarled.

Sprinting side by side, Aspen passed the keys like an Olympic gold medalist in the relay race. She didn't hear the locks disengage, but when she reached the passenger side of the car, the door popped open with a yank. She flung herself inside as Dainty fired up the engine. The debutante stomped the accelerator with a lead foot. The car powered from zero to fifty in mere seconds, generating enough momentum to slam the passenger door shut.

Behind the wheel, Dainty gasped for breath. "I've had more experience at this kind of thing."

Not that Aspen paid much attention. She twisted in her seat, put the headrest in a chokehold, and tried to see out the rear windshield, but the sight of dust and debris boiling up from the ground obscured all but the jagged teeth of Kirk House.

The company car bumped over the cattle guard and onto the highway. Tires screaming, it went into a slide and fishtailed across

the two-lane road. Physics be damned, a combination of angle, torque and velocity slung Aspen back into her seat; inertia kept her in place. With Dainty behind the wheel, small wonder they weren't pulling a couple of g's.

"What was that?" Aspen panted.

"How the hell would I know?" Dainty snapped, clearly operating under demonic possession.

"It's okay to be scared."

"Not me." Dainty, sporting a diabolical countenance, gave a vehement head shake. With her eyes locked on the ribbon of road unfurling before them, she hadn't let off the foot feed since they slid out onto the highway. "I only ran because you were screaming."

"I wasn't screaming. That was you."

"Hey, I have a great idea. How about we don't tell anybody?"

But Aspen was thinking, *Now why didn't I think of that?*

It took an awkward exchange of several *What the hell?* looks, a few heart-pounding minutes, and a couple of miles of real estate between them and Kirk House before they expelled sighs of relief.

Dainty spoke first, once again posing a question that neither of them really was

to know the answer to. "What was that?"

"Probably a coyote. Maybe two." Aspen bobbed her head, as if doing that trivial act would make it so. She didn't like thinking about the alternative. "I told you about my dog. That I caught one stalking him yesterday."

"I thought you lived in the city?"

"Yeah." Like anybody cared. She knew Dainty was just buying time, trying to figure out a reasonable explanation for that ungodly scream of the damned.

"Oh —" Dainty drawled out the dawning realization. "So is that why you got arrested?"

"How do you know that?"

"We all know it."

"That effing bitch." Rochelle with her multiple personality disorder. "Now I have to kill her."

"Not Rochelle." Dainty cast her a sideways glance. "Tig."

"Tig?" Said on a whoosh of air. "How'd he know?"

"Yeah, Tig." Dainty said with an emphasizing head nod of her own. "I heard him yukking it up in the break room with Chopper Deke."

Nice.

Not nice.

Chopper Deke, the resident perv. Now there's an unholy alliance.

"I wouldn't worry about it." Dainty shot her another sidelong look. "If you're going to be a serious journalist, you'll probably get arrested at least once in your career. I myself have been arrested," she said, as if she'd won the Nobel Prize and had learned to be self-deprecating about it. "Not that I actually did any hard time . . . I managed to get myself un-arrested." Her eyes dipped to her breasts, perfect and curvy beneath the cashmere sweater. "These aren't here just to feed babies," she added, as if disclosing a secret as deep and dark as the Masonic handshake. "They got me a date with the cop who arrested me," she added in a sing-songy voice. "Not that he'd ever admit that's what attracted him to me. But men are shallow."

Aspen supposed it was true that, rather than brains, the average woman would opt for beauty, boobs, and a set of buns that clamped together tighter than a wind-up, cymbal-clanging monkey, because the average man could see better than he could think with his penis.

Listening to Dainty's confession was fine, since neither of them wanted to talk about the reason they found themselves sitting in a greasy spoon attached to the only convenience store within miles.

"We should alert Reggie. Tell him not to come." Aspen pulled her phone out of her pocket and placed it on the table while she tugged off her gloves. But she really wanted to say, *Save yourself.*

"He'll think we're scared."

"*Hello* — we *are* scared."

They commandeered one of the booths at the back of the grill's snack area, with Dainty occupying the bench seat that faced the door. Each time the little bell above the entrance tinkled, Aspen found herself glancing over her shoulder to see who'd come in. There were mostly truckers and other motorists patronizing the store.

Nothing to get jumpy about.

The bell jingled.

Reggie? There was still the possibility that he'd started down to Kirk House without calling to check their status.

Not this time.

A pack of Goths swarmed in wearing black trench coats and dark clothing, like a page straight out of Columbine — times five — only without all the trampling, screaming and mass hysteria. They fanned out across the aisles like marauding Vandals, gathering items off the shelves with the intensity and fury of locusts.

Behind the counter, a sparse-haired elderly man with a creased, weather-beaten face watched them with a cruel stare, like Stalin overlooking the troops at the May Day Parade. Aspen suspected the video camera mounted on the ceiling and aimed at the cash register either didn't work or didn't have a tape in it since the clerk rested one calloused hand protectively against the till. In his rickety condition, he couldn't have stopped the thugs from looting the store if he'd wanted to. But extended summer visits to Aspen's grandparents' farm had taught her that just because rural folk tended to be simple, salt-of-the-Earth people, that didn't make them stupid. Like her grandparents — God rest their souls — this whiskered old geezer'd developed his cunning streak early on. And she figured the hand he'd concealed in the pocket of those hayseed denim overalls was wrapped comfortably around the butt of a small handgun.

Coming here had been a bad idea.

Wishing she'd worn a watch cap, Aspen slunk down in the seat like a cartoon character. Hair the color of bonfire flames wasn't easy to hide, especially in high humidity, and the mouthy little Goth girl she'd run into earlier glided in with them. Only this time, she'd blackened her eyes with face paint to form two large spheres. Spheres with what appeared to be tentacles coming out of them, drawn on with dark liner.

Maybe she intended them to look like spiders. Spiders with an eyeball in each center. Either way, it looked creepy.

"I just figured out who you are." The voice came from behind and to the right. "You're the TV reporter. I knew I'd seen you."

Busted.

Dainty beamed. "How nice that you'd notice me. Even though I only did that one broadcast. But thank you."

"She's not talking to you," Aspen said, clench-jawed, in a ventriloquist's voice. She pulled herself up from her slumped position and gave the Goth girl a bland smile. "Hey. How's it going?"

By way of an answer, the girl turned to her shoplifting friends. "Look, it's the TV chick I told you about."

Ghoulish eyes peering out from pasty faces turned her way in a collective shift. Throat-clearing rumblings came from the other side of the snack area.

"Wicked cool," said a disembodied voice.

Another voice rang out from the pack.

166

"Yo, Paper Cut. You want anything?"

The girl from Kirk House shook her head.

"Paper Cut?"

"My Goth name. What's yours?"

"Aspen Wicklow. I'm the new anchor for
—"

"I said I know who you are." The attitude returned as she pulled a phone from her dress pocket and stabbed the keypad with dark-lacquered nails that poked through fingerless black gloves. "Your Goth name is *Lustful Curiosity.*" Her gaze shifted to Dainty. "Who are you?"

"Dainty Prescott."

"For real? That's your name?" She chuckled without humor. "Dude, that sucks." Slim fingers stabbed the keypad a second time. "Your Goth name is *Bludy Obsess.*"

Clearly repelled, Dainty scrunched her face.

"I'm willing to call you Paper Cut," Aspen said. "I'm even willing to let you call me Lustful Curiosity. But only if I know your real name. Otherwise, like all good things, this conversation has come to an end."

"That's rude."

"We're done. I don't waste time on people who refuse to identify themselves."

The girl did a quick lean in. "Susanna. Susanna Epps," she hissed. "I told him you saw me out there today. I had to. He said this might happen. That you were a sharp cookie. Please don't say anything around my friends."

"Why's that?" Dainty challenged.

"Easy, Dainty," Aspen soothed. To the girl wanting to be known as Paper Cut, she said, "What do you mean: *'He said this might happen'?* Who's 'he'?"

The girl's expression turned fearful. "It'll all come out in due time. Seriously — don't use my name." The Goths had stopped milling about, and started to merge into a pack again. A newfound urgency tinged her voice. "I'm begging you. I'll explain later."

"What's wrong with now?" Dainty again, super-miffed.

"Really. You'll get me killed."

Without warning, a crescent of Goths closed in on their table, making quiet assessments behind serious, reproachful faces.

"They're wicked cool," Paper Cut announced, animated with excitement and full of false cheer. "These are the TV people I told you about. This is Lustful Curiosity. And this is . . ." She cast Dainty a furtive look.

"Bludy Obsess. Pleased to make y'all's acquaintance."

As if telepathically aligned, Aspen and

168

Dainty shared another simultaneous thought: *Not!*

Giving her friends a wan smile, Paper Cut said of the Goths, "They thought I was scamming them, when I told them I'd met you." To Aspen, she said, "Are you on your way to the haunted house? Because that's where we're headed. It's a full moon, and we want to do a séance. Can you think of anything more wicked cool than that?"

"Yeah," Dainty murmured, "the sound of a gunshot."

The bell overhanging the front door tinkled.

Reggie strolled in looking like hell. He must've seen the Crown Victoria parked outside and stopped in to pick up more Red Bull. Reggie lived on that stuff.

Aspen viewed him in stages — muddy high-tops, hairy ankles, then furry legs with scars on the knees, and camouflage fatigues that had been hacked into shorts. The rumpled T-shirt beneath his long trench coat had a WBFD decal ironed on the chest where a pocket should've been, and the lanyard around his neck that held his credentials hung hopelessly lopsided.

Apparently she wasn't the only one having a bad hair day. Despite the ponytail and backward ball cap, Reggie's oily, unmanageable mess had taken on a life of its own — like Medusa with a rubber band.

He held up a skinny arm and flared his fingers. "What's shakin'?"

Aspen shot Dainty a lethal glare. True, she didn't have a clue as to the goings-on in this place, but if the old adage about safety in numbers meant anything, maybe now would be a good time to return to Kirk House.

"Over here." She waved the photographer closer. Instead of moving into the makeshift dining area, he pointed to a set of coolers lining the walls. The glass door swung open and he grabbed a four-pack of the energy drink before heading over to their booth.

Poor bastard. Thinks we're making new friends.

Wonder if he'll pick up on the panic vibes.

"Yo." Reggie greeted the Goths with a hand sign. Apparently, this was a magical gesture, because the unpleasant tension that had gradually become palpable immediately subsided. "So, you ladies ready to roll?"

She looked at him hard but he didn't seem to get the message.

Paper Cut hung back. She caught her friends' attention and jutted her chin at Aspen. "She wants me to ride with them."

It was a real *ad-lib* moment. Like being

singled out in a Method acting class, only without the possibility of getting a good grade or landing a plum role. And, oh yeah, these people could conceivably kill you.

An obvious leader emerged from the pack. He wasn't as big as some of the other toughs, but his presence was as overshadowing as a wall cloud. If not for an ominous deadness shrouding his eyes, the blue-black Mohawk, black Victorian clothing, and the silver lightning bolt piercing one brow would've invited ridicule. Pin-dot pupils looked like ice-pick tips. Aspen instantly felt the burn of his laser-like stare. The man possessed crocodile chromosomes, and those genes had assigned him the ability to pick up on her pheromones of fear.

"Oh. Em. Gee," Dainty muttered, "it's *Betelgeuse*."

No kidding. Before the night was over they'd probably need the services of a bio-exorcist.

Paper Cut thumbed at Aspen. "She doesn't remember how to get there, so she asked me to ride along."

Reggie nodded. "Wicked cool. Let's roll."

As the Goths cleared out, some heading for the cash register while others ferried their stolen snacks to their vehicles, Aspen and Dainty gaped.

Paper Cut said, "Let's go." She patted the air in a downward motion. "And be cool."

Out in the company car, Aspen slid into the driver's seat while Dainty and Paper Cut jockeyed for position to see who'd ride shotgun. One by one, Goths pulled out of the parking lot and headed down the highway with the taillights of their vehicles receding into the darkness. For a moment, Aspen thought Dainty had decided to become the bigger person by letting Paper Cut ride in the front seat. When the intern got into the back and unthreaded her belt from the loops of her tailored wool slacks, it turned out that good manners had nothing to do with the decision.

"Just so you know," Dainty said with authority, "if you make one move to harm either one of us, I'll wrap this belt around your neck and hang you over my sink like a kitchen witch."

Aspen's eyes cut to the rearview mirror.

"Seriously," Dainty said with emphasis, "who the hell are you?"

"Stop it. She's just a kid."

But Paper Cut was too busy inching her hand up the hem of her black dress to protest.

"Oh my God, she's got a gun," Dainty screamed.

With lightning speed, she lassoed Paper Cut's neck with the belt, wrenching it tight enough to pin the back of the Goth's head against the headrest. Dainty hadn't counted on the girl's quick reflexes. She'd somehow managed to jam her fingers between her skin and the angry bite of leather, enough to gasp out an explanation that left them momentarily speechless.

CHAPTER FIFTEEN

"I'm . . . a . . . cop."

Then Paper Cut's body went unexpectedly limp.

Dainty jumped back, releasing her hold on the belt.

"Oh my God, you killed her," Aspen said. Shocked into silence, they exchanged terrified glances. "Do something."

"What do I look like — a nurse?" Dainty snapped.

"No, but you didn't look like an assassin, either, until now."

A twitch of movement that started near Paper Cut's eye radiated down to her jaw. In seconds, she was gasping for breath, clawing at her neck and sputtering, "Air."

Aspen hit the electric-window button, and the glass slid halfway down.

Dainty struck the Goth in mid-back with her fist.

"What are you doing?" Aspen yelled.

174

"Trying to help."

"She didn't swallow anything, you twit. You nearly strangled her."

"Don't call me a twit. I am not a twit. You're the twit."

"I'm not the twit."

"You're both twits," said Paper Cut, who'd almost completely recovered except for the rapid intake of air gulps and an angry welt on her throat, now visible beneath the dome light. "Have you lost your mind?" she said over her shoulder.

"Talk fast," Aspen said.

"My name's Susanna Epps. I'm an undercover officer —"

"Bullshit." That coming from the former debutante.

"I'm working a case for Sheriff Spike Granger —"

Ha.

Spike only had one female deputy — Sheila — and he didn't think much of her. Aspen shut her eyes, assaulted by the unbidden image of Granger with that tramp on his lap, still seared into her mind from earlier in the day. Her eyes rolled up in their sockets. With a stinging slap to the back of the skull, Dainty encouraged them to snap back into place, yanking her out of the past and into the present.

"Ow, ow, ow. Did you just hit me?"

"No."

"Yes, you did." Aspen looked to the Goth for confirmation. "You saw it, right?"

"Would you two put a lid on it?" Paper Cut massaged her neck, wincing under the pressure of her own tender touch.

"Show us your badge," Dainty demanded.

"I'm not crazy enough to carry a badge. You think I want to get killed? Do you even know what 'undercover' means?" Eyes lined with black face paint dipped to Dainty's breasts. "Oh, yeah, I'll bet you do."

"What's that supposed to mean?" Dainty yelled into the hormonally charged air.

"Knock it off." To the Goth, Aspen said, "Got any ID?"

"Not on me."

"You don't work for Spike. He only has one female deputy and her name's not Susanna."

"I'm Sheila. I'm assigned to the task force."

"You're Crazy Sheila?" Embarrassed, she quickly apologized. "I'm sorry. That's what he called you. He said he only hired you to get the EEO prick over in Personnel off his butt."

"He hired me because I can pass for a teenager. They needed to put someone into

176

the high school. He put the paperwork together and sent it over to the school. Next thing you know, I'm enrolled. The principal's the only one who knows."

"Why'd you say your name was Susanna Epps?"

"That's the name on my UC DL — my undercover driver's license. It says I'm fifteen."

"Why don't you carry it?"

"There's a guy in the group whose dad's a cop. UC licenses come from the Texas Department of Public Safety. They start with certain numbers, like encoding, so if you're stopped by the highway patrol the state trooper realizes you're UC, assumes you're on a case, and doesn't out you."

Aspen had heard of this. "Why should I believe you? You told me *your* dad was a cop."

"That's before I realized you were Granger's girlfriend. Then I remembered. I was there the day you came down with a camera guy to interview him about the overcrowded prisons."

Aspen would've corrected her. Would've said she *used* to be Granger's girlfriend, but Dainty had pulled out her cell phone and started stabbing the display screen with a fingertip.

"What're you doing?" Aspen and Paper Cut chorused.

"Making a call."

It took a few beats for Aspen's short-term memory to kick in. Earlier in the evening, when they were talking about getting arrested, Dainty'd mentioned her boyfriend was a cop.

Paper Cut's eyes resembled bivalves with legs. She sat through the silence with an occasional blink.

Dainty said, "Hey gorgeous-and-talented, *c'est moi.* Hey, do you know a chick named Susanna Epps?" Her words came out soft and kittenish, but her face went suddenly hard. "What about Sheila? She's supposed to be on the task force." And then, *"What?"* She practically shrieked the word.

Everyone exchanged awkward glances.

"Right," Dainty said, her voice slightly subdued but returning to normal. "I remember. Okay. Love you. Bye." She clicked off her phone and stared at Paper Cut. "Oh. My. God." Her gaze cut to Aspen. "I choked an undercover cop." Then she flopped against the backseat and wailed, "Oh my God. Ohmygod, ohmygodohmygod."

"Tell her it's all right," Aspen urged the Goth.

"It's all right."

"Ohmygod, I'm going to jail and my mug shot will look as bad as yours."

Aspen rather doubted it.

Building on her exasperation, she addressed the undercover Goth. "Would you do something, please, or I'm going to have to climb back there and beat the living daylights out of her?"

It took several minutes for Dainty to calm down. But once she did, they listened in stunned silence as Paper Cut, aka Susanna Epps, aka Sheila of the Sheriff Granger variety, filled them in as to how, because of her size and youthful appearance, she'd been assigned to infiltrate the Goth group. As a *baby bat* — a newcomer to the Goth scene — the members weren't entirely comfortable with her, and watched her closely.

"Do you remember that girl the authorities found eviscerated a few months back?" Paper Cut asked.

Aspen had only a vague recollection.

Three months before, she'd been in the middle of finals at the University of North Texas. Then Gordon hired her to fill the investigative-reporter position vacated by Stinger Baldwin. Anything else that happened during that time period melded into a big, fat blur.

"I'm not familiar with the details."

"No? I would've thought Sheriff Granger filled you in."

She shook her head.

"The victim was a Goth," Paper Cut said. "A *pregnant* Goth. Nobody seems to know what happened to the newborn."

"And you think one of them did it?"

"I don't know. The Goths were using Kirk House as a hangout long before I came on the scene. Can we please go? The guy with the Mohawk — Plex Rominus — he doesn't trust me."

Aspen started the car. They'd already taken too long, and she had no intention of getting anyone killed tonight or any other night.

180

CHAPTER SIXTEEN

Right before Aspen pulled off the main road and into the driveway leading up to Kirk House, Granger's deputy issued a stern warning.

"Once we get out of the car, you don't know anything about me. To you, my name's Paper Cut. We're not friends. You gave me a lift; I gave you directions. *Quid pro quo.* That's it. You ever see me again, you don't know me. You see me in uniform, you don't know me. You see me with Goths, you sure as hell don't know me." Distress puckered her lips.

Aspen felt a thrill of terror. Harsh truths should be glossed over. Now that the jig was up, it was hard to remember that only hours ago, Paper Cut had made a believable fifteen-year old.

"I want to keep in touch."

"No." Big head shake. "You don't."

"I do. Sex, drugs and death are three of

the four media food groups. There's a story here, and I want an exclusive."

"Get your information from Granger."

"I can't. I'm no longer with him."

"Since when? Five o'clock this afternoon? Because I heard you were having dinner at his house."

Aspen shook her head. "He has someone else."

"Who told you that?"

"I saw her. He's carrying on with another woman."

"You're wrong."

"No. It happened today. I caught them together."

"Then he's an idiot. Look, I have to scram. Hanging out with you is compromising my safety."

Reggie had already arrived in the ENG van, WBFD's electronic newsgathering vehicle, and was setting up to shoot video. Equipped with a microwave beam capable of transmitting news live on the air for up to sixty miles, the ENG van came with spools of cable, an input-output panel with connectors, an editor — two tape machines joined together so scenes of video filler known as B-roll could be edited into a news package to be shown in conjunction with the live reporter — and an extendable mast to raise the transmitting antenna in order to send the video signal back to the receiver located in Fort Worth.

At the moment, Reggie was unspooling cable, and since this involved a bit of preparation time, Aspen used the opportunity to juice more information out of Paper Cut.

"She's blonde . . . the lady he was with. Long hair like a palomino, legs like a racehorse. Pretty."

"He's into you, okay?"

"I know what I saw. What I'm asking is, whether you've seen her before?"

"Sounds like the woman on that flyer he distributed."

"What flyer?" Aspen watched for Goths straying from the pack, but that still didn't satisfy Paper Cut.

"One of you keep an eye on the back window. I don't need any of these dirtbags sneaking up on me." Her dress had ridden up slightly. She disappeared below the front dash long enough to readjust the leg holster and smooth the fabric back down. Then she popped open the lock, opened the door and slung out a leg. As she alighted from the vehicle, the last thing she said was: "You're wrong about Granger. If he made you a promise, he'll keep it, or die trying."

The door slammed shut and she moved away from the car, into the shadows and past the trees. The next time they noticed her, after Reggie had turned on the camera light to get a quick reading, she'd assimilated into the pack.

Dainty crawled over the seat and landed on the passenger side.

"What in the hell have we gotten ourselves into?" Aspen whispered, still caught up in the spell.

"I don't know," Dainty mouthed without sound.

"Am I the only one wanting to pack up and go home?"

Without taking her eyes off the Goths, Dainty shook her head.

"We're in way over our heads," Aspen said softly.

"That's the understatement of the year." Dainty nodded, still dumbstruck. "Did you bring a gun?"

She wanted to tell her that the PD had confiscated her gun. That they were keeping it as evidence until her trial. And that the only thing she had in the event they needed a weapon was her car keys and pepper spray.

"We need a gun," Dainty said in a hushed whisper.

"A big one."

What they really needed was to get Reggie. To make like a shepherd and get the flock out. Let the cops handle it. Catch the two A.M. movie and report back to Gordon that the so-called screams that had been reported were not an urban legend, but were actually the quavering cries of the *Canis Latrans* — or "singing dog" — keeping in touch with their coyote kin.

She made this suggestion to Dainty.

"Fine by me."

"Go tell Reggie there's nothing to report. That we're ready to go."

"You go tell him."

"Fine," Aspen said through a huff of air. "We'll both go tell him."

As they made their way up to Kirk House, Dainty caught her by the arm. "How do we get out of here without those misfits realizing something's wrong?"

"I get your point. We'll do a fake broadcast without mentioning the screams. Then we'll invite the Goths to be on TV. Everybody wants to be on TV, right?" Aspen nodded along with her monologue as if doing so would lend legitimacy to her claim. "Maybe we'll ask them if we can video their séance."

"Have you lost your ever-lovin' mind?"

"Scratch the séance. We'll do the fake broadcast, get Reggie, and go."

Aspen wished Dainty had never planted the *Blair Witch* idea in her head. The pseudo-broadcast with a backdrop of Goths was scary enough without the seeds of little stick people suspended from tree branches germinating in her mind. By the time they wrapped up, she half expected to turn around and see one of the Kirk brothers materialize in the corner of the house, nearest the window he'd been shot through. If one of the Goths had held a flashlight beacon up to his face, she would've run screaming for the car and never looked back.

A half hour later, they wrapped up for the night. Reggie called Aspen over while he packed up the ENG van. "Heard you did a little time in the slammer."

"Does everybody know?"

"Not everybody. There are people living in caves in Afghanistan who haven't heard."

"Can we not talk about it?"

He ignored the question. "My grandfather has a ranch in west Texas. Coyotes are always killing sheep. Did you know an adult coyote can bring down a calf? And a pack of them can bring down a full-grown cow?"

She didn't know that.

"Some of those counties out there get government funds to pay out bounties."

She wished Tarrant County had such a

program. And that she could collect a bounty big enough to pay the tab for her arrest.

"My grandfather kills 'em and sticks their heads on the fence posts."

"What — as a warning to other coyotes?"

He shrugged. "It's just something he does. Last time I talked to him, he was paying twenty-five dollars to anyone who'd deliver both ears of a coyote."

Aspen winced.

"People around here don't realize what they're capable of. They'll eat anything. If their food source dries up, they'll eat plants and nuts and berries. They wreak havoc on the deer population. And they love to eat the baby fawns."

"Oh, stop. I can't take it," Aspen said, doing a little face scrunch.

"No, really," he said. "What you did was a good thing. You should get an award. Just last week, my grandfather's boxer went outside right before bedtime. He saw a coyote coming up near the house and took off after him. My granddad's dog was going to kick its ass. He got about twenty feet from the coyote, and five more came out from the trees. That boxer retreated like the French."

Reggie turned out to be a wealth of

information. Perhaps he could testify on her behalf as an expert witness.

"That's how they operate. They send the Mata Hari of coyotes in to lure dogs away from safety. Then the pack jumps them. Pretty grisly."

Remembering the horrible pitch of Stir Fry's screams made her gorge rise, and she didn't need to hear any more.

Reggie finished packing up the ENG van while Aspen and Dainty headed back to the company car pretending nothing had gone wrong. Aspen wanted to glance over her shoulder in search of Paper Cut to make sure Granger's deputy was safe, but she didn't dare. The camera lights had long been extinguished, leaving nothing but an eerie glow from a dozen or so candles beneath the light of the opalescent moon. The crunch of gravel underfoot brought Aspen a sense of relief. She liked the sound of it, especially knowing such noise would act as a deterrent to all things slithery.

Even though she and Dainty were locked safely inside the Crown Victoria with the motor running, the low-lights on, and the front of the car pointed toward the gate, Aspen couldn't shake off the feeling that they were being watched — and not in a good way. It wasn't until Reggie started the

ENG van and turned on the headlights that the tension drained from her shoulders. She knew the meaning of "siege mentality" and this had been a good example.

When Aspen pulled out of the gate, bumped over the cattle guard, and eased onto the roadway with Reggie hugging the bumper, Dainty made an observation that put the knots back in her shoulders. "Hmm. That's weird."

Aspen cast her a sideways glance. "What's weird?"

"Did you notice that BMW parked in the ditch back there?"

Her heart jumped. "Get a pen and paper. Do it now. Get ready to take down the license plate." She practically slapped Dainty with every word she spoke. Then she pulled a mid-highway U-turn and drove back toward Kirk House.

But when they reached the culvert where Dainty had last seen the car, it was gone.

So was the candlelight.

Chapter Seventeen

After wrapping up at Kirk House, Aspen dropped Dainty off in the parking lot. She waited until the intern climbed into her silver Porsche and started the engine before driving the Ford around to the back of the building and parking it in one of the fishbone spaces that had recently been repainted. Since Gordon had made things easy on the talent by having the fleet of pool cars all keyed the same, she locked the car and dropped the key into her purse.

After arriving home in her own car, she pulled out the clothes she'd selected for her broadcast debut and hooked the hangers over the molding above the closet door. Then she lay down on the bed and closed her eyes, intending to stay only long enough to process the experience at Kirk House. When the alarm went off a few hours later, she realized she'd slept in her clothes.

Before showering, she checked her answering machine. Sure enough, the pulsing red dot indicated she had messages.

She pressed the button.

"Darlin' —"

She stabbed the Delete button with her finger. Oops. Sorry. Not.

The tone for the next message sounded.

"Darlin' —"

Delete. Oops again.

Another tone, and she thwarted the third call from Spike. "Four times and you're a stalker, buddy."

The tone sounded and the next message took its place.

"Miss Wicklow?"

She winced. Harriet Ramsey, director of Tranquility Villas.

"It's your father again. We caught him having sex with one of the female residents —"

Aspen sniffed in disgust. The management at Tranquility Villas should rejoice that these dalliances were with women. There'd been a time when the word around town was that Wexford Wicklow could get aroused by just about anything.

"Deal with it." She punched the Delete button.

Call number five came from Spike. As soon as he spoke her name, she sent the call into the ether.

The sixth call came from Loquita Hendrix, also from Tranquility Villas. "Sorry to bother you, Miss Wicklow, but it seems your father paid one of the residents to perform a striptease . . ."

Since this message captured her interest, she listened to it all the way through. Then she made a call of her own. Because of the late hour, she got Harriet Ramsey's voice mail.

"Hello, Mrs. Ramsey, this is Aspen Wicklow," she said with put-on sweetness. "I'm sorry about those pesky staff cutbacks, but when I placed my father in your care, you and the rest of the employees promised that things would be just like they were when he lived at home. And I really want to commend you for fulfilling that promise. He was boinking women back then, too, before my mother showed him the door, so I'm sure he's very happy there. Thanks a bunch." She infused fresh cheer into her voice. "Oh, and tell Mrs. Hendrix that I said thanks for the phone call, but I don't think my father should have to pay extra for entertainment. My understanding is that Tranquility Villas is all-inclusive. But, hey — maybe he forgot. You know he's pushing eighty, right? If you don't like it, teach him a card game."

She dealt with the rest of the messages, delete, delete, delete. Then, she primped and dressed to the nines.

The new wool dress she'd purchased in a tropical weight still had the manufacturer's tags on it, and the tags gave the color as sea-foam green. Gordon insisted the females wear gem tones in solid fabric on-air — no prints except for ties and scarves — because, according to him, those were specific fashions that photographed the best. Misty Knight was allowed to wear pretty much any color she wanted while doing the weather except for green. Gordon said it interfered with the chartreuse background of the chroma key wall and made her look like a disembodied head with hands and legs.

The male anchors still wore suits in muted or dark colors, but the boss let them pretty much choose their shirts and ties. Anything below the waist didn't matter because the clothing the anchors wore couldn't be seen beneath the desk. The previous night, when he announced the "Breaking News" teaser, Steve Lennox had on a pair of drawstring pants beneath the put-together, on-air look. In short, it was all a façade. Smoke and mirrors.

Once Aspen finished dressing and pronounced herself acceptable, she ran fresh water in Stir Fry's bowl out of habit, then caught herself. She no longer had a dog. He wouldn't be coming back. Finally, she set the burglar alarm — a gift from Spike — and locked up the house, waiting beside the nearest window until the little green diode on the security system turned red. With a quick glance around to ensure her safety, she hurried to the Honda and drove toward Interstate 30 with the daily newspaper resting in the seat beside her.

A short time later, the Honda's headlight beams swept across WBFD-TV's parking lot, illuminating the area enough to perform a quick visual scan the way Spike had instructed her. Instead of using her reserved space, which had previously been Bill Wallace's but now had her name stenciled on the wall above the concrete stop, she backed into a random space earmarked for staff parking.

Out of the car, bathed in the orange glow of sodium vapor streetlamps, Aspen mentally gave herself the all-clear sign and locked the Accord. Shoe-horned into a pair of low-heeled Ferragamos, she wouldn't have to run for her life. For now, she felt secure.

She caught her reflection in the driver's

194

window and thought she looked intelligent with a copy of *The Dallas Morning News* tucked under one arm. Before heading toward the TV station's main entrance, she did another visual sweep of the lot and was treated to a view of WBFD's meteorologist, doubled over and heaving next to her silver Audi.

"You okay?" Aspen called out. She took a few steps in Misty's direction, but the honey-blonde weathergirl waved her off. Probably swilled down too many Hurricanes at the corner bistro the night before. Misty had a well-earned reputation as a boozer.

Aspen turned toward the entrance and did a double take. Her eyes narrowed into a squint.

What the . . . ?

Is that a midget stuck to the glass?

She did a tight eye blink.

I'm hallucinating.

A cigar-smoking dwarf in a trench coat and deerstalker hunting cap with fold-down earflaps in a houndstooth weave had his nose and hands pressed to the glass entry like a suction-cupped plush toy. Since the station didn't unlock its doors to the public until eight o'clock weekday mornings, any guests scheduled to appear on the morning

broadcast were instructed to use an unmarked back door with a peephole.

Judging by the row of miniature hand
smudges, he'd pressed himself against each
pane for a better view before affixing himself
to the door. Which probably meant the
rotund character blotting his oily nose
against the glass had no legitimate business
at the studio at four o'clock in the morning.

A little head jerk shook the cobwebs out
of her mind. The man was still there.

*So what's a dwarf — oops, little person —
doing at Channel Eighteen?*

More weirdness at WBFD.

Just once, could I have a normal workday?

She approached the portico with visions
of a perfect news segment disintegrating in
her head. Actually, what she'd had in mind
for her first broadcast on the job as WBFD's
youngest anchor ever wasn't so much disintegrating as it was going straight to hell.

From the moment Gordon gave her the
anchor position — after she'd managed to
snare the attention of CNN with WBFD'S
Public Defender segment on prison overcrowding during her whirlwind gig as an
investigative reporter — she thought that
her troubles were over. That she'd awaken
to the chirps of cartoon birds swirling
around her head, tying satin ribbons in her

hair. But, no. So far, she'd spent the night in jail, found out the man she'd fallen in love with had a bimbo on the side, and gotten the crap scared out of her at a shell of a house where nobody lived, by disembodied screams coming from people she couldn't see . . . yep, she'd landed the plum job, fallen asleep and awakened right back here in Aspenland.

The guy by the door leered at her.

With a chipper "Excuse me," she swiped the keypad with her card, only to have the little fellow attempt to follow her in.

"I'm sorry, but we don't open until eight o'clock." Flashing a polite but detached smile, she body-blocked the door. "You'll need to come back during regular business hours."

He spoke in a helium-balloon voice. "I'm here to see Rochelle." Alcohol fumes carried on the breeze.

Aspen's nose clamped down in self-defense. "Do you have an appointment?"

"Don't need one." Indignant, he balled up a pudgy fist and jammed a Vienna-sausage thumb into his chest. "I'm her boyfriend."

Before Aspen could stop, she barked out a laugh. Rochelle stood five-feet-eight and only liked men who reminded her of Dirty

197

Harry. Not little bitty short guys with backs wide enough for a saddle.

He jammed his hands on his hips. "What's so funny?"

"Nothing," she lied. "I'll let her know you're here, Mr. . . . ?"

"Bumgardner. Ulysses S. Bumgardner."

She found the introduction so howlingly funny she bit her lip to keep from cackling. Ulysses S. Bumgardner epitomized the consequences of a pub-crawler weekend. Without waiting for the pneumatic door actuator to shut on its own, Aspen pressed the glass until the lock clicked shut behind her.

The lobby had an airy feel, due in part to its thirty-foot ceiling and the spiral staircase leading up to the mezzanine where the production staff had their offices. As she walked in and glanced to her left, she should've seen Rochelle LeDuc, the brunette, stylishly dressed, fifty-ish secretary-slash-office-manager buzzing around the desk. On a normal day, regardless of the temperature, Rochelle would've had her dark hair upswept in a chignon and her personal fan in her hand, airing out her cleavage as well as the perspiration dotting her forehead.

Instead, Aspen did a double take.

The teakwood nameplate for Rochelle

LeDuc had been removed, replaced with a hand-lettered length of poster board folded into an upside-down "V". It identified the middle-aged, blowzy blonde, wearing what looked suspiciously like Rochelle's flowing wrap with the collar tilted up past her neck, a silk scarf covering her bouffant hairdo and a pair of Jackie-O sunglasses, as Phaedra Peramos. Standing behind the desk in her long overcoat, the woman could've been mistaken for a member of the Gestapo.

Aspen angled toward the desk, pretending to be taken in by the cheap disguise. "Excuse me, ma'am, but can you tell me where I might find Rochelle LeDuc?"

"It's me." Rochelle spoke in the rich, whiskey voice of a drag queen. With hostility crackling all around her, she lowered the sunglasses enough to peer over the top. "But don't call me Rochelle. I'm Phaedra. Phaedra Peramos. I'm Greek."

A scary silence passed between them. Without turning around, Aspen thumbed at the entrance. "Does this pathetic attempt at being *incognito* have anything to do with Mr. Bumgardner?"

"Who?" Glossy red lips curled into a sneer.

"The dwarf stuck to the glass."

Rochelle gave an aristocratic sniff. "I'm

sure I don't know what you mean."

Aspen sighed. Almost within days after she hired on at the news station, she'd suspected a decline in her own mental health would eventually come. She half expected to see and hear things other people standing nearby couldn't. The Wicklows had no family history of mental illness that might suggest a genetic predisposition toward schizophrenia, but her first month at the TV station had been enough all by itself to push a normal person to the brink of insanity.

She decided to test the theory. "There's a dwarf — or maybe he's a midget — stuck to the entry door, Rochelle."

"Shhh." The secretary ducked her head.

"Wait — did you just shush me?"

"Don't say my name." Readjusting her upturned collar enough to shield her face, Rochelle looked up with a blank, chilling expression.

"Don't pretend you can't see him. Mr. Bumgardner says he knows you."

Rochelle scrunched her face as if she'd bitten into a lemon. "Is that his real name?"

"No, it's Grumpy. I'm pretty sure he's not Happy or Bashful."

Sick humor went over Rochelle's head. "Are you certain the name's not DeVito?"

She cast the man a furtive glance.

Aspen hooted. "How'd you meet this guy?"

The contours of Rochelle's face hardened. "He was express-mailed to me from hell." Something painful and ugly seemed to be going on behind the dark glasses, because she flinched. "I need aspirin."

In lieu of sympathy, Aspen unleashed a donkey-bray laugh. Getting one-up on Rochelle rarely happened. "Just how drunk were you?"

Rochelle patted the air in a downward motion. "Can you get any louder? I'm not sure the producers heard you upstairs." She gently pressed her fingertips against her temples. "Anyway, you should be more compassionate. Firecrackers are going off in my skull."

"What'd you do, give him your phone number?"

"I don't remember."

"Oh, for heaven's sake. Haven't you had enough excitement for one year?" She was referring to the beginning of sweeps month when Rochelle went on a vigilante spree in an attempt to find the man who raped, bludgeoned and left her best friend's daughter for dead. For her trouble, Rochelle took a blow to the head with a tire iron before gunning down her assailant in the parking lot of Wild Dick's Bar and Grill.

Ever since the crowbar upside the head, Rochelle hadn't been her usual self. Which should've been a good thing now that her short-term memory was shot. If she couldn't remember what infuriated her, she couldn't hold a grudge. Unfortunately, the incident didn't produce a kinder, gentler Rochelle. Rudeness and sarcasm still dominated her personality.

Back to the problem at hand. Or, rather, the one stuck to the glass.

The persistent little fellow had pressed himself against the door, smashing the side of his face into it until it resembled Silly Putty. So did his splayed, starfish-like hands.

"You should do something before Gordon discovers your stick-on Elmer Fudd doll."

"Knock it off," Rochelle snapped. "I wouldn't make fun of you."

Already did.

"Give me the mug shot." Aspen held out her palm in demand.

"I don't have it."

"Where is it?"

"I threw it away." A claw hand shot out and gripped Aspen's wrist. Rochelle's fingertips tightened around her painfully. Desperation tinged her voice. "You've got to help me. Tell him I don't work here. Tell him I got fired. Tell him I've gone to live in a leper colony, and he should be tested for his own good."

Aspen sucked air. "You didn't sleep with him, did you?" When Rochelle didn't deny it straightaway, she got an ugly visual and spent the next few seconds shaking out her fingers to slough off the risqué images. "Ugh, ugh, ugh."

"Lower your voice." Rochelle glanced around to see if anyone was watching. "How should I know? The last thing I remember is giving him my number. Now are you going to help me, or not?"

Aspen snatched up a pen and scrawled "Rochelle got fired" on a piece of paper. She strode over to the glass doors with purpose in her step, and held up the sign for the dwarf to read. Gimlet eyes narrowed. Then he scowled. She gave him her best palms-up shoulder shrug.

"I'm sorry," she mouthed without sound, not adding the obvious: *I'm sorry my coworkers are undiagnosed schizophrenics, bipolar or borderline personalities.*

He turned his back on her. A moment later, the main line rang at Rochelle's desk. Simultaneously, a stumpy arm raised a cell phone to his ear.

"Don't answer it," Aspen warned.

Too late. Rochelle had already picked up.

"WBFD-TV," she announced in a hushed voice. Instant recognition blanched her face. Realizing her mistake, she winced, then launched into one of her low-grade, foreign accents that sounded more Italian-to-English than Greek. "Rochelle LeDuc? That lush? She no longer works here. They had to fire her."

Short pause.

"I don't care what you think. It's true." She looked around in a panic. "And her name's not Rochelle." Another pause as her brow knitted. "I don't care what she told you. That woman was fired for . . . embezzlement . . . yeah, that's it. Embezzlement. She stole a half million in company funds and flew to Belize." Rochelle set her jaw. After a short pause, she opened her mouth, and her cheesy accent slipped away. "Well, Jimmy crack corn, and — you guessed it — I don't care. The point is they can't extradite her so she won't be coming back. You should watch more TV. I think she's featured on *America's Most Wanted* this week. Who am I? My name is Phaedra Peramos. I'm Rochelle's replacement."

Aspen didn't wait for the scorned suitor to walk away. She had an early-morning appointment with Gordon, in his office, at five-thirty, and didn't want to be late.

As she tip-tapped across the marble floor toward the office with *J. Gordon Pfeiffer* stenciled on the door, she viewed her boss in strips, through vertical blinds twisted partially open behind the long glass wall. Seated at his big desk, he held the Metro section of the newspaper up to the light. From her place in the doorway, she caught sight of her flaming red hair in the photograph of a feature story the *Fort Worth Business Press* printed describing her meteoric rise from investigative reporter to anchor. Inwardly smiling, she gave the molding a light knuckle rap.

The station manager leapt to his feet, bounded over and swept her inside along with a good-natured greeting.

This was a rare event, catching Gordon sporting a friendly grin. Most days, he could be found pacing the length of his office with his face permanently flushed, mostly from belting back shots taken directly from the bottle he stowed in his bottom desk drawer. Or, from yelling behind closed blinds until the inner walls vibrated. But today was different. Today, the newspaper article reported that WBFD no longer held the last-place ranking in the Metroplex. Out of sixteen television stations, the one run by J. Gordon Pfeiffer had pole-vaulted into the third-rated slot.

Thanks to yours truly, Aspen Wicklow. Who'd gotten here through pluck and luck, and a teensy-tiny bit of help from Rochelle . . . and — oh, what the heck — she was a big enough person to give credit where credit was due . . . and so thanks also to Spike Granger, without whom she wouldn't have snared the attention of CNN.

Gordon motioned her into one of the new cowhide-covered guest chairs. After CNN purchased footage from her story and the check cleared, he gave Rochelle a proper budget to redecorate his office. She went for a Texana theme with a deer-antler chandelier, a longhorn hat rack and lots of leather. With the money she saved using a suspect furniture source (read: fence), she purchased an oil painting of bluebonnets by Porfirio Salinas (read: stolen) and positioned it above the wall behind the client chairs where the boss could see it.

"How'd it go last night at Kirk House?"

"Reggie shot the house — no screams, but plenty of Goths. Apparently it's become a hangout."

"I see. So how's our little celebrity?" Gordon asked with the gusto of a proud papa.

He thumped the newspaper with his finger. "Nice story. Did you read it?"

Ever critical, his eyes narrowed as he scrutinized her outfit. Of course, the best part of it happened to be the part he couldn't see — the *point d'esprit* teddy from Victoria's Secret — a gorgeous swatch of silk lingerie that fell more into the category of *objet d'art* than undergarment. Nothing caused her to exude elegance or transformed her personality the way slipping into a satiny concoction of fabric and lace did. Wearing such a fabulous one-piece would almost be worth getting hit by a bus and dragged six blocks so the world could see what she had next to her skin.

When he said, "Ready to host the morning broadcast?" she knew her debut outfit passed muster.

"I'm nervous, but I can do it." She'd been shoring up her confidence with pep talks all weekend. No matter what popped up on the teleprompter, no matter how bad the storyline, she wouldn't become emotionally involved. Or misty-eyed. Or break down in sobs at the first mention of tragedy.

Deliver the news.

It was just that simple.

"Oh, there's one other thing before you go on air . . . have you seen a copy of *The*

Dallas Morning News?"

"I have one, but I haven't read it yet. Why?" She glanced down at the paper she'd carried in with her.

"Why don't you leave it with me?" he said, not altogether good-naturedly. "You can pick it up after your show."

She handed it over.

"Break a leg."

"Thanks."

He stood, ushered her to the exit and swept her out. As soon as the door clicked shut behind her, she could've sworn she heard the *thunk* of a newspaper landing in the trashcan.

Chapter Eighteen

Inside the studio, the first hour of Aspen's debut broadcast went without a hitch. Most of the time, she settled back in her chair at the anchor desk, waiting for the producer to cue Misty Knight to give the weather update, or Steve Lennox, who handled the morning sports broadcast.

Misty had positioned herself in front of the green screen, a blank chartreuse display screen the technical people called the chroma key wall. The screen was painted bright green because the color was the furthest pigment from skin tone — with the exception of the Hulk. The video camera was pointed at the screen where the meteorologist would stand. According to the cameramen, who liked to awe new employees with painstaking explanations of the green screen's mechanical workings, the video signal went through the video production switcher and a special circuit called a chroma keyer would pick up on the green color. Everywhere the camera registered the green color, the keying circuit would substitute another video signal in place of it. In the case of Misty's weathercast, a weather map was substituted.

The explanation confused Aspen until Reggie, who'd turned out to be her favorite photographer, positioned her in front of the blank green screen by way of illustration, and fed into the production switcher a video of an orgy at a famous area swingers' pad. When cameramen included it in their "Stupid Outtakes" video and showed it at the annual Christmas party a few weeks before, the intricate workings of the chroma key wall suddenly made sense.

At the moment, Max, the station's other rising-star cameraman, had fed a weather map into the system for the viewing public. As the on-air talent watched Misty pointing out invisible air currents and temperatures for the Metroplex, moving her hand in a sweeping flourish as if she could actually see the graphics behind her, in reality the puffy cumulous clouds, wind current arrow and lightning bolts appeared on a nearby monitor. Looking sharp in a tailored red suit, Misty gave a head toss that sent her highlighted hair flipping back over her shoulders.

Few of WBFD-TV's viewers would've guessed that earlier, she'd been in the parking lot heaving her guts out.

Over the past several weeks, her behavior had become unpredictable. Steve Lennox, Aspen's morning cohost, complained about heavy objects being hurled at him from inside Misty's office as he walked down the corridor. Even Gordon had found her snappish. About the time Misty's irritable personality scab healed over, Rochelle would pop in to pick at it. Now, the weathergirl fussed with the waist of her jacket, sucking in her stomach and pressing her hands against the buttons.

"Do I look fat?" she asked of the room at large.

Nobody commented on her second-skin skirt. "Well, do I?" she demanded with the petulance of a five-year-old.

A disembodied male voice floated out from behind one of the cameras. "Don't feel bad if you put on a few holiday pounds. Count your blessings. Fat people are harder to kidnap."

Misty whipped around. Steam practically coiled from her nostrils. "Who said that? Show yourself." When nobody owned up to the observation, she branded him a coward.

"This is a serious question and I expect a serious answer. Do I look fat?"

Echoes of "no" resounded through the studio. The weathergirl locked her attention on the camera lens and addressed the viewers with a chipper lilt.

"What does the work week have in store for you? Well, we have pretty strong winds possibly gusting up to sixty kilometers — what the hell?" Her smile slipped away. Hands dropped to her sides in frustration. It was like watching a person with bipolar disorder plummet, without transition, from the manic phase directly into the depression stage. Hand on hip, she clipped her words. "What's the damned deal with the metric system? You know I don't understand that. Where'd you bozos get this information — Canada? Damn it, I hate Canada." She abruptly looked down at the remote in her grip. "What the hell's wrong with this clicker?" She raised her hands in disgust and stormed off the set with the mike still activated. "Can we come back to me later?" A sigh huffed out. "Did I mention I hate Canada? Stupidest white people on the face of the Earth."

Her words carried a certain amount of hang time.

Aspen sat in stricken silence. Undoubtedly, Misty's recent distaste for Canadians had an indirect tie-in with being unceremoniously dumped by a Dallas Stars hockey player; but no matter what happened in the personal lives of the on-air talent, Gordon expected them to conduct themselves like professionals. Now, for no good reason, the morning broadcast had gotten off to a rocky start.

"And . . . we'll come back to the weather in a moment." Looking for help, Aspen shifted her gaze to her cohost and infused a chipper lilt into her tone. "What's going on in sports, Steve?"

"Well, Aspen, I'm glad you asked." Decked out in a blue blazer with a red-and-blue rep tie, few would guess a pair of Bermuda shorts exposed Lennox's hairy legs. He flashed a mouthful of veneers at the camera. "Last night's baseball score — what? Did I just say baseball? I meant football. I got my balls mixed up." Realizing his mistake, he said, "Damn it. Come back to me later." To no one in particular, he yelled, "Which one of you cretins monkeyed with my copy?"

While they went to a commercial break, the producer skulked over and shoved a script insert into her hands. Aspen did a quick review before he cued her for the drive-time broadcast, scouring it for words like "tragedy," "dead," "grisly," "beyond recognition," or similar words used in conjunction with children, animals or the elderly. The leadoff story was —

Oh, no. Not this.

How would she ever get through this without bursting into tears? It was the story from last night's "News at Ten" show. Two unidentified assailants had gunned down a young couple in a Dallas County suburb.

She scanned the page for details. *Pulled into their driveway after a shopping trip . . . ski masks . . . pump shotgun . . . killed husband . . . blew off wife's arm . . . wife fighting for life in hospital . . . two children and a baby on the way.*

A familiar burn started behind her eyes. She ripped her gaze from the script and fanned her face. This was how it always started: eyes burning, chin quivering, voice cracking . . . and then guts-out wailing.

She couldn't let Gordon see her puddling up. Gordon hated crybabies.

"What's wrong?" Lennox gave her a slit-eyed look.

"Allergies." She pinched the bridge of her nose and fluttered her lashes enough to beat back the tears.

Across the room, one of the production assistants opened the back door to the studio. A swarm of children swirled in, ignoring his bid for quiet. Abruptly, the studio echoed with the raucous buzz of merriment.

In the midst of calamity, she tried to foist the breaking news off on Lennox by sliding the page on top of his pile of notes.

"Hey — wait a minute." He reared back his head.

Halfway to panic, she said, "Rock, paper, scissors."

"All right." Lennox counted, "One, two, three," as each pounded their palm with a fist.

Lennox flat-handed paper. Aspen scissored her fingers through the air.

She gleefully squealed out, "Yes. Scissors cut paper. You lose." She glanced back at the monitor and was treated to a wild-eyed view of herself.

The producer cued her with a *Westward-ho!* motion.

"And, it's back to me." Said wearily. "Let's take a look at traffic, where we have a multi-car pileup. We go now, live, to Chopper Deke." She fixed a smile on her face and stared at the camera expectantly. "Deke?"

The demented grin of Chopper Deke, a helicopter pilot during the Vietnam War, popped up on the monitor with Aerial

Patrol captioned in the bottom left corner of the TV. As the dagger-eyed, leathery-faced, crew-cut jarhead dipped low and buzzed a couple of cars on Beltline Road, a split screen image appeared to show which Dallas and Fort Worth arteries were clogged. Above the *whuppa-whuppa-whuppa* of rotor blades, Chopper Deke angled hard right. The aircraft lifted back up like a spider on a wind current.

Flying shotgun with Chopper Deke, Traffic Monitor Joey screamed, "This just in from the *'You need help department'* — can somebody down there get this guy evaluated when we land? *If* we land?" He shook out a barf bag, lowered his face into it and hunkered his shoulders.

Cut to Aspen.

She injected false cheer into her presentation. "And now let's see what's up in the weather department. Here's Misty Knight again. Misty, what does the weather have in store for us?"

The camera cut away to Misty, standing in front of the blank chartreuse screen surrounded by a group of bleary-eyed elementary school children. The cameraman zoomed in on a close-up of a speckled child, then panned back to the weathergirl. The viewing audience had just been treated to an outbreak of chicken pox, which Misty had apparently overlooked.

"Thanks, Aspen." Misty launched into a sweeping hand gesture. "We'll climb to the lower sixties this afternoon, and this very low air mass over here is going to cool things off. There'll be more changes in the weather this week — *ha!* No kidding. What'd you expect, you're in Texas, for God's sake." Her posture straightened. The tension in her face relaxed and the furrow that had formed in her brow snapped back into place. Her demeanor returned to that of a professional. "All that coming up in a few minutes."

It was like watching a schizophrenic having a psychotic break. You didn't want to watch, but you were powerless to stop yourself.

Aspen checked the monitor. The weather broadcast had been cleared for one of their advertising sponsors. Without warning, Misty went ghetto on them. "Who wrote this? Was it one of those interns from SMU? I'm working with a bunch of idiots." She glowered at the speckled child. Realization dawned. "Oh, shit. Are you kidding me? Is that chicken pox? Get away from me."

Cut to commercial.

Aspen drooped in her chair. Excising a

molar with plastic utensils would've been easier than delivering the news this morning; yet her cohost sat, relaxed, exchanging small talk with the cameramen. It was almost as if they were doing a parody of the news. Now that WBFD had jumped to the third-rated slot in the Metroplex, jealous employees from competing stations would see this broadcast and have good reason to call them third-rate.

She took her lead from Lennox. Briefly, they sipped scalding coffee from cups they'd stowed beneath the desk. Across the room, the makeup girl blotted Misty's face with a tissue before retreating out of camera range.

Abruptly, the anchors straightened and assumed a professional air. With the diseased child now herded off to one side, Misty rounded up the kids in front of the blank screen. "Remember what we practiced yesterday," she said in a tone that bordered on threatening.

The producer cued her.

WBFD's weathergirl turned her grimace into a bright smile — fake, but luminous. "Isn't this exciting?" She clapped her hands together, then looked into the camera with the electrifying stare of a psychopath. "This morning we have a few budding meteorologists from Mrs. Schmidt's first-grade class

— get down. Yes, you, little boy. I'm talking to you. What the hell? Did you just pee on the floor? God, I hate kids."

Misty stomped off the set with her mike still on. The anchors couldn't identify who she was talking to, but her voice came in loud and clear. "Did I just say that? Well, I do. Little bastards. Whose idea was this . . . Rochelle's? I'm having her killed — is this mike still on? Where the hell's Gordon? I can't work with chimpanzees."

Aspen caught an advancing blur out of the corner of her eye.

The sound of Rochelle's name had brought the dwarf out of hiding. He burst forth from the throng of first graders, brandishing a Saturday night special.

Kids went slack-jawed. Then they screamed. The teacher, who'd turned as white as plaster of Paris, shepherded her charges into a tight ball and hovered over them in a protective stance.

Misty, oblivious to the danger, strutted back into view and resumed the weather forecast. "Where were we? Ah, yes. What does the workweek have in store? Well, if you're worried about catching the flu this season, here's an idea for you. Move. Shun other people. Become Amish." Aqua-blue eyes widened in alarm. "What the hell's going on? I just disappeared off the screen. You make it look like I'm talking to myself. Which one of you idiots pushed the wrong button?" Her voice went suddenly shrewd. "Wait a minute . . ." She raised a hand to her forehead, shielding herself from the canned lighting overhead. Squinting, she peered into the depths of the studio. "Who's the troll? Is this a joke?"

Staring in crazed panic, Steve Lennox pointed to the gun-wielding dwarf. The monitor framed a close-up of Rochelle's angry suitor. To Aspen, Lennox hissed, "Say something."

Terror washed over her. Where was Gordon? She darted a glance at the studio doors.

Nothing.

And the children — Aspen's breath went shallow. Her heart beat like a savage fist.

Usually, Misty's cringe-worthy bouts of intermittent explosive disorder cast a pall of apprehension over the cameramen and on-air talent. Not this time. Once Misty tuned up like a howler monkey, the dwarf's attention was riveted firmly on her. The man's concentration seemed so disconnected that he appeared almost autistic. While the teacher seized the opportunity to quietly shepherd the first graders off the set, Aspen looked around for anything she could use as a weapon to defend them. She saw only cups of hot coffee.

She spoke with more command than she felt. "We interrupt this broadcast to . . . announce that . . . WBFD-TV has been taken hostage. We're coming to you live from our studio where a man has just pulled a gun on the morning anchors . . ."

Misty's gaze flickered to the floor. She let out a scream. "Oh my God — is that a cockroach? Somebody kill it. Reggie — come out from behind that camera this instant and kill the damned thing. Jesus, it's got antennas bigger than most of the penises I've seen."

Chilled by her own mortality, Aspen tried to recall something Spike once said: *More victims survive if they humanize themselves to the perpetrator.* Voice quivering, she tested the theory. "Why are you doing this?"

"I told you" — the spurned man's face flamed — "I want to talk to Rochelle."

"Please put the gun down." Her voice grew thick, as if her tongue had been injected with Novocain. She pressed her knees together to stop the shaking. Even beneath the heat of the directional lights, the temperature seemed to drop twenty degrees.

"Get Rochelle out here." The man's face flamed beet red.

Aspen darted a glance across the studio. Off to one side, concealed from the hostage taker by a thick cotton velvet acoustical curtain hung to block out noise and light from the set of doors directly behind it, Rochelle and Gordon seemed to be hatching a plan. Aspen's pulse throbbed in her throat.

"We have someone looking for her," she said, distracted. "Please put down the gun. Nobody's going to hurt you. And we don't want to get hurt either."

For the first time, the dwarf noticed that the majority of his hostages were missing. He began to rant. "Nobody else moves, or I'll kill her." He pointed the gun at Aspen's head.

An explosion of chills rained down her body. For a moment, the studio blurred before abruptly coming back into sharp focus.

Rochelle's voice boomed in surround sound. "Don't hurt any of these people."

The overhead lights seemed to dim.

"Rochelle? Is that you?" The dwarf looked around, as if trying to pinpoint the location of a voice piped in from the spirit world. "Show yourself."

"No damned way. Put that gun down. The

cops are on the way."

"If you don't come out here and talk to me, I'll kill the redhead."

Aspen slumped weakly against the desk. She scribbled "Ulysses S. Bumgardner" across her notes and slid them over to Steve. In what sounded like a voice-over at a golf tournament, Steve Lennox reported more breaking news.

"Coming to you live from the studio of WBFD-TV, where the morning anchors have been taken hostage by Ulysses S. Bumgardner, a . . . spurned suitor of one of our employees —"

"I heard that," Rochelle yelled. "Don't make me have to come in there and beat you bloody. He is not a suitor. He's a stalker."

The dwarf let out an anguished cry. "You said you loved me."

"I most certainly did not. We met in a bar, for Pete's sake. Even if I did let my mouth overload my brain, you can't hold me responsible for anything I said under the influence of alcohol. I must've been plastered. You can't hold a drunk responsible for what they say just before they pass out."

"You can't have sex with me and then toss me out like yesterday's garbage," he wailed.

Lennox sat up straight. "You had midget

sex? How does that work?"

Beneath the anchor desk, Aspen stepped on his toe.

"Shut up, Steve, you sexually ambiguous, blow-dried putz." To Ulysses S. Bumgardner, Rochelle made an emphatic declaration. "I did not have sex with you. Stop saying that."

"I'm trying to visualize this." Lennox again, staring at his hands as he molded them into finger people and tried to fit them together like sexually active toys.

"Oh, no," Rochelle moaned. "It's coming back to me. That's disgusting. Lord, make it stop."

Lennox fueled the fire. His voice went low, almost conspiratorial. "How does one have midget sex? Do you need a chair? Who gets to be on top?"

Blood whooshed between Aspen's ears. Surrounding sounds went tinny and distant. Aware of her thudding heartbeat, she spoke through clenched teeth. "Shut up before you get us killed."

Still off-camera, Rochelle gave a dramatic sigh. "That's it. I'm joining AA. Now put that gun down and give yourself up. The cops are on the way."

"No," he squawked. "I demand you come in here and talk to me right this minute, or

I'll kill this woman."

"Do what you have to do."

Betrayed, Aspen went rigid. This was it. This was how they'd find her — keeled over in a heap with blood pooling near her ear, Reggie zooming in for a close-up of congealed brain matter . . .

The lights went out.

Aspen grabbed her coffee cup from under the desk and swung it hard. It connected with flesh as Steve Lennox grabbed her by the scruff of the neck and yanked her out of the chair. Both anchors fell to the floor and rolled beneath the desk.

Then things got Western.

The crack of a bullet flashed orange. It pinged against a can light and ricocheted off who-knows-where. Shards of glass tinkled down like a melody struck on a xylophone. Somewhere beyond the anchor desk, a violent scuffle broke out.

The flip of a circuit breaker echoed through the studio, and the lights abruptly came back on.

Rochelle had the dwarf in a headlock. She lifted him inches off the floor until the fight drained out of him. His body went limp. The cheap derringer clattered to the floor. His nose dripped crimson where Aspen had bloodied him up with her coffee mug.

225

A dozen patrolmen swarmed the studio. Each officer jostled for position. At least four of them grabbed limbs and clothing as they took custody of Ulysses S. Bumgardner.

Rochelle straightened her blonde wig. "Show's over," she snapped, then prissed out of the studio.

Aspen and Steve peered over the desk like alligators peeking over a log.

Gordon yelled, "Everybody back to work. Misty, quit bitching and give the damned weather report. And knock off the cursing before the FCC yanks our fucking license, damn it."

So Gordon expects us to act like this is business as usual?

Ha. As usual from the funny farm.

The picture on the monitor panned from police hauling out the gunman to Misty Knight. She'd shirked her tasteful blazer for a Dallas Stars jersey with what appeared to be the universal "No" sign painted on it by an angry fan, and a backward ball cap.

"Good morning from WBFD-TV, I'm Misty Knight, bringing you the *'In Your Face'* weather forecast for the Metroplex. For those who've just joined us, the elementary-school brats we had on earlier are gone, so I'll be rapping the weather

226

today. Give me a beat, Reggie."

Behind the camera, a lanky silhouette grunted out gorilla noises to a peppy cadence. Misty bobbed up and down at the knees like a float on a fishing line.

"I'm here today to tell you howdy,
And our skies are not so cloudy.
If you missed the fanfare, we almost got
  shot;
I'm callin' OSHA 'cause this place ain't so
  hot.
The sky's hazy, but the weather's clear;
Think I'll go out and have a beer.
I need a raise 'cause this place sucks;
If management won't pay, they can just
  get fu—"

The screen went black, and the rest of her routine was censored out with a high-pitched bleep.

Steve Lennox said, "That's lame."

Misty whipped off her ball cap and threw it on the floor like a gauntlet. "Screw you, Lennox. You think you can do better? Where's Gordon? I want my own bodyguard."

The producer cut to Aspen. He twirled his finger in the universal *Wrap it up* signal.

She wrenched her face into a somber

227

expression. "That's all for this morning. This is Aspen Wicklow coming to you live from WBFD-TV, the station that'll go through hell just to bring you the news. Hope you've had fun and we'll see you back here at noon if we don't get our license yanked."

The signature music trailer came on, overhead lights dimmed and the local cutaway faded to black as the morning program switched to the station's national affiliate.

A combination of relief and adrenaline swept through her. In one fluid movement, Aspen rocketed out of her chair, ripped off her mike and threw it on the desk.

"Where's Rochelle?" Ways to commit murder without getting prosecuted raced through her head. "What's this 'Do what you have to do' business?"

CHAPTER NINETEEN

Aspen found the secretary in the break room, sitting at a bistro table with vapors from a cup of hot-and-sour soup snaking up her nose. Using the little hot-mustard packets that came with the take-out order, she was spelling out swear words across the thin film congealing on top of the soup, and bracketing them, artistically, with squiggly designs.

" 'Do what you have to do'?" Aspen shrieked.

Rochelle barely looked up. "Let's not get riled."

"Easy for you to say. You weren't the one with a gun to your head."

A look of boredom settled over Rochelle's face. "Gordon and I devised a plan. I was just ad-libbing until he cut the circuit breakers."

"You could've gotten me killed."

"That's a bit harsh, don't you think?" she

229

asked with a blank, scary expression.

It took a few seconds for Aspen to realize she'd been staring down at her own hands. She'd formed them into a circle in order to gauge whether they'd fit around Rochelle's throat before she actually tried it.

Beyond their view, shoe heels clicked against the floor tiles.

They tabled the conversation long enough to shift their attention to Misty, who'd strutted in pulling at her skirt and muttering. "Damned dry cleaners. Shrunk my favorite suit. I ought to sue." She plunked two coins down the chute of the soft drink dispenser and banged a fist against one of the selection buttons. A loud clunk followed a rolling rumble, and an aluminum can slammed against the opening. Misty picked up her Diet Dr Pepper and snapped open the tab.

Looking directly at Rochelle, she asked, "Do I look fat?"

Aspen held her breath. She hadn't counted on a dicey situation developing in the hormonally charged break room — like the time Henry VIII had his fifth wife killed for continually reminding him of a right turn he made in London when he should've gone left.

Rochelle gave Misty the once-over. After an uncomfortable pause, she said, "No. You don't look fat."

"Really? Because I was thinking about try-ing acupuncture to lose weight."

"Let me know how it turns out." Rochelle again, feigning interest.

For a few seconds, the weathergirl smiled in satisfaction. Abruptly, her mouth went slack. She studied Gordon's office manager with cold scrutiny. "Have you ever had any work done?"

"No. I happen to have good skin, and I stay out of the sun. But if it ever needs to be tucked, sucked or plucked, I'm all for it."

Misty gave her a skeptical nod, pivoted on one heel and sashayed off.

Aspen leveled her gaze. "I think I just saw a pig fly past the window."

"Big deal. She's going to do what she wants to do without any input from me." Looking bored out of her mind, Rochelle went back to her cup of soup.

Then Chopper Deke walked in and slot-ted a couple of coins into the soda machine. With his spiky-moussed hair sticking up and a demented leer on his face, he pressed the soda selector. Crazed eyes slewed to Ro-chelle. "Hey, I've got Viagra."

"I've got Uncle Guido. And Uncle

Guido's got a thousand acres and a back-hoe."

Chopper Deke's drink rumbled down the chute and hit the stop. Crestfallen, he leaned in, picked it up and stomped out of the break room.

Frustrated and unnerved after the morning's events, Aspen wanted to escape the madness. She wished she could talk to Spike. To recount the horrible morning and have him wrap her in his big, brawny arms and promise her everything would be all right. He might be bald, middle-aged and myopic, but he was the most interesting person she'd ever met and for some strange reason, he seemed to have a soft spot for her, too.

Until yesterday.

Rochelle must've read her mind. "I have about ten messages from that law dog of yours. You should call him back."

"I'm not calling him."

Rochelle glanced up from her soup and gave Aspen a hard look. "Trouble in paradise?"

"Like I'd tell you after you almost got me killed."

Rochelle slipped her hand into the pocket of her jacket. She pulled out Granger's business card and turned it over. "He was here," she said, holding it at an angle so Aspen could see his home phone and cell numbers written on the back. "Said I should call him if I heard from you."

"Don't you dare," Aspen snapped. "So what'd he say?"

Rochelle offered her upturned palms. "That was it. He came here looking for you yesterday afternoon, and when I told him you were out on assignment, he left his card and asked me to call when you came in. He looked like hell, did I mention that?" She pushed back her chair and rose from the table. "I'm guessing the lipstick smeared on his neck and collar wasn't yours."

"You can't breathe a word of this." Aspen took Rochelle by the hands and squeezed until the secretary winced.

"Never." Rochelle's gray eyes lit up like directional beacons.

By the time Aspen finished the tawdry tale about the blonde with the trout lips suction cupped to Granger's neck, Rochelle was bobbing her head with ideas.

Then she played devil's advocate. "There could be a perfectly logical explanation for what happened. Why don't I look into it for you? It's the least I can do for nearly getting you killed."

"Ha. So you admit it."

"Anyway," Rochelle went on, "I know people."

"What people?"

"People who know people. Six degrees of separation, and all that."

Three hours before the noon broadcast, while Aspen showed Rochelle photos of Kirk House in the privacy of her office, Gordon flung the door open and burst in, rumpled, and gasping for breath.

"Wicklow — we have a situation." He looked at her, grim-faced. "The Dallas SWAT team's outside. They want you to come with them."

She reviewed her mental checklist of recent crimes. There was that incident at the grocery store where she'd accidentally dropped a couple of cans of tuna, then inspected them for fresh dents and returned the tins to the shelf, effectively swapping them for ones without dents. And the clandestine removal of a little plastic packet with a spare button and extra thread from a jacket identical to one she'd purchased at the same store one week before. And there was that thing Rochelle taught her to use on telemarketers who violated the "Do not call" list — slamming down the phone after screaming, "Ohmygod, somebody just did a drive-by on my house."

Not exactly death penalty offenses, right?

She ran through a mental checklist of reasons that might excuse her from leaving with the police and only came up with one. "I have to do the noon broadcast."

Gordon said, "I already tried that. They said they'd have you back before then."

"I don't understand." Aspen gulped. "I didn't do anything." She lowered her voice. "Is it about what happened yesterday? The . . . you know . . ." She couldn't bring herself to talk about the arrest. Her bottom lip quivered. "Why would Dallas SWAT want to talk to me?"

Gordon raised his hand to her. "Don't you dare cry. I can't stand crybabies."

Rochelle, who'd been amazingly quiet during the drama, came to her rescue. "He's not going to hit you. Truth is, Gordon's a big ol' softie. If you cry, he'll cry. And then he'll never be able to keep the photographers in line." In an uncharacteristic move, she slid an arm around Aspen's shoulders and squeezed.

"That's crap and you know it." He took a deep breath and let it out on a long exhale. "They're trying to talk a jumper down from the top deck of the Timmons Building."

He was messing with her.

She reminded him that the upper deck of the Timmons Building had been permanently closed to the public more than thirty-five years ago, after the last suicide victim swan-dived over the rail.

"Well, apparently, the guy talked his way up there. Something about replacing burned-out light bulbs; hell, I don't know." Gordon shrugged. "What I do know is, the cops are asking for you."

This made no sense. "Didn't you tell them I'm an anchor now . . . that I'm no longer an investigative reporter?"

"Apparently, they don't give a tinker's damn whether you're the carnival sideshow, since the fellow they're trying to talk down asked for you personally. Claims he knows you."

"I want to talk to the police." Aspen pushed back from her desk and moved, zombiefied, out the door and down the hallway. A couple of burly, jack-booted, ninja-looking men in dark clothing stood near the front door.

"What exactly do you want from me?" she said to neither in particular.

They exchanged eyebrow-encrypted messages. Then the smaller of the two emerged as their spokesman. "We have a possible jumper on the roof of the Timmons Building."

She was already shaking her head. "I'm not going on a rooftop that happens to be one of the tallest buildings in downtown Dallas."

"He says he knows you. That you're the only one he'll talk to."

"Anyone could say that. What's his name?"

"He won't say. Our print guy lifted latents off the door handle leading up to the rooftop, but it could be hours before we get a match through AFIS."

"Enough of the cop-speak," Aspen said. "Talk to me in plain English."

"Our fingerprint technician took latent prints — the kind you can't see with the naked eye until dark powder is brushed over them — but using the Automated Fingerprint Index System, where they're run through a database, takes a long time even if you put a rush on it."

Made sense.

"Are you in contact with this man?" she asked. "Because I'm going to need a name."

Gordon, who'd come up from behind, seconded the notion.

The SWAT members conferred on their portable radios. Then the apparent leader moved to Rochelle's desk and made a phone call. He gave the person at the other end the lowdown, repeating the pertinent parts of their contact with Aspen, and from that contact, learned the name of the jumper.

"Heath Strawn?" Her voice broke upon sounding his name. A serpent of nausea coiled in her gut. "Are you sure?"

It was if the air pressure had changed. Physically, she was standing in WBFD's marble foyer, but in her head she was back at the university, in American Lit, exchanging longing glances with the campus hottie.

"Ohmygod. I'm going to be sick."

CHAPTER TWENTY

Down in Johnson County, over at the high school, the bell rang. Then the mouths of the exits burst open, disgorging hundreds of school kids on their way out to lunch.

Granger didn't have to ask how to get to the principal's office. He knew the way. After all, he'd done his fair share of time there.

The principal, Harvey Thomas, had been around way back when, and had put in enough years to retire. Despite their rocky start, Granger and Thomas had become fast friends. Five years ago, when the gangs started to flourish and the drug trade moved into the high school in a big way, Thomas came to Granger to see about putting an undercover officer in the school.

They struck a deal. Using the blind-taste-test theory, Granger would get the school's transfer forms and doctor the paperwork, but the new student would only enroll at the beginning of each semester, at the same time everyone else enrolled. It was safer for everyone concerned, including Harvey Thomas, if nobody knew.

"You owe me lunch," Granger said good-naturedly.

"I owe you a lot more than lunch. How you doing, cowboy?"

It was the one habit Granger couldn't break Harvey of. Everybody was "cowboy" whether they liked it or not.

They ended up at Sue's on the Square, a homey café across the street from the courthouse, furnished with pieces of cast-off furniture, gingham curtains, wall art you couldn't have given away at a swap meet, and cloth napkins. None of the contents matched, but that only added to the charm. People came for down-home cooking, just like Mama used to make. Hearty food and camaraderie.

When Granger and Thomas walked in, there were shouts and raised hands all around. They took a table near the kitchen that Sue kept cleared in case the waitresses wanted to grab lunch during their shift, or when Granger showed up, whichever happened first.

Granger ordered the blue plate special, which consisted of chicken-fried steak — a thick cut of beef Sue hammered with a meat tenderizer until it was the size of a salad plate, breaded in a mixture of flour, corn flakes and another cereal that Sue kept secret — real mashed potatoes with cream gravy, and fresh green beans with salt pork. Dinner rolls, too, and it was all made from scratch.

Principal Thomas ordered the chef salad with fat-free dressing, and both men drank sweet tea. "What's on your mind, cowboy?"

"Need a favor."

"I'll see what I can do."

Granger told him about needing the use of the gymnasium for two nights, tops. One to set up for the magic show and rehearse, and one to put on the fund-raiser.

Thomas winced. "Our kids have games, cowboy. They have practice."

"Can't they have practice somewhere else?"

"Highly irregular," he said, as the waitress stopped by with their lunch plates. Principal Thomas scowled at his salad next to Granger's feast. "Cholesterol." He unfurled his napkin and placed it in his lap, then reached for the salt. "It'll happen to you, too, cowboy."

"We're all gonna die of something, Harvey. *Cause of death* might as well be Sue's chicken-fried steak."

"I heard that," came a high-pitched voice from the kitchen.

Granger sobered. "I need this, Harvey. I'm getting my ass beat in the polls. You know Neil has deep pockets. He can outspend me. Give me the gym. I'm asking for two nights." He held up two fingers. "Two. If I don't get reelected, you don't have to mess with me again."

They cemented the deal over a piece of pie, the way a lot of Texas deals were made. Handshake and a generous slice of home-made pie. Chocolate meringue for Granger, coconut meringue for Principal Thomas. And an extra slice of the state pie of Texas in a to-go box for Granger: Southern Pecan.

Granger picked up the tab and left Sue a big tip, even though he figured it ought to be the other way around since he knew the secret ingredient for the chicken-fried steak coating was Kellogg's Special K.

On the way back to the high school, within the confines of the patrol car, they talked about the good ol' days, and the bad new ones. Before he let his friend out at the curb, Granger made an inquiry about a certain student who'd been giving his men problems.

A girl about fifteen or so. Maybe sixteen.

Ran with the Goths. Ought to be a fresh-man. Maybe sophomore. Went around town all dressed in black. Juvenile delinquent, on probation for Minor in Possession.

A kid named Susanna Epps. The Goths called her Paper Cut.

"You know the kid I'm talking about, don't you? Misfit? Chip on her shoulder? Hates the world? We're keeping an eye on that one."

"Yes, I know her." Harvey gave a curt nod. "My teachers tell me she's flunking every class except music."

"Music?" This genuinely surprised him. "What — she's in the band?"

"Nah, she won't join the band. Not cool. But they say she has an aptitude for the sax."

"Does she make it to class every day?" Granger asked, but he was thinking, *Well, butter my butt and call me a biscuit.* "Because her daddy's doing time down at the Ferguson Unit, and her mama works at a strip club over in Dallas. She told her probation officer there's nobody to take her to school, so I just wondered."

"I think she drives herself. Has a little rattletrap Daihatsu Charade. Bought a permit for it at the beginning of the year."

Granger feigned surprise, snapping his finger to show his memory had been jogged.

"That's right. Got a hardship license." Of course he knew about the car. It'd been awarded to the SO in a drug forfeiture case. "Now I remember one of my boys telling me he wrote her a ticket."

"What's your interest in this girl?"

"Aw, nothing really. She gives a couple of my deputies a hard time. I just wondered if she's getting to school on time."

"I wouldn't know, cowboy. Girl didn't show up today. I've got the truant officer out looking for her now."

CHAPTER TWENTY-ONE

Heath Strawn's claim to fame — back when Aspen attended North Texas State University with him — started with a golf scholarship. But his white-blonde hair, lean, tawny body and Dresden-blue eyes brought him even more notoriety as a campus hottie than his number-one spot on the golf team. They took a few classes together and, for a while, they were tight. Then summer school ended and she only saw him at school functions, or on news clips run at the university's TV station.

Now they were destined to meet again.

On the drive to the Timmons Building in downtown Dallas, tires droned against the asphalt, lulling her into a near-hypnotic state that allowed her thoughts to free-associate. Why would a successful athlete like Heath Strawn want to do himself in? Got dumped? Didn't win the green jacket? Accountant took a permanent vacation to a country without an extradition treaty? Even worse, would she find him poised to swan dive from the rooftop, or did he expect to be talked down off the ledge by a friend?

At the sight of a tower belonging to a rival TV station, she preferred to fret over who'd do the noon broadcast if she didn't get back to the station in time. The idea of Gordon picking Tig Welder to sit in for her chapped her no end. From the moment she'd hired on at WBFD-TV, the station's star investigative reporter had tried to undermine her success. And even though Gordon told her he was going to fire Tig, he hadn't. Because even though she hadn't seen him milling around the station, his Hummer was still parked in his reserve spot.

In the distance, the Timmons Building rose from the landscape like a monolith with a pyramid on top. The Dallas landmark was situated near Dealy Plaza, the grassy knoll where shots rang out during the Kennedy assassination. At the top of the tower, a three-level structure designed to house an observation deck, a full-service restaurant, and a cocktail lounge remained open to the public. But the pyramid topper, whose aluminum struts held close to 300 lights that burned most of the evening hours and could be programmed to flash different patterns for light shows, was strictly off limits.

The restaurant's revolving floor made the dining experience particularly memorable. Tables lined the glass wall, and the eating area rotated clockwise on what amounted to a conveyor belt. It took nearly an hour to complete a revolution, but the wait was worth it: It allowed patrons to experience a 360-degree view of the Metroplex.

Aspen had been there only once. But revolving floors and twinkling skylines weren't the most memorable part of the dining adventure branded in her mind. For her, the trip to the Timmons Building would forever mark that inauspicious occasion where the love of her life unceremoniously dumped her for a stripper called Satin. In retrospect, she figured Roger had picked the place to diminish the likelihood of her resorting to street theater in the presence of Dallas's elite. The hallmark event careened into mind as if it had occurred yesterday.

"There's something I've been meaning to talk to you about."

He'd pulled a small box from his blazer. Silly her, thinking he was about to give her a ring. When she opened it, the smile died on her face.

The ring turned out to be her house key.

"For God's sake, Roger, the least you can

*do is have the common decency to tell me
why you're dumping me."*

"Just remember — I didn't want to hurt you."

"Out with it."

*"Fine. You want to know the real reason?
You're just not that interesting."*

The tactical officer broke her reverie.
"Looks like your people are already here."

Sure enough, WBFD's electronic newsgathering van was parked at the scene.

The tactical officer threaded the unmarked
police car between a marked patrol unit and
the ENG van, enough for Aspen to glimpse
Tig threading a mike through the but-
tonholes of his shirt. She sighed in relief.
Tig wouldn't be filling the noon anchor spot
after all. Max, Tig's photographer, had
already strung the cable and hooked his
camera to the input-output panel on the
van. As Tig finished getting miked-up, Max
turned on the camcorder; its overhead
beacon lit up the investigative reporter.

Aspen scrunched her eyes. Tig must've
gotten one of those spray-on tans at the tan-
ning salon. Instead of the light washing him
out, his complexion glowed with an unnatural orange hue more suited to the skin
of a pumpkin.

A SWAT commander approached the car
and opened her door. "Aspen Wicklow?

Come with me." He took her by the elbow, helped her out of the vehicle, then ushered her over to the tactical squad van. "We threw a phone out on the deck. He wants to talk to you. Whatever you do, be careful. One wrong word and he could jump."

She gave him a slow, incredulous eye blink.

So now you're making it my fault?

She didn't even have time to learn SWAT protocol before a negotiator thrust a telephone receiver at her.

Her voice trembled. "Heath? Is that you?" Lifting her gaze, she shielded her eyes from the glare of the morning sun and spotted an ant-sized figure standing on the west side of the tower.

A voice came across the line, tinny and distant. Aspen forced her index finger into her free ear to block the surrounding noise. Apparently Heath Strawn had his own problems hearing. After a few unsuccessful tries, he demanded she come to the top of the tower — the part closed to the public — and talk face-to-face.

She bosomed the phone, clutched the commander's sleeve, and said, "He says he can't hear me. He wants me to come up there."

Already, the commander was shaking his

head. "Too dangerous. He could pull you out there and take you with him."

Fine by her. The commander had only said aloud what she'd been thinking.

"We can get you on deck, but you don't want to get any closer than fifteen feet. If he wants to make physical contact, instruct him to step away from the ledge. Make *him* come to *you.*"

Fair enough.

The negotiator took the telephone from her. "Don't go anywhere," he said into the mouthpiece with the gallows humor of a seasoned veteran. "We're coming up."

Nearby, Tig Welder pressed a mobile phone to his ear. Clearly, he was talking to Gordon. "So if he throws her to her death, does that mean I get the anchor job?"

CHAPTER TWENTY-TWO

When Aspen reached the top deck with the SWAT commander, she assumed the man curled up like a tortellini on the outer ledge was Heath Strawn, but it was hard to tell from a distance. He wore a dark knit watch cap pulled down over his ears, and had an industrial-sized box of light bulbs that he'd no doubt brought in as a prop to gain access to an otherwise off-limits place. A pink Princess phone lay near his head. His eyes were closed as if he'd decided to catnap.

"How'd he get in here?" Aspen said.

"Conned the cleaning crew."

Her voice dissolved into a whisper. "What do we do now?"

"In a perfect world, I'll dial the number and he'll pick up. Hopefully." He eyed her up. "Then you'll talk him off that ledge and convince him to come inside . . . hopefully."

"What if he refuses?" If not for the wind gusts reddening her old friend's cheeks, he already looked dead. "I don't want the responsibility." Fear turned to panic. "I didn't ask for this. And I damned sure don't want to get blamed for it."

"You're the best chance we have of talking him in. Besides, if something goes wrong, FD's standing by with a rescue net."

More cop slang. She lifted an eyebrow.

"Fire department," he explained. "Think of it as a trampoline. Only from this height, all it'll really do is keep all his body parts intact. He'll likely be deader'n Hogan's goat if he jumps." The commander had one of those gunfighter gazes that suggested she didn't have the right to object. That the plan had already been put in motion. "You ready?"

Panic gripped her. "What if I say the wrong thing?"

"Then it's *Goodnight, Irene.*"

For a trained negotiator, he obviously wasn't listening. She couldn't do this. She'd botch the job. In desperation, she clutched his sleeve. "I don't even know him, really. We only had a couple of classes together four years ago."

Not true. Well, okay, partially true. They'd shared a couple of kisses beneath the mistletoe that first Christmas at a frat party. To minimize her exposure, she'd left that part out. A lie by omission. Guilt set in.

"You're the only one in the gene pool he asked to speak to. Since you have the inside track, that puts you a rung up from the negotiator. I'll put you on speakerphone so I can monitor the call, but I'll stay off to the side where he can't see me. If you need help, we'll do cue cards. You know cue cards, right?"

Reflexively, she caught herself nodding. Like reading off a teleprompter.

"When I give you the signal, push redial."

Got it.

This would be easy. Like conversing with an old friend.

A bat-shit crazy old friend.

She stood, marooned, as the commander slipped out of sight. Moments later, he gave her the green light, an "OK" sign formed with his thumb and index finger. Then he made his hand into a phone and put it up to his ear.

Aspen realized she'd been holding her breath and let out a deep exhale. Armchair quarterbacks were always looking for someone to point the finger at. If Heath jumped, she'd be the goat. She couldn't shake off the chilling sensation that this horrible event was turning into another fly-on-the-wall documentary about herself.

What would Rochelle do?

Probably wrestle the bullhorn away from the commander and yell, "Snap out of it, you damned crybaby."

Rochelle operated under a pretty unorthodox, yet effective, code.

She lifted the receiver and pressed redial. The phone purred in her ear a few beats ahead of the actual shrill.

Heath Strawn's eyes popped open. He squinted, then lifted his hand to block out the sunlight before reaching for the receiver. "Aspen. Nice to see you again."

"Heath." Her eyes welled. "How are you?" Okay, that was stupid. They hadn't brought her here for idle chitchat, and she didn't care to prolong the agony of the frightful experience playing out before her eyes.

He hoisted himself up on one elbow. "Considering I've got a headwind blowing straight up my ass, I'm exceptional. How about you? I've been seeing a lot of you on TV lately. I was planning to phone after you did that piece on the serial killer, but I got busy. Hey — remember that Christmas party at the Kappa house?"

"Come inside and talk to me. It's hard for me to hear you clearly with the wind and all."

His mouth angled up in a smirk. "No can

do." He raised himself to a seated position and slumped miserably against the aluminum scaffolding.

"Heath . . ." A flash of white caught her eye. A section of poster board flashed up from across the room. It read: *Ask what he wants.* "Heath, why am I here? You could've just called me. We could've met for coffee. What's so bad that you had to climb onto a ledge to get my attention?"

"That's a very good question." He carefully maneuvered himself to a standing position. He'd worn a sheepskin-lined jacket, and the wind was whipping the flaps back. His shirt ballooned. Pant legs unfurled like flags. "I watched you on TV earlier. Congratulations. You handled that pretty good — but, then, why wouldn't you? I read all the newspaper stories about you. The ones about the dead girls. Candy Drummond. She used to give you grief. I never slept with her. I know you thought I did, but I didn't."

Thanks for clearing that up.

"Personally, I never thought you had it in you to be an investigative reporter. You always had your head buried in books. But, hey — now you're the anchor, right?"

"Heath, let's talk inside. Please." This time, she gambled on the truth. "I'm afraid."

"You? Scared?" He barked out a laugh.

255

With a shake of the head he added, "You can't be scared and hear what I have to say."

"I don't understand."

"I asked for you because you're the most fearless person I know."

The words carried a bit of hang time.

Fearless?

He only thought that because he'd probably watched her involvement in death-defying situations during sweeps month. What he hadn't seen in all that frightening footage was Spike Granger off to one side. So it was Spike, not her, who should be called fearless. Come to think of it, this would be right up Spike's alley. People respected him. She could almost hear that smooth country drawl cajoling, "Get on in here, son, and get yore bidness straight."

"You weren't scared last night." Heath's voice broke into her thoughts. "You can't be scared. If you're scared, she'll kill you, too."

Last night? This made no sense.

How could he know where she was last night? And who was *she?* Aspen asked him that very question.

"Dolly Hastings."

The name tumbled through her head without recognition. She was about to ask him to explain when another cue card shot

up. It read: *Dallas atty. Family law. Total bitch.*

"The attorney who practices in Family Court? How do you know her?"

"You might say I did some work for her."

For the next few minutes, Aspen didn't need any prompts. The "who, what, when, where and why" of her journalistic training kicked into high gear. By way of explanation, the so-called work Heath did for Dolly Hastings amounted to heavy-handed collections. She tried to imagine him popping up at a client's workplace, demanding money, and couldn't wrap her mind around him passing himself off as a bruiser and a thug.

"Do you still work for her?"

"Have to. You quit, you die."

Crazy talk.

"Heath . . . what do you want from me?"

He laid out his request in plain, uncomplicated terms. He wanted her to tell his story. To shame the cops into putting Dolly Hastings away so she couldn't hurt anyone else.

"I don't understand. Can't you please come inside and let's talk about it? I know people who're pretty high up in law enforcement. They might be able to help if I knew what brought you here."

"Dolly and I killed a man."

That siphoned the oxygen out of Aspen's lungs. She fought the urge to glance at the

257

commander.

"I have it all documented here." With one hand pressed against the scaffolding for balance, he tucked the receiver between his chin and shoulder, and pulled a file from the back waistband of his pants.

"You should take that to the police."

He gave a vehement head shake. "I need someone I can trust. That's you, Aspen."

"We'll find you a good lawyer."

"You know as well as I do . . . they'll have to send me sunlight in a milk bottle because I'll never again see the light of day. I'll die in prison."

He was still standing on the ledge with the phone receiver in one hand and the documents in the other.

"Please, Heath, come inside. Let's talk it out."

"This is how it has to be."

"You're scaring me." A thin squeak escaped her lips. Tears blistered behind her eyeballs.

"You weren't scared last night."

What?

"You weren't scared out at Kirk House."

She sucked air. How could he know that?

"You weren't scared at Tiny's Drive-In, sitting there with that little blonde."

She caught herself panting. "I don't

understand. Where were you?"

"Watching."

"You followed me?" Her voice shrilled. Okay, this was just flat creepy.

The commander held up another sign: *Calm down.*

"I don't understand," she whimpered.

"You saw me."

"I didn't."

"Yes, you did. That's why I called for you. I thought you recognized me."

"Recognized you?" He must've been concealed behind one of the aisles, because the only people she saw were the clerk, a couple of random customers, and the Goths.

No.

Fresh chills ricocheted across her skin.

No, no, no, no, no.

He unhanded the scaffolding and tugged off the watch cap. A blue-black Mohawk poked up from his scalp.

Plex Rominus.

That's you?

The face paint, the hair . . . the dagger eyes?

She tried to recreate the image of the Goth leader in her mind.

Without warning, the door leading onto the top deck burst open.

Tig rushed in with Max in tow, there to

259

shoot breaking news.

Heath gaped. His hand came up in slow motion, eyes shielded by the file folder. He recoiled with a backward step.

In less than a split second, he realized what happened.

Pages from a legal pad fluttered on the breeze like canaries, swirling past the ledge on an air current.

And as Heath Strawn followed them down, Aspen rushed to the ledge and forced herself to watch.

CHAPTER TWENTY-THREE

While the SWAT commander was busy jacking up Tig and Max, Aspen found herself with the keys to the ENG van. With a promise to give a written statement if the Dallas PD would permit her to leave long enough to present the noon broadcast, she pulled away from the crime scene and headed down Commerce Street. As she drove toward the grassy knoll, sheets from a yellow legal pad rolled like tumbleweeds across the lawn.

Aspen slammed on the brakes. Horns blared. Drivers swerved. She curbed the van, got out and started snatching up yellow pages before they blew across the interstate. Once she'd collected everything within reach, she returned to the van and circled the block. The decision paid off. She gathered up at least a dozen more sheets, then continued the drive a mile to the east and collected several more pages.

She was pushing the envelope now, running out of time. No way could Misty Knight run the noon broadcast alone. If this morning was an indicator, the woman was heading for a nervous breakdown. Steve Lennox — now he could manage alone, but he wasn't scheduled to work, and he had the bad habit of turning off his pager and shutting off his phone while he slept, effectively putting him out of commission.

With one hand on the steering wheel, she rummaged through her handbag, pulled out her mobile phone, and speed dialed her co-host.

No answer.

Her heart drummed. So much for Plan B. Steve probably went straight home after the dwarf fiasco and curled up with a bottle of Jim Beam.

In her panic, she got a creepy visual of Gordon, sitting behind the anchor desk, sweating like a pig and "going Misty" on the viewers. *"This just in — an exclusive you'll only see on WBFD. Today, we're hiring for an anchor, an investigative reporter, and a photographer position because these fuckers didn't take me seriously when I said the cardinal rule of journalism is* 'Never become part of the story.'

"In other news there's shit going on over on

the east side of Fort Worth . . . people can't get along, so what else is new? And over in Dallas, well, who gives a tinker's damn? I'm a Fort Worth boy, born and raised, so I guaran- damned-tee *you, I sure don't . . .*"

She imagined him posing in front of the weather map. *"You expect me to stand in front of a blank screen and talk about cloud cover? Where are the pictures? What are these ar- rows supposed to mean? Damn it, where's the teleprompter? Oh, that's it? Well, roll it closer. I can't see the text.*

"Okay, people, we have weather. What kind of weather, you ask? How should I know? Go outside and look around if you're that inter- ested. You'll have just as good a shot at figur- ing out what's going on as our girl Misty."

She checked the digital clock in the dash- board and realized she had less than ten minutes to be in her seat, and exactly zero minutes to scan the broadcast notes. She'd have to wing it.

With seconds to spare, she flung herself through the door sporting stun-gun hair, and spotted Rochelle standing at her desk, minus the earlier disguise. At the sound of Gordon's disembodied voice echoing through the receptionist area, she skidded to a halt.

Heath's papers could end up being used

263

as evidence to bring down a lawyer. She needed to ditch them before Gordon saw the legal proof in her clutches. She had an uneasy feeling that by holding onto the documents, she'd violated Cardinal Rule number three: Don't break the law. Translation: Don't end up in a body-cavity search. Gordon didn't want to pay off any lawsuits.

She didn't relish putting the boss in the position of having to make an executive decision to turn the documents over to the cops. Until she determined whether their exclusive news value outweighed their evidentiary value, they should be stored in safekeeping.

At the last second, she decided against giving the papers to Rochelle to hold for her. What was she thinking? Why not just throw a grenade in the henhouse?

She sprinted past Gordon, who was pacing the length of the studio, cursing to high heaven during the last of several car commercials scheduled to air prior to the news. The crisp pinpoint oxford he'd started out in that morning had sweat rings the size of radial tires beneath the arms, and his sleeves were rolled up to his elbows.

"What the hell, Wicklow?" he bellowed, palms up, meaty hands outstretched. Perspiration stippled his forehead. Beads of sweat glistened atop his balding head. His face flamed crimson, but the veins corrugating in his neck relaxed.

The studio was in chaos. She slid into her seat and gathered the script placed in front of her. She sat motionless as the makeup girl, on standby, rushed up. As the girl blotted Aspen's face and dusted her cheeks with a light coat of bronzer, the hairy arm of an unseen helper crooked around her neck and fastened a microphone to her clothing.

"When you're done," Gordon announced in his sportscaster voice, the one that projected across the room and hung in the air a good ten seconds after the words stopped coming out, "in my office, front and center." His voice trailed him out of the studio. "Damned *prima donna* bullshit . . . people trying to give me a heart attack . . . can't take any more of this." Followed by one of his innocuous grumblings about posting bail.

The musical theme leading into the noon newscast played in the background. Reggie, the resident beatnik, manned the camera. One of the show's producers counted her down. "And, three . . . two . . . one. You're on the air."

A red light not much bigger than a pin dot glowed on Reggie's camera. Split-screen images of her face, shot from different vantage points, appeared on the monitor, along with skyline views of Fort Worth and Dallas. The skyline faded. A frontal view of herself from the waist up popped up on the monitor.

Then Aspen lost her mind.

She shoved her papers aside and ignored the text scrolling down the teleprompter. Instead of leading with the cruise-ship disaster in the Gulf of Mexico, the top story most of the other stations would be airing, Aspen fixed her emerald gaze on the camera lens and mentally psyched herself up to report the latest local catastrophe.

Okay, so it hadn't been cleared by Gordon. But it was exclusive news, right? And that's what people tuned in for. That's why their ratings had soared during sweeps month. And viewers loved her.

Trusted her.

And wanted to hear the truth from her.

"Good afternoon. I'm Aspen Wicklow, with a WBFD exclusive that'll only be found here on Channel Eighteen."

Gordon burst through the doors. Rubber-soled shoes squeaked to a stop. The sides of his hair resembled Brillo pads hot-glued to his head.

"A local man fell to his death from the

266

Timmons Building earlier today, despite the fact that Dallas police were on the scene attempting to talk him down." She gave a slow exhale. The fear that had built up while Heath Strawn balanced precariously on the ledge seemed to follow it out.

She blinked back tears. This was a mistake.

"Go to commercial," she said, but the producer shook his head and pointed his finger at her as if to say, *You picked the fight; now deal with it.*

"Oh, who am I kidding?" she announced to potentially millions of viewers. "This job just plain sucks."

Gordon's beady, X-ray eyes bulged until they looked like two Saturns with white rings circling his irises.

"Okay, here's how it is, people." Aspen traced a fingertip beneath each eye, wiping away tears and flicking them aside.

Gordon chanted a low, familiar mantra, "Don't go folksy on me, don't go folksy on me, don't go folksy on me. Oh, hell . . . she's going folksy on me."

"I was there. At the Timmons Building. The guy was a friend of mine. I can't release his name because his next-of-kin haven't been notified." She wiped the back of her hand across her nose and sniffled. "It was terrible. You can't imagine how it feels to be

267

talking to someone you cared about, and they just disappear off the side of the building, right before your very eyes."

Gordon mumbled, "Oh, shit. Here we go. Somebody have Rochelle get me a drink. A stiff one. No ice. Just bring me a bottle. Anything that doesn't have a skull and crossbones on it."

"I know most of you can't understand what I'm going through right now" — she stared pointedly at Gordon — "but we were friends, you know?" She looked at the camera beseechingly. "And since I can't tell you who he is, I'll tell you what he was like."

Gordon groaned. "Forget the drink. Bring me my gun."

The producer said, "It's not worth killing yourself over, Gordo."

"It's not for me, you idiot. It's for her."

Rochelle appeared with a flask and he practically jerked her arm out of its socket. She whispered in his ear and he calmed noticeably.

"Heath —" Aspen faltered, realizing her mistake. She'd said his name and now she had to recover. "He was such a talented athlete. He had the kind of good looks that made a girl catch her breath when he walked into a room. But he was nice, too. All that attention didn't go to his head. He was one of the most approachable men I've ever met, and if you asked, he'd give you the shirt off his back . . . no, you wouldn't need to ask; he'd just do it."

Goaded by Gordon's curious gaze, she continued. "So you can see why I'm heartsick. I'm the one he asked for at the end. So, right now, people, I don't —"

Gordon muttered, "Why does she do that — people, people, people?" He swiped an arm through the air. "Talks to the damned camera like she knows all these sons-abitches. Why can't she just read off the damned teleprompter like I pay her to?"

Rochelle leaned in and bent his ear.

"— really give a flying flip about some boat floating around out in the Gulf of Mexico with a bunch of sick people on it. If they're not from here, then they ought to be quarantined. Don't we have enough problems here at home, without inviting an epidemic onto our shores?"

Gordon, still deep in the throes of conversation with Rochelle, spoke in a low-level hum. "When she gets off the air, fire her."

He stormed off the set.

Aspen sniffled.

To the camera, she announced, "Well, I'm all better now," and huffed out a sigh. "Had to get that off my chest. Sorry about the meltdown. But those of you who've lost special people in your lives understand."

Stinger Baldwin, Tig's nemesis, appeared on the monitor with his mike tilted close to his lips, waiting to be cued from out in the field.

Aspen read off the teleprompter. "In other news, frightening new information on a pit bull who climbed its owner's fence and mauled a five-year-old boy . . ." She grabbed her stomach. "Are you kidding me? I think I'm going to be sick. Who slipped this into my copy? Why didn't somebody warn me?" She caught herself sounding like Misty and cut herself off. With a dignified tilt of the chin, she said, "We go live to Stinger Baldwin."

Cut to Stinger.

"Can somebody get me a wet cloth?" Aspen asked.

The makeup girl appeared like a genie. "You're wonderful. That speech was so moving. You had us all in tears."

She wanted to tell her not to worry about it happening again. That Gordon was madder than a hatter, so she probably wouldn't be around after today. She looked at the broadcast schedule to see where they were on the rundown.

Reggie muttered something unintelligible.

She cupped a hand to her ear and strained to listen through the ear fob. "What? You're making me do the *Love Boat* story? But I already told them about it."

She got a shrug for her protests. As Stinger Baldwin wound up his report, she waited for him to cue her with his chipper finale. "Back to you, Aspen."

She sat, rigid, with the look of a hardened professional riding on her face. Stinger signed off and she glimpsed herself on the monitor.

"In other news, a cruise shit —"

Oh, dear God, these mistakes are contagious.

"— Goodness . . . did I say that? Sorry. A cruise ship floating under the Lithuanian flag is anchored out in the Gulf of Mexico while doctors on board — hey, where'd my picture go? This isn't . . . Ohmygod. Are those baby harp seals being bludgeoned to death? I'm not reporting that. What — are you people just trying to make me cry? What happened to the *Love Boat* story?"

She'd gotten a taste of why Misty had gone berserk earlier.

New footage appeared on the monitor.

"Ah, yes. There we go. Having a few little technical difficulties today, are we?" She segued back into the story. "Hundreds of people who got sick on a cruise ship are believed to be contagious with a possible outbreak of . . . what? You're pulling the story? I'm lost."

She stared at the blank teleprompter, giving an occasional lizard blink of confusion.

A series of commercials ate up the time: two car dealerships, a casino, and a Texas lottery advertisement. Weary and sad, and believing herself in the midst of her final broadcast for WBFD, she decided to go out with a bang. Soon, she'd be on the list of the world's shortest books: *Famous Redheaded Broadcasters.* Clearly, today was *not* the day she'd be headhunted to CNN.

The lotto commercial ended, and the producer finger-pointed her way.

She fixed her gaze on the teleprompter's blank screen and rolled her eyes.

"Do you play the lottery? I don't. No way. I'll keep my dollar, thank you very much. Do you have any idea what the odds of winning are? Practically zilch. Not to mention . . ." She flapped her hands in frustration. "I mean . . . take a good look at the people who are buying these things, will you? They don't even have enough money to clothe themselves properly, but they're out buying lottery tickets and a twelve-pack? You've gotta be kidding. And I'll bet you every blessed one of them has kids who're probably going hungry because these insensitive jerks are using family funds on the lottery that could be better spent on food. I mean . . . don't even get me started. What a travesty."

Having gotten that off her chest, she smiled sweetly. "On the brighter side of today, let's see what the weather has in store for us. Misty?"

Misty Knight appeared on the monitor looking like she'd swum ashore from the *Love Boat.* Her cheeks were pale and her face drawn, but she launched into the weather report like a pro. She finished with a cheery, "So if you don't like the weather, move. We've got too damned many people here anyway." She snapped her fingers. "Hey, I've got an idea . . . those of you who're sitting around complaining, why don't you head for sunny Mexico? Come to think of it, I heard Mexico's pulling out of the next Olympics. Well, I'm not surprised, since anyone who can run, jump or swim has already crossed the border into the United States."

Gordon staggered in, pale-faced.

Misty's cheeks flushed crimson. "Maybe we can start an exchange program, what do you think?" Sarcasm oozed. "For every thousand Mexicans invading our borders every day, why don't a hundred of you rednecks drive your pickup trucks down there and wreak havoc on Mexico? Personally, I think . . ."

Gordon gave the signal to pull the plug on her.

Misty was still on a rant, but the meteorological segment went off before anything more volatile hit the airwaves. Only the staff heard her vent about how much better things would be if each state would empty out their death row inmates and ship them to Iraq.

"That's right." Her voice took on the upward spiral of a maniac. "Take them all out to the desert and dump them into hostile territory with AK-47s and a canteen of holy water. Those who make it back get a pardon. Those who don't — well, what the hell? They were going to die anyway. Right?" Wild-eyed, she added, "Damned straight."

Aspen suspected she'd been drinking.

WBFD went to commercial — *to what else?* — the Texas lottery. Misty sauntered up to Aspen at the anchor desk and high-fived her.

Gordon walked into camera range and stood, hands on hips, spectacles on nose, and menaced them with a glare. "You ladies don't hang out together when you're not at work, do you?" he asked, in a way that suggested their answer should be no.

They exchanged awkward glances.

"Because I don't advise it. Your bad habits are rubbing off on each other. And I don't want you hanging out with Rochelle, either."

The commercial faded out with a familiar jingle.

Cut to Aspen. "We're all out of time. That's our report. Tune in later this afternoon for more exclusive footage you'll see only on WBFD, the station that'll go to hell and back to bring you the news."

And cut.

She pulled off her mike. "I know, I know. Front and center."

As she stepped away from the anchor desk, Reggie strolled cautiously up beside her. "Nice knowing you."

Under her breath, she asked the question that was on everyone's mind. "Has security been called to escort me from the building?"

CHAPTER TWENTY-FOUR

Unbelievably, Gordon behaved like a gentleman when he swept Aspen inside his office and motioned her to a seat on his cowhide sofa. With Heath's notes folded up in her handbag, she found herself stroking the rust-colored spots on the hide, grazing her fingertips along the grain of the fur, wanting to take in all the senses and sensations of her first and last day as WBFD's news anchor, for posterity's sake.

He leaned back in his chair and peered at her through thick lenses, possessing all the characteristics of an ocular lie detector, studying one's movements and facial expressions, listening to the timber of one's voice, searching for signs of deception.

Then he delivered breaking news of his own. "Rochelle said the phone lines are jammed."

This is it.

Here it comes: "Clean out your office and

don't come back."

Her eyes slewed to his wastebasket. "Can I get my copy of *The Dallas Morning News* back?"

"No. Did you read it?"

A head shake.

"Well, don't."

"Why not?"

"Because there's an article about you. And a photo." His words carried a bit of hang time.

Aspen winced. They'd gotten her mug shot. "Look, Gordon, you've been really good to me —"

"Rochelle said that newspaper fellow wants to do a follow-up interview with you about the jumper."

"I really don't feel like talking about it right now, if it's all the same to you."

"I hate crybabies." He shook his head. "I just don't get it."

"I can't help it. That's how I'm wired."

"Maybe you can explain it to me."

"What? Why I feel others' misery?"

"No — explain why the stupid cows who watch this program can't seem to get enough of it."

She gave him a dedicated eye blink. The morning call-ins were positive.

"Do you have further business to conduct

at the police department?" Gordon asked.

"They want a written statement."

"Tell them to go hump themselves."

"What if they subpoena me to testify before the grand jury?"

"I'll post your bail."

I'll bet.

"That's not why I called you in here," he went on, grim-faced. "Apparently, the Dallas PD placed Tig and Max under arrest for interfering in the Heath Strawn matter."

"Are you posting their bail?"

"Not bloody likely. Here's what I want you to do . . . call that SWAT commander and tell him the only way you'll come down and give a full statement is if they release Tig and Max without filing charges against them."

"But you just said I should tell them to . . ." She dropped her gaze. "You know."

"Oh, I don't expect you to give them a statement," he added. "Just make them think you will so they'll release my employees. Then when it comes time, you invoke your Constitutional right not to talk to them. Simply decline to cooperate."

"They'll lock me up," she said in a panic. "Can't I take a member of the legal team with me? Then every time the police ask me anything, the lawyer can instruct me not to answer."

Gordon beamed. "Even better."

"I don't understand what they want from me. The commander was there the same time I was. Why can't he just put what he saw in his report and be done with it?"

"A very good question. I'm thinking this has something to do with a set of papers the dead man had on him."

That sucked the wind out of her.

"Have any documents come into your possession?"

Her eyes darted around the room in search of an escape hatch. Gordon's drill-bit gaze bored into her with such heat she felt a sting of pain.

"On second thought, maybe I don't want to know. Because if you did come across something like that, we'd have an exclusive. And you know how I feel about exclusives."

When Aspen came out of Gordon's office, Rochelle waved her over. The woman had a finger hooked into the neckline of her knit top, airing out her cleavage with a hand-held, battery-operated fan, and appeared to be placating a caller. She looked up miserably and scowled.

"Uh-huh, okay, sounds good." During a long pause, she clicked off the fan and set it on the blotter, pulled her sack lunch out of the drawer and emptied the contents onto her desk. "Uh-huh," she said again. "Fantastic. Let me get my credit card."

"Rochelle," Aspen hissed, but the maladjusted assistant halted further conversation by flashing the universal *Wait-a-second* symbol.

Rochelle crumpled the paper bag at the neck until only a small area that she could blow into remained. She picked up the receiver and spoke.

"I've got that card number for you — wait. Ohmygod, no. Don't come any closer." She pulled the phone from her ear and carefully positioned it on the blotter. Introducing a new level of drama into the mix, she launched into an eerie whine. "Please, I'm begging you. Put down that gun." Then she blew into the bag and popped it. Snatching up the telephone, she panted, "I've been shot. There's blood everywhere. The room's blurry. I can't see. I think I'm . . . I think . . ." She clattered the receiver back into its cradle. Swiveling her chair around, she picked up the personal fan, clearly pleased with herself. She clicked it on, aimed it at her face, closed her eyes, and tilted her head back. "May I help you?"

"You're a cruel woman. What is it this

time? Telemarketer? Vacuum-cleaner sales-
man?"

"Donation request for gun-control legisla-
tion," she said, trance-like.

Nice.

Again, not nice.

"You wanted to see me?"

Rochelle's eyes popped open and she
stared up from behind thickly mascaraed
lashes. Eyes as gray and translucent as ice
fixed Aspen in their gaze.

"Yeah. A Mrs. Ramsey just called from
Tranquility Villas. She said they caught your
father playing naked Twister with some of
the female residents."

Aspen sighed. The people of Tranquility
Villas might as well get used to it. This
would go on until the day Wexford Wicklow
died.

"And your boyfriend called."

"He's not my boyfriend."

"Fine. Then Dirty Harry called."

Rochelle meant Granger.

Before she could tell Rochelle how she
wanted her to handle future calls from
Spike, Gordon stepped out of his office and
locked the door. Hat in hand, he strode
toward them in a dead heat.

"When will you be back? Better, still,
where are you going?" Aspen said.

Gordon never broke stride. "I'm going to see a man about a dog."

"Are you bailing Tig and Max out?" she called out after him.

"Just Max. Best damned photographer I ever saw. If I don't do it, one of the other stations will. Bunch of piranhas, you ask me." He whipped around and jabbed a finger into the air. "About those papers, Wicklow . . . if you have them in your possession, you'll eventually have to turn them over to the law. Better make a copy."

He disappeared through the glass doors, slapped the fedora on his head and walked down the sidewalk next to the hedges, toward the car pool. It had all the makings of watching a shark fin slice through water.

"I guess I'll need copies," Aspen said.

Rochelle didn't lift a finger. "Let's just run the ambulance right up to the front door, shall we? Make them yourself." Wordlessly, she opened a drawer, pulled out a book on the art of lock picking, and fanned herself with it.

Aspen sighed, exasperated, and slunk back to her office. She grabbed her purse and ambled over to the copier. Midway through making copies of Heath Strawn's death notes, the machine locked up. Unable to finish, Aspen headed out the door. Even though she knew they'd probably keep her there the rest of the afternoon, she drove straight to the Dallas PD to give them a statement and turn over the evidence. Well, not *all* of the evidence . . . just the part she'd managed to duplicate.

CHAPTER TWENTY-FIVE

Crazy Sheila was nothing if not dependable. In the short time she'd worked for Granger, she'd never been late and she'd never called in sick. Before he agreed to put her into the high school, Granger made a deal with her that she'd call in every afternoon — without fail — when the school day was over. Until today, she'd checked in with the precision and regularity of a Swiss timepiece. So even though the school day wasn't over yet, Granger's gut told him something bad had happened.

First, he checked his cell phone directory and called one of the deputies she'd reportedly become chummy with in the academy. The deputy denied having seen her. Then he called one of the jailers who knew her pretty well. The jailer hadn't seen her since the day before.

There was probably nothing to worry about, Granger thought, but just to be on the safe side, he dialed up Sheila's ex-husband, Blaze Clarke, a certified public accountant, at his tax firm. Even though they'd divorced over a year ago, they were on amicable terms. According to Crazy Sheila, Blaze didn't like the idea of her being in law enforcement, and he'd done everything he could to undermine her success in the academy. Once she graduated from cadet school and Granger realized what an asset he'd stumbled onto because of her keen intelligence and youthful appearance, she lasted only a week on street patrol before he pulled her in and sent her undercover. At the time, it'd been too much for straitlaced Blaze to accept.

From the CPA's receptionist, Granger learned that Blaze Clarke hadn't reported in to work. Nor had he bothered to call to let anyone know he wouldn't be in. But, hey, the receptionist chuckled, wasn't that one of the perks of self-employment? To be able to take the day off whenever you wanted? Not to mention the staff was a lot more relaxed without the boss around. No, the employees at Blaze's CPA firm were hardly chomping at the bit to see him. Type A personalities like him worked all the time and tended to be slave drivers. At this rate, he'd work them into an early grave.

Out of ideas, Granger sent a couple of deputies out to Sheila's house to nose around. If they didn't find her there, she could be just about anywhere.

Twenty minutes later, the deputies reported back to Granger. Sheila's car wasn't in the driveway. Neither was her ex-husband's. Which didn't mean one or both cars weren't in the two-car garage. But the garage door was down, the single window blocked by junk, and no one answered the deputies' knocks at the front door.

Granger instructed the dispatcher to put out a BOLO — *be on the lookout* — and prayed to God that she surfaced under her own steam. Before leaving the office, he informed Lucinda that he had business in Fort Worth that might last all afternoon.

Monkey business.

Aspen had given him her extra house key when she flew to New York City to be on a CNN broadcast several weeks before, and since she hadn't returned his calls and demanded it back, he made the trip in his personal vehicle, a white pickup truck. He'd loaded the bed with old Christmas lights that had been stored away in his attic, pieces of lattice, an armful of wooden posts, a multipurpose metal washbasin, a ball of twine, and his tool kit. On his way out of

286

town, he made one last stop at the largest grocery store in the area and bought every last produce box full of grapes they had in stock.

His project took three hours to complete, and when he could no longer wait for Aspen to come home, he scrawled out a note and left it on a small bistro table in her backyard with a rock on top to secure it.

He returned to the office by four-thirty, long enough to make contact with the jail and have one of the deputies on the evening shift transport Buster, belly-chained and in leg irons, over to the high school gymnasium. Then he drove there himself. All the kids had gone home for the day, which was fine by him. He wanted to look over the setup to get an idea of what sort of trappings Buster would need in order to put on his magic show, and for Granger to have a successful fund-raiser.

So far, the sheriff had decided to enlist the help of a few parents whose little kids recently performed in a recital for Miss Mary's Dance 'n Prance. There was nothing like a handful of talented little munchkins to draw a crowd. He'd have deputies stationed at the door with absentee ballots, just in case some of the spectators wanted to vote early. And who would they vote for?

Why, him, of course. After all, hadn't he just treated them to the best gosh-darned magic show ever?

Of course, a lot of this depended on Buster. But Granger had promised to talk to the judge on his behalf — after the show.

They'd need to post signs at the intersections near the high school with arrows pointing the way, so that out-of-towners could find it. He'd station Lucinda at the door to sell tickets to the event and the reception afterward, and have Crazy Sheila in tights and a turquoise-sequined leotard borrowed from one of the high school gals from the Dance 'n Prance recital, since Crazy Sheila would be the pretty lady Buster would saw in half.

If they could find her.

Granger's gut clenched. He hadn't lost an officer yet, and he damned sure didn't want to lose Crazy Sheila. He'd never met such a daredevil.

Seating would be first come, first served; but they'd trot in metal folding chairs for the overflow. Principal Thomas said they'd haul out the protective surface they'd stored away for events such as these, and lay it over the basketball court.

He saw all this in his mind: the seats filling up with spectators; Buster backstage, wearing the tuxedo Granger planned to purchase with his own money. Until the show started, the inmate wouldn't be able to take more than little geisha steps.

Granger would get there early to inspect the boxes his deputies were building for the disappearing act, and the box Crazy Sheila would lie in when Buster bisected her. They'd have a straitjacket hanging on a seamstress's mannequin. They'd also have two fifty-gallon drums, one with lockable hinges on the lid and an identical container with the bottom cut out and reattached at the seam so the escapologist could kick out the lid and "disappear" once the drums were switched.

"Hey, Spike."

At the sound of his name, Granger looked around and saw the deputy steering Buster across the gymnasium floor.

"If you'll get your man here to unlock these handcuffs, I'll show you where we ought to place the props. Can you get me a couple of those clothes racks — the kind with wheels on them? I need about three of them with curtains so we can roll them around and hide some of these boxes."

Granger ignored him. To the deputy, he said, "Don't even think about uncuffing him." To Buster, he said, "We already talked about this. You'll remain unshackled while performing onstage, but between acts, you'll stay trussed up like a Christmas turkey. And just so you know, I'm positioning deputies at every exit, with orders to shoot, just in case you get a wild hair and make a break for it. The last thing I need is for you to escape during the performance."

While Buster sulked at this news, Granger conjured up a picture in his mind. He could almost hear the din of voices rumbling through the gym — locals having a good time, old friends getting reacquainted, inquisitive strangers making new contacts.

Granger gradually became aware of his temperature spiking. Now, he remembered. Without adequate ventilation, the backstage temperature became sweltering. They'd need to have the AC turned on several hours before people arrived.

He left the deputy to watch Buster while he ducked behind the heavy, cotton velvet curtain in search of a couple of box fans. The drama department used this area for school plays. Granger opened the door to a room that held props. He glanced around, found nothing of interest, turned around and pulled the door closed.

When he looked up, Dallas Ostrander was standing in front of him in a full-length fur coat as platinum as her hair. She bore a striking resemblance to the ice queen.

"What are you doing here? You're not supposed to be back here, Dallas."

"What about you?" she challenged him. "Are you supposed to be back here?"

"I'm looking for fans."

"I'm a big fan."

"Not that kind of fan. The kind that blows."

"I blow." In a provocative move, she pursed her lips. For a second, Granger thought she might whistle a tune. But before anything came out, she lifted a manicured finger to her mouth and sucked.

"Electric fans." Granger didn't want to encourage her.

"It is a little hot in here," Dallas conceded. "Do you have any bottled water?"

Granger had toted in a six-pack of bottled water. Buster had one and the deputy had one, so that left four. He pointed her toward a wooden stool.

As she walked away with a sway in each step, he checked out her shoes. High heels. Expensive ones, too. When she turned to face him, she was unscrewing the cap on her water bottle. But instead of raising it to her lips, she opened her fur coat and stepped out of it. The wrap crumpled to the floor

291

like a dead polar bear.

Dallas had forgotten her clothes.

With each step toward him, she poured water over her naked form, starting with her breasts.

Chills crawled over Granger's torso. If anyone came back here —

Perspiration broke out across his forehead.

His ex slinked toward him — touching herself?

He blinked in disbelief. His groin stirred.

Then common sense took over. "If you don't put your damned coat back on, right this second, I'm going to arrest you."

But Dallas just laughed, a musical, child-like giggle. "You can't arrest me. It's not against the law to go topless — only to show your genitals and I haven't done that, yet. The carpet doesn't count."

She came within reach of him. Glanced at his crotch and said, "Ooooh, does Spikey-Wikey likey?" She showered her face with the last of the water and tossed the bottle aside. It rolled beneath the curtain, out of sight.

"I want you out of here."

"Really? I want you right here."

"It's not going to work." He held out his hand like a traffic cop to distance her. "I don't know what you're trying to pull, but whatever it is, you're not going to pull it with me."

The deputy called out to him. "Everything all right back there, Sheriff?"

"Everything's fine." To his ex-wife, he said, "Put your coat on or I'll haul you out of here naked as a jaybird. How do you think Neil would like that?"

"You're no fun," Dallas said. Jasper eyes thinned. "Fine. If you don't want to play with me, I'll take my toys and go home."

She was talking about her breasts.

Her absolutely perfect, luscious breasts.

She picked up her fur coat and slipped back into it. "You sure?"

"I'm dead positive."

He expected her to look good walking away. Hell, she even looked hot flipping him off. But the last thing Granger expected to see when he came out from behind the curtain was Dallas Ostrander in a lip-lock with Buster Root, and Buster's eyes rolling up so far back in his head he could probably see his sinus cavities.

Granger yelled, "Get him away from her."

The deputy stepped in and separated them, sweeping Dallas off to one side as he pulled Buster beyond her reach.

"You want to file charges?" Granger asked Buster. "That's simple assault."

Buster shook his head.

"Son. Of. A. Bitch." To Dallas, he said, "Lady, don't you *ever* fuck with my inmates again. You hear me?"

Instead of answering, Dallas flashed him a huge smile, and sashayed across the basketball court with her heels clicking against the floor.

It was then that Granger noticed the petite blonde, dressed in the school's colors, sitting in the bleachers, hunkered over her laptop with her head bent in concentration. She had a face carved out of marble, and the kind of diabolical smile that made men's hearts skip a beat. She seemed vaguely familiar. But at the moment, he couldn't place her. He'd met all the new teachers, and he thought he knew most of the kids. Hell, he'd watched them grow up. But this gal? This little heifer was smokin' hot. So how was it he couldn't place her?

He touched the brim of his Stetson, *Howdy.* Then he turned his attention back to his deputy. "Get him back to jail," Granger growled. "I'm not done with you yet. Come straight to my office after you lock him up, and be ready to explain to me how that woman managed to get back there without you saying anything."

Then he stomped out the door ahead of

them, listening to Buster's chains rattle against the basketball court's pale maple floor with each tiny geisha step.

He was only a few blocks from the office when the screaming deputy radioed in his location. "I need backup. Buster Root just escaped."

Granger whipped the unmarked cruiser into the intersection, stomping the accelerator until he felt the sole of his boot against the floorboard. He headed in the direction where Buster had bailed out of the patrol car and taken off on foot.

He wanted to kill Dallas Ostrander.

But first, he wanted to inflict as much pain as possible, dump her cold, dead corpse on a stack of mesquite logs, light it and send her straight to hell in a bonfire. He didn't need to ask what that lip-lock she'd planted on Buster had been about.

He knew the answer with one-hundred-percent certainty.

That's how she'd slipped him the handcuff key.

CHAPTER TWENTY-SIX

After spending more than six hours at the Dallas PD, the last thing Aspen wanted to see when she arrived home around seven-thirty that same evening was Rochelle's lipstick-red Nissan Z parked in her driveway. When she didn't see Rochelle's silhouette in the car, she assumed the woman had broken into her house.

The last time Rochelle had come here, she'd almost lost her life — they both had. The mechanic had ambushed Rochelle, tied her up, duct taped her mouth, and then lain in wait for Aspen to get home. She should've realized something was out of order. The house had been eerily quiet.

Not so tonight.

Her stereo had been turned on and turned up, and Italian opera numbers that didn't come from her collection spun out of the CD player and leaked out through the door.

She opened the door and let herself in to

smells of marinara sauce. Stir Fry's empty crate, visible from its place in the living room, sent a lance of misery to her heart as she followed the aroma into the kitchen. From the doorway, she could see her small bistro table draped in a red-and-white-checkered tablecloth, with two place settings of spatter ware in a soothing shade of blue. A small bouquet of wildflowers was hydrating in a simple crystal rose bowl. A bottle of wine chilled in a nearby ice bucket.

These items did not belong to her.

It was almost as if she'd inadvertently walked into a neighbor's house.

Rochelle saw Aspen and grinned. "Oh. It's you."

"What are you doing?"

Rochelle had opened a bottle of wine, and poured a new glass full before topping off her own. "Here. Drink this."

"No, thanks."

"Trust me, you'll need it."

"What's this all about? Why are you in my house?"

"In due time, my pet. In due time." Rochelle walked over to the CD changer and pushed a button. The music of Tuscany filled the kitchen. "Follow me."

Aspen obliged, trailing Gordon's assistant to the guest bathroom.

"Here's a gift. Put it on." Rochelle handed her a box.

"What?"

"Aspen, I swear." Exasperation tinged her voice. "Didn't you ever have someone surprise you so completely that it left you speechless?"

"I don't like surprises."

"That's because the surprises you've been getting lately are of the bogeyman-behind-the-door variety. This is different. This is the good kind."

"No — I really don't like surprises."

"You'll like this one."

Aspen gave up. Handed Rochelle her half-empty glass and retreated into the powder room. She closed the door and, for good measure, locked herself inside.

What had Rochelle done?

For all she knew, this could be Chucky-in-a-carton.

She slowly lifted the lid. Pulled back the tissue paper to reveal a folded piece of white cloth that was almost as sheer as the wrapping. When she shook it out, she was looking at a peasant blouse. The tag was missing and it appeared to have been previously worn. When she lifted it to her nose and sniffed, it smelled of floral detergent and fabric softener. She dug further into the box and found an item stitched from gauzy purple cloth. Shaking it out, she watched it unfurl from its own weight.

This was a broomstick skirt — or peasant skirt — the kind you laundered and wrung out in your hands before tying pieces of string around it to ensure that it crinkled during the drying process.

Crinkle-cloth. Yeah, that was it.

For several seconds, she stared at her confused face, reflected in the mirror. Had these things been Rochelle's? It was hard to imagine Rochelle hanging out in anything this casual, even cooped up in her own home with no expectation of drop-in company.

Surely there was more.

She draped the clothes over one arm and dug through the tissue paper, bypassing what appeared to be a scarf. At the bottom of the box, she came across a card. It rested on a pair of cheap black flip-flops, the kind you'd find in the seasonal section of the drugstore. She pulled out the thongs, dropped them on the floor and turned the card over in her hand.

It had been typed, and read: *"I may not be able to spirit you away to Italy tonight, but I can give you the next best thing."*

So that was it. Rochelle, ever the enigma,

trying to do something nice for a change.

Maybe this was a theme dinner with spaghetti and meatballs. She loved spaghetti and meatballs.

Or lasagna. Rochelle made the best lasagna.

She watched herself brighten and grinned back at her reflection. Rochelle had probably made lasagna and brought it over for dinner.

As she slid out of her dress and slipped the peasant blouse over her head, she wondered whether Rochelle would be dressed in similar clothing when she returned to the dinner table. She stepped into the skirt and pulled the elastic waistband over her hips, then smoothed the fabric until it hung just so. She tried it several ways: blouse in, blouse out, blouse tucked back in. Either way, it didn't look so hot. Then she remembered the scarf.

When she tied it around her waist, the costume — if that's what this was — looked perfect.

She folded the green dress — it would have to be dry-cleaned — and placed it beside a stack of hand towels.

What the heck? This could be fun.

She took off her Ferragamos and slipped on the thongs, gave her hair the once-over and pronounced herself ready as ever.

She walked back into the dining room but didn't see Rochelle. She continued through the kitchen, calling her name.

"Out here."

She couldn't see Rochelle beyond the screen door but she did glimpse twinkling lights in red, white and green.

What?

She felt a smile break across her face.

She took the porch steps down to the patio with the music of Tuscany filtering through the leaves. Houseplants in terracotta containers had been brought in, along with several ficus trees. Some sort of canopy had been put together, and those twinkle lights were everywhere.

Then she heard water, like the sound of a distant waterfall or an outdoor pond. She rounded another corner and stopped dead in her tracks.

There was Rochelle, just beyond an archway of grapevines — complete with grapes — standing next to a washtub, holding their glasses of wine.

"I don't understand."

Rochelle gestured toward the tub — full of grapes. "This is for you," she said, handing over the hastily scrawled note, done in the kind of penmanship that might interest a psychiatrist for the criminally insane.

It read: *"It'll be just like Lucy and Ethel. Only without Ethel."*

"I don't understand. Did you write this?"

It took a few seconds for the moment to sink in.

"I think you're supposed to take off your shoes and step on in," Rochelle said with a grin.

"But I —" Aspen's throat caught. "What made you — ? How'd you know — ?"

"Not me, sweetie. Dirty Harry."

"Spike did this?"

He must've bought a hundred pounds of grapes.

She pulled up the skirt hem and put a foot into the tub. It squished. Then she stepped the rest of the way in with the cool night breeze ruffling her hair.

Rochelle raised her glass in a toast. "May you never run out of grapes to stomp — or men's hearts to stomp on."

Aspen's chest tightened. Her nose burned, and tears blistered behind her eyeballs. "Did you put him up to this?"

"Not at all. I only furnished the clothes and the meal."

"You plotted this with him?"

"No. It was totally his doing. He left me fifty bucks to pay for the ingredients and pick up a few plants at the nursery. Don't thank me. I'll dance at your wedding."

"Rochelle," she said warily, not wanting to say there'd be no wedding. "I know what I saw."

"From the sparks of conflict rise the flames of desire. Blah, blah, blah. Your words are wasted on me."

Aspen ducked her chin and smiled.

It touched her, the trouble he'd gone to in order to fulfill a fantasy. They'd been talking about taking a trip together and she told him that as soon as she built up enough vacation, she wanted to go to Ireland, the homeland of her father's people. Or Paris. Then Spike vetoed Paris, so she said she could see herself in Italy, stomping grapes. Tears blurred her vision.

The next time she saw Spike — and she realized that she *would* see him, even if it was only for closure — she wouldn't tell him that she'd only remarked about stomping grapes in Italy because she'd watched *I Love Lucy* the night before and the scene stuck in her mind like a song you can't get out of your head. He'd gone to so much trouble to please her.

"Aw, look at you having fun. See? Told you you'd like it."

"Did he make the food, too?"

"No way. That's where I came in. Nobody makes Italian like I do."

"I don't know, Rochelle. Spike's a pretty good cook," she said, still squishing grapes underfoot.

"*Ha.* I'll pit my Italian cuisine against his anytime. One of these days I'll challenge him to a cook-off. By the time he finishes eating my spaghetti, he'll be forced to admit his food tastes like economy class on Air Cambodia."

Then Rochelle seemed to have an epiphany. "I almost forgot. This came for you while you were out." She rummaged through her purse and pulled out a pink message slip. "Now let's eat."

Aspen read the note, written in Rochelle's psychotic penmanship: *Spike's having a fund-raiser. Be there. All will be made clear. Call office tomorrow betw. 2–3. Ask Lucinda to put you through.*

"Rochelle." Aspen held the note as if she had a mouse by the tail. "Who's this from?"

"I asked, but she wouldn't leave her name. She kept talking about a paper cut."

CHAPTER TWENTY-SEVEN

The next morning, Aspen studied Heath Strawn's notes between broadcasts. She learned plenty from the entries. In short, Strawn accused Dolly Hastings of running a black-market baby operation. She preyed on young pregnant girls over the age of eighteen, bribing them with money that allowed them to live high on the hog until their babies were born. But after Dolly financed the irresponsible lifestyle of one such girl, the teen — a Goth — reneged on her promise to give up her newborn for adoption and ended up dead in a ditch.

Aspen couldn't believe what she was reading.

Dates, times, and places. If she had copies of this information in her possession, imagine the powderkeg the Dallas PD would have if they found the remaining pages. She picked up the landline in her office and dialed the SWAT commander. From that contact, she learned that five additional pages had been retrieved.

"I'd like to make a deal," she said.

The short answer was, the Dallas SWAT didn't make deals.

"I think I can help." With the remaining documents now photocopied, Aspen could turn over the remaining evidence. But first she needed a favor. "If you'll fax me copies of those pages, or scan and e-mail them to me, I'll make an on-air announcement that there's a reward for anyone who finds more of these sheets and turns them in." The words popped out before she could stop them.

"Tell you what," he challenged, "if you get those papers over here in the next half hour, I won't file charges against you."

She tried to imagine what Gordon would say if he'd landed himself in the same predicament. When it mattered, Gordon played hardball.

"I just realized I must've been mistaken. These notes are tonight's news script. I can't imagine where those papers went," she said coolly. "What if I can't find them?"

Ten minutes later, Rochelle brought a six-page fax back to her office. Now she could fill in the blanks. She spent some time looking them over, jotted down a few notes and headed down the corridor to the studio.

Miked up and ready to give the morning broadcast, Aspen settled into her chair and waited for Traffic Monitor Joey to give the morning traffic report. But when the commercial ended, the cutaway to Chopper Deke revealed that Traffic Monitor Joey had been replaced with Traffic Monitor Dainty.

Aspen's jaw dropped. Her eyes slewed over to Reggie, who was sucking down one of his energy drinks and looking bored out of his mind. He picked up on her confusion and wandered over to the anchor desk.

"Joey quit. Gordon had to send somebody up in his place."

"Since when do we pair up interns with Chopper Deke?"

"Since Joey demanded combat pay and didn't get it."

Across the room, Misty barked out a laugh and gestured at the monitor where poor Dainty heaved into her barf bag.

"Gordon ought to get rid of Deke. He's psycho."

"Do you have any idea how hard it is to find a helicopter pilot who wants to work for this penny-ante station?"

Misty, who must've thought she had more time and wasn't expecting the TCU intern to throw up her guts, hurried over to the green screen in time to position herself in front of it. The producer, apparently thinking he'd have to do the weather forecast himself, passed a dramatic hand across his brow, flinging invisible sweat into the air. He counted her down: three, two, one.

Misty blinked at the camera. She held an envelope. "Okay, people. Anchors aren't the only ones who get fan mail." She stuck a thumbnail under the flap. It made a ripping sound as she dragged it the length of the letter. Spreading the serrated envelope apart with her fingers, she tugged at a sheet of paper and shook it out. On a split-screen monitor, VIPIR — short for Volumetric Imaging and Processing of Integrated Radar, the most advanced radar for broadcasters — showed a total of three inches of rainfall on the scale.

Her jolly smile slipped away. The sudden downturn of her lip telegraphed disappointment. "This guy wants to know how to tell when we're going to have severe weather." Her hand dropped to her side. "Oh, give me a break, will you? Just look at the screen. Wherever you see a line where two different colors meet, if you're in that area, take cover." The fan mail fluttered to the floor. "Let's make this simple, shall we? If I'm ever up here talking and you see red on the

Doppler weather radar, run. If we have testicle-sized hail or larger, run. If you see a funnel cloud, run. As for today, it's all to the east of us. So don't worry about getting wet."

Reggie, who'd momentarily slipped out the studio door, returned with a Dr Pepper. He mouthed, "It's raining," and did a little downward-falling finger-flutter to show it was pouring.

A public service message ran for the next thirty seconds, followed by three more sponsor ads. Then Aspen read from the teleprompter. "One woman's battle with City Hall turned ugly this afternoon when eighty-year-old Agnes Loudermilk chained herself to the front door of the old Cattle Driver's Hotel — naked. Loudermilk, who ran the hotel when it was reputed to be a brothel over fifty years ago, is protesting the building's upcoming demolition and says she won't leave until the city agrees to sell the property to the Historical Society for a museum. Stinger Baldwin is on the scene with a report. Stinger?"

A clip of the former madam popped up on the monitor. Viewers were treated to a close-up of Agnes, topless, looking like she had a pair of flesh-toned knee-highs with a tangerine dropped into the toe of each one hanging from her chest. Passersby reacted with horrified looks, like the ones on the faces of Polish refugees in old war movies.

Stinger said, "Aspen, for the past several hours, Mrs. Loudermilk has been exposing more than just her political views. She's kept her promise to identify local politicians she claims patronized this former house of ill repute, and you can hear her yelling names from beneath the awning . . ."

Censors scrambled to bleep out words. "Mayor, you pin-*bleep,* I'm the one who broke you in when you were nothing but a pimple-faced, pimple-*bleep* little prick. And Councilwoman Samuelson, your husband used to be my best customer. And don't try to cover for him — I've seen his *bleep* up close and it has a strawberry mark shaped like the state of Florida on it. Why, I knew your father and it's a damned wonder you even got born because I've seen his *bleep,* too . . . that old thing was so small I had to use a magnifying glass to find it."

Unfortunately, the piece on Agnes Loudermilk turned out to be the best part of the broadcast.

Before they cut to a guest interview Steve Lennox had prepared with the Texas Rangers new left-hand pitcher, Aspen honored her promise to the Dallas SWAT commander and asked any viewers who might have found the rest of Heath Strawn's papers to take them directly to the Dallas PD. After the wrap-up, she returned to her office and went back to her copies of Heath's notes. She picked up a pen and tablet and began to create what amounted to a timeline of terror.

By the end of her workday, Aspen had learned that, while in her mid-twenties, fifty-something Dolly Hastings had been a suspect in the murder of her common-law husband and the attempted murder of another boyfriend shortly thereafter; underwent a ten-year stint on probation that caused the state bar to lift her law license; reinvented herself after she got her law license back, only to again become a suspect in the unexplained death of a client at her home, the hanging death of a building contractor who'd been putting an addition on her office, the murder of her pregnant secretary's husband, and the attempted murder of her pregnant secretary.

And, if Heath Strawn could be believed, the murder and evisceration of a pregnant Goth girl.

Around two in the afternoon, Aspen called the Johnson County Sheriff's Office and asked for Lucinda. When Lucinda came on the line, she asked to be put through to Sheila.

"We don't have anyone named Sheila working here."

Then it dawned on her. Like *Mission Impossible,* Lucinda had probably been told to deny Sheila worked there.

"Then put me through to Susanna Epps."

"I'm sorry. We don't have anyone named Susanna Epps who works here."

"Then put me through to Paper Cut."

Silence stretched between them.

"I can't do that," Lucinda said tentatively. "Who'd you say is calling?"

"I didn't."

"No one by that name is here."

"Can you clarify that statement for me: She's not there at the moment, or she's not there yet, or she's not going to be there at all?" Aspen didn't intend to have a dialogue tinged in snippiness, but what was it about these law-enforcement types that made them act so paranoid? She tried once more to get a straight answer. "Look, she called and left a message — Paper Cut, Susanna Epps, Crazy Sheila — whatever. I'm supposed to call her back between two and three o'clock. She said to ask for Lucinda. That's you. And that you'd help put me through to her."

"Wait. She got a message to you?"

Oh, so now you know who she is? "That's correct."

"When did she call you?"

"I don't know. Someone else took this down. It looks like maybe four or five yesterday afternoon."

"Oh, my stars. Just a moment."

It was all very Deep Throat.

The next thing Aspen knew, she'd been forwarded to another line. When Spike answered, she slammed the phone in his ear.

In less than a minute, her cell phone trilled. Instinct told her it was Spike. But an unfamiliar number popped up on the digital display so she answered it.

"Hello, darlin'."

Well, hell. "Don't call me."

"I'm returning *your* call."

"I didn't call you."

"Then why'd Lucinda put you through to me?"

"I was looking for someone else."

"I doubt that."

"I was."

"Who?"

"Crazy Sheila." She could almost hear his booted feet coming off the desk, and the chair snapping into an upright position.

"How do you know Crazy Sheila?"

"None of your business. You're not the boss of me."

"Listen to me, Aspen," he growled in his roughly textured, no-nonsense, *I mean business* tone, "we've been looking for Sheila since late yesterday afternoon. There's a BOLO out on her. Now, if you know something, you need to spill it."

The Spike Granger she'd known and loved had vaporized, replaced by his alter ego, Spike Granger the confession extractor.

"What do you mean, you're looking for her? She works for you."

"And she's missing."

Oh, no. The weight of this news struck like an anvil dropped from a cliff. "Does this have anything to do with the Goths?"

"What do you know about the Goths?" he demanded.

"I'll tell you, but you have to share what *you* know. I'll be at your office in twenty minutes."

CHAPTER TWENTY-EIGHT

Granger hung up the phone. He had no intention of swapping so much as one damned kernel of information about this investigation with Aspen, even if he did want to throw her down and make mad, passionate love to her. This was an official police investigation, and his deputy's safety might be jeopardized. So, no, he did *not* plan to share information.

Before she showed up in her little black-and-blue houndstooth suit that fit better than a sprayed-on tan, he'd wanted to grab her and pull her inside his office, back-kick the door closed, and sweep everything off the desk. She was a sight for sore eyes. But when she strutted in all *Let's Make A Deal,* the desire to clear off the desk evaporated. Now, he just wanted to bend her over his knee.

"How do you know Sheila?" he asked. "And let me take a look at that phone message."

"Not so fast," she said, flaunting her advantage like a boa of ostrich and marabou feathers. "I'll tell you what I know, but then you have to share what you know about the Goths. And about Kirk House."

This took him aback. "What do you know about Kirk House?"

They each held part of the puzzle. If she wanted the rest, they'd have to work together.

"That's where I met her," Aspen said. "Now I have a question for you. Why the Goths?"

"Drugs. Let me see the message."

She handed it over. When he finished reading it, she said, "What's with Kirk House?"

"It's a hangout."

"I get that." Said facetiously. "What else?"

His eyes thinned into slits. "We found a dead girl near there a few months ago."

"You think it's somehow tied in?" She pulled out a spiral notebook, then flipped to a fresh page and poised her pen to write.

"Maybe."

"What was her name?"

"It's not your turn." *Parry and thrust.*

For the next few minutes, they sat staring at each other in a standoff; her across the desk from him, seated in one of his comfy leather guest chairs; him behind the desk with his elbows on the blotter and his fingers steepled.

"My deputy's missing. If you're holding back anything that'll help us find her, you need to give it up now. Now, Aspen. I'm not fooling around. Her life may depend on this."

"I get an exclusive."

"Fine. But not until the whole investigation's over. You can have your story when the indictments come down. Or if we find her dead in a ditch. Whichever comes first." He didn't mean it to happen, but his voice cracked. And from the expression on her face, she heard it.

He rose from the desk and snatched his hat off the wall peg. "Let's go."

"Where are we going?"

"For a drive."

They were inside the unmarked patrol car, several miles from the SO and headed out to Sheila's house, when Granger said, "Ellie Canfield. Her parents and I went all through school together. She was a good girl. Then she fell in with the Goths." He slid her a sidelong glance. "Rumor had it she was pregnant, although her mama will deny it to her dying day. But the principal thinks so.

The autopsy confirmed it."

"What happened to her baby?"

Eyes on the road, he shook his head.

"Is that the reason you put Sheila in the high school?"

"Susanna. Don't say Sheila again. Understand? We're calling her Susanna."

"Is that why you put Susanna in the high school?"

"One of the reasons."

"And the other reasons?"

"Already said. Drugs."

"Do you think Ellie Canfield was killed over drugs?"

"I don't know what I think anymore. Instead of becoming clearer, it's more screwed up than ever."

Aspen looked around. The last of the city lights played out, and now they were driving into the countryside with only the moon, the stars, and the headlights on the patrol car to guide them.

She said, "Where are we going?"

"To Sheila's."

"I thought you said to call her Susanna."

"If you're talking about Goths, you're talking about Susanna. That's the distinction. Right now, I'm worried about my deputy."

They drove in scary silence. When they

arrived at Crazy Sheila's, Granger cut the
headlights and shut off the engine. "Stay
here. I'll have a look around."

"You're not leaving me out here."

"You'll ruin your shoes."

"You're buying me another pair."

He gave a derisive grunt, pulled out the
flashlight stuffed between the two seats, and
turned on the handheld. The police radio
crackled to life. "Stay behind me."

"So you can stir up the snakes so they can
get me?" Her tone said, *I don't think so!*

"Fine. Then stay beside me. And keep
quiet. Don't slam the door getting out." As
he alighted from the unmarked car and
carefully clicked the door shut, Aspen followed suit. They surveyed the perimeter
from their place near the hood.

"Ever been deer hunting?"

She shook her head.

"Too bad. This is a lot like deer hunting."

"How so?"

"Make a bunch of noise, you scare off the
deer. Now, come along." He headed toward
the house with Aspen a half step behind.
When they reached the door, Granger
stepped off to one side, pulling Aspen so
hard he nearly toppled her.

"No need to manhandle me." With an
aristocratic sniff, she jerked her arm from

319

his grasp.

He hadn't meant to be so rough. And he didn't like the look she'd given him when she pulled away because he couldn't read her expression in their dimly lit space. He didn't trust his own judgment while standing alone with her out in the boondocks. And yet the dazzled look she'd gotten when he put his hands on her suggested his touch had thrilled her. So he was probably losing his mind. Even worse, her presence left him floating in the abyss. Not good, since his job was to protect her.

"A lot of cops have died standing directly in front of a door," he snapped, dodging her glare and the blame. "I reckon they were no match for the blast of a shotgun through the wood." He rang the bell. They stood off to one side for thirty seconds or so before he rang it again. Then he jabbed the button like he was putting out Morse code.

Nothing.

"Hear anything?" he asked.

She shook her head.

"Me neither. Let's check around back."

"Does she have a dog?"

"I'm guessing no. If she did, it would've been barking by now." He paused for a second. "How's your dog?"

"That's what I came to tell you about the

other day. That dog you pawned off on me got me arrested."

"What?" Granger stopped in his tracks. "Fine. I'll come get him."

"No need." Her voice cracked. With a soft gasp, she buried her face in her hands. "He's dead."

Well, hell. "Wait for me back at the car." With eyes focused on their surroundings, he dug into his pocket for the key. Urgency gripped him. Damned women. They were still about as foreign a notion to him as the Dead Sea Scrolls. One would probably get him killed, but it by-God wouldn't be tonight.

"No." She brushed away tears with the back of her hand. "I'm fine."

But her bottom lip looked like it weighed fifty pounds and said, *Not fine.* He wished she hadn't told him about the dog, because he already had enough horror shows reeling through his head. Who did that? Stood around a potential crime scene looking like he was grabbing his whanker through his pants pocket?

I mean, Granger thought, *you're out in the middle of frickin' nowhere, your deputy could be inside that house carved up like a twenty-dollar steak, and* — oh, wait! — *your girlfriend decides to turn you into her own personal wail-*

ing wall, and all of a sudden you're leaking like a sieve and plugging bullet holes with your fingers. No thanks. Better to go it alone.

"Where you go, I go," she said with a little hair toss.

He knew her so well that her tone of voice told him precisely what he suspected. Aspen Wicklow would go to hell and back to get a story.

CHAPTER TWENTY-NINE

"How do you know the dog's dead?" Granger froze near the back porch.

It was a rhetorical question, and Aspen knew it. He was just trying to make her feel better . . . to hold out hope and behave until they could get back to the patrol car and talk it out. Granger may have been a country boy, born and raised, but Aspen had visited her grandparents' farm enough times to know a coyote's hunting technique like the back of her hand — stalk, attack, crush the neck in its jaws, render the prey immobilized and helpless. Then carry it off to be eaten later.

Aspen swallowed hard. "I'll tell you about it some other time," she whispered. "What're we looking for back here?"

"It's where Sheila's bedroom is."

"How do you know?" The words were hot-wired to her tongue, and she regretted them as soon as they rushed out.

"I know the guy who built this subdivision. All of the floor plans are the same out here. The only reason the houses look different is because they flip-flopped them. Now be quiet."

She stood beside him, stewing in her own juices, hating the way her mind ran rampant with suspicion. Had one bad experience because of Roger's cheating ruined her trust in all future suitors? But she'd seen Spike with that leggy blonde suction cupped to his neck, so why not a pseudo-Goth?

The accusations that wanted to fly were instantly halted when Granger held up a hand. "Hear that?"

Another head shake.

He raised his fist and hammered it against the window frame in the kind of unmistakable police knock that precipitated every raid she'd ever seen in gritty cop movies. Granger yelled, "Johnson County Sheriff. Open up."

Then he fell silent. Straining against the whispering breeze, he listened. Abruptly, he inclined his head toward the window. "Hear that?"

Another head shake.

"Well, I did." He called out Sheila's name in the eerie twilight. Then he waited a few seconds before grabbing his handy-talkie and radioing in their location to the dispatcher. He requested a unit to start their way. Then he turned to face her. "Here's your choice. I'm going back to the car for a master key. You can either stay put, or go with me."

Aspen gaped.

Master key?

So you have been here before.

Bastard. I knew it.

"Then stay put." He un-holstered one of his Colt .45 Commanders and handed it to her. "By the powers vested in me, you're hereby deputized. If you see something move, and you don't know what it is, shoot it."

"Yeah? That's what got me arrested."

Before heading out of sight, he said, "It'll take me less than two minutes to get back here. Do not shoot me. Understand? No matter how much you'd like to."

She didn't expect to giggle. It wasn't funny and she still harbored a grudge.

"One more thing," he said, before walking around the corner and disappearing from view, "I love you."

Maybe Rochelle was right with her pep talk — that he'd love her if she had an ass like a forty-dollar mule.

She started counting: *One-Mississippi, two-*

Mississippi, three-Mississippi . . . inwardly panicking when she reached the two-minute mark. Then she heard the crunch of dry grass underfoot, just before Granger rounded the corner carrying a twenty-pound maul.

Ahh . . . the master key.

He holstered the Colt and gave whoever was in the house one last chance to open the door. His knock went unanswered. But this time, Aspen heard what Granger had heard — a thin moan, coming from inside the bedroom.

He ordered her to stand back, but he needn't have bothered. She'd already given him a wide berth, stepping aside to put herself out of range. After tucking the flashlight into his waistband, he wielded the sledgehammer.

It sounded like the Earth opening up as the door cracked open, taking the molding inside with it.

"Sheriff's Office. Come out with your hands up."

The moan increased in volume and pitch.

"Watch the door," Granger said under his breath, propping the sledgehammer up against the nearest wall. Then he drew his weapon and pulled out the flashlight. "I'm going in."

"Right behind you."

"Don't shoot me in the back."

She hooked a finger onto the leather gun belt of his double-rig, taking side steps like a crab in an effort to discourage would-be intruders from getting the jump on them. As he drew her further into the house, her heart skipped. Blood whooshed between her ears.

Red and blue lights flashed in the distance — Granger's backup, running Code-Two.

As he cleared each room with a sweep of the flashlight, he flipped on the light switch and illuminated the area. Then they reached the bedroom.

Granger twisted the doorknob and flung open the door. The flashlight beam swept across the room. "Oh, no."

When he slapped on the light switch, Aspen sucked air. And promptly wished she hadn't. The stench of urine filled the room. Her nose clamped down in self-defense.

A shirtless male, dressed in tight leather pants, lay dead on the floor, clutching a flogger in a death grip. Postmortem lividity had set in, creating pale, blotchy skin on his back and mottled reddish-purple coloring on the areas of his body making contact with the floor.

Sheila wasn't dead.

But she probably wished she were.

Granger holstered his weapon. Then he took his other gun from Aspen and holstered it, too. When he stepped aside to take a closer look at the deceased, Aspen saw what he'd seen when he first hit the room with the beam of light.

Sheila lay on her back with her right hand cuffed to one metal rod of an iron headboard, and the other hand tied with a necktie to the opposite metal bar. Legs splayed, her feet were similarly restrained with ties knotted around spokes in the bed frame's footboard. She lay naked from the waist up, except for a black harness that separated her breasts, and black crotchless panties that did precious little to cover the waterfront. Silver bullrings had been fastened to her nipples, and red welts lashed her thighs and breasts. Her face was fully covered with paper-white makeup, except for the black spidery drawings that ringed her eyes. Black-lined lips were stretched to accommodate a ball gag.

While Aspen stood riveted in place, with her mouth opening and closing like a big-mouth bass, Granger whipped out a tiny key and unlocked the handcuffs, as if he were an OB-GYN accustomed to seeing exposed coochies. Then he cut away the neckties with his penknife while Sheila tried to remove the ball gag. Her arms must've gone heavy and her hands numb, because she pleaded with her eyes.

Aspen unhooked the buckle. As for this masochistic need-to-know mentality? Well, she could do without.

Granger said, "This your ex?"

Sheila nodded, working her jaw and swollen tongue.

"Consensual?"

Sheila nodded without meeting his gaze.

"What happened?"

"If it's all the same to you, Spike, I'd like to get my robe."

"Sure," Granger said.

A commotion that began at the back door worked its way inside the house. For a moment, Granger seemed to have forgotten about the backup unit he'd radioed for. "Stay with her. I'll handle this." He left the room, closing the door behind him.

"Where's your robe?" Aspen said, distracted.

Sheila jutted her chin toward the closet. She leaned over and picked up one of the pillows off the floor, removed the pillowcase, and used it to wipe off her face.

"I'm so embarrassed." The tips of her ears had turned red, and she had trouble moving her jaw.

Aspen found a housecoat and handed it over. "What happened?"

"My ex is — *was* — a kinkster. Role-play, stuff like that. He handcuffed me to the bed. How was I to know he'd drop dead on me? I've been like this for twenty-four hours, unable to move, unable to call for help, strangling on my own drool."

That was putting it mildly. Not to mention the smells.

Aspen said, "That must've been awful."

Crazy Sheila shrugged into her bathrobe. "What I want to know is, what took him so long to break down the damned door?"

When Aspen found Granger outside, he was standing in front of the patrol car holding a tactical baton. He looked like King Kong with a toothpick.

"That was nice, what you did," Aspen said on the ride back to the SO.

"I'm just glad it was me who found her that way. If it'd been one of my men, it'd be all over the department. Some of these guys are like the town crier."

"Not this. The grapes. It was sweet."

"I'd take you there if I could. But I can't afford the time while the election's coming up on me."

"It didn't have to be Italy. I would've settled for Paris."

"I believe I made my feelings clear on that one."

"I don't understand why it'd matter if we went there for a week." *Listen to yourself . . . talking like you have a future with this man.*

"Because I told you I didn't want to go there at all."

Sounds like he's still game.

Is he still game?

"You're so stubborn," she said.

"And you're not?"

"So if I wanted to go for a week, and you didn't want to go there, period, would you at least entertain the possibility of a compromise by spending one day there?" Inwardly, she held her breath. This wasn't about a trip to Europe. This was code for whether they could have any kind of future together.

"Tell you what — if you find a travel agent who can get me the Hitler package, I'll agree to it."

"Hitler package?"

"That's right, the Hitler package. Hitler was there for twenty-four hours and saw the Eiffel Tower and Notre Dame. That's enough for me."

CHAPTER THIRTY

During the drive home to Fort Worth, Aspen pondered the question Granger left her with.

"So, are we together, or not?"

"I need time to think about it."

Then he'd said, *"Kiss me,"* and leaned closer.

Even though she'd given him the Heisman, seeing him had churned up those warm feelings she'd stuffed away. But the images of the blonde that were branded in her head would take more than a ride in a patrol car to drive out.

She had time to grab a few hours' sleep before dressing for work and heading off to the station to deliver the morning show.

If Granger had an unsolved homicide that might somehow be linked to Kirk House, maybe the way to get a handle on this tangled mess was to think outside the box. First, she checked the computer's search engine for realtors in the Metroplex and typed "horseshoe logo" into her search terms. Then she pared the possibilities down to only the surrounding counties and came up with Lucky Realty. It was almost too easy. She called the company and spoke to the realtor. From that contact, she learned that Cynthia Kirk, mother of the two victims and the only living survivor at eighty-three years old, lived at Tranquility Villas.

Aspen's eyes almost popped from her head like champagne corks. What were the odds?

But, hey, she reasoned, she'd tried to find the best rehab and care center for her parents. And the Kirks had tons of money and could afford it. Why wouldn't Mrs. Kirk want the best in the area, too? Inwardly, Aspen grimaced. Even the best nursing homes were bad.

After delivering the morning news, she drove to Tranquility Villas Care Center to meet Mrs. Kirk. With the luck of the Irish, she could sneak inside without running into Mrs. Ramsey.

Tranquility Villas, a taupe-colored stucco building at the end of a cul-de-sac, was less than three miles from Aspen's house on the west side of Fort Worth. Outside, the lawns were immaculately groomed, with flowerbeds planted in bright hues. This month, purple and yellow pansies filled them. Inside, the floors were kept polished to a high luster. Visiting areas painted in Wedgwood colors had matching sofas, a baby-grand piano in one corner, and plenty of fake ficus trees positioned near the windows. Oriental rugs had been used to break up large areas into smaller ones. As nursing homes and rehabilitation centers went, it was probably the best Fort Worth had to offer.

Aspen pulled into the parking lot and used the rearview mirror to check her freshly powdered nose. She cast a couple of furtive glances at Mrs. Ramsey's corner office, the one with two sets of windows that faced different directions. That setup gave her the optimum chance to watch whomever entered and exited the front doors, as well as checking out goings-on in the parking lot.

On almost all of Aspen's previous visits, Mrs. Ramsey had been on the telephone. Which was mostly a good thing. Today, she wasn't sitting behind her desk — which turned out to be an exceptionally good thing.

The electronic doors slid back and Aspen walked in.

Not so good.

"Miss Wicklow." Harriet Ramsey was standing just inside the door and off to one side, concealed by a large cane plant. "We need to talk."

Yikes. The woman had probably been lying in wait for her since she'd pulled into the parking lot. "I'm not here about my parents," Aspen said with put-on sweetness.

"Well, since you're here, and since your father was caught naked in the pool last night, we need to talk."

"Is that a problem?"

"What? Being naked in the pool? I should say so. Miss Wicklow, your father's done everything he can to expose himself to these ladies. These are nice, well-bred widow women that come from good families. I'm talking Fort Worth's social elite. We're expected to provide a safe environment for them."

"How many of them complained?"

"What?"

"The number of complaints, Mrs. Ramsey. How many widows complained? Or was it just the staff that brought this problem to your attention?"

"The staff."

"And these nice, well-bred women from good families — are they women without legs?"

"What? No. Of course they have legs."

"Well, unless they're amputees, or he's invading their rooms to pull his shenanigans, these nice ladies can get up and leave if they're offended."

"Miss Wicklow, you can't be serious."

"I'm very serious. Did you ever stop to think maybe some of them would *like* to see a naked man walking around here? Did it ever occur to you that maybe they *miss* seeing a penis? That it might actually be refreshing to see a man with TMDD Syndrome — which, by the way, stands for *Too Much Damned Dick.* For that matter, don't you think if it *really* bothered them — I mean *really, really* bothered them — that they'd bring their complaints to you instead of you getting them from the staff?"

"Well, I . . ."

"And you have to admit, Mrs. Ramsey, that it's a sight to behold. There are statues over in Italy with appendages that look like nubs compared to my father's. So why not just let the ladies look? They're clearly not as bashful as you think. It's like commerce. My father has a product to sell, and these widows want that product. He's just giving the people what they want."

An elderly woman using a walker hobbled past. She cut her eyes to Mrs. Ramsey and looked out from behind a stub of gray lashes. "Bring back naked Twister."

A cluster of ladies in pearls and diamonds who'd been loitering at the fringe of the lobby yelled out to the director.

"What about naked Monopoly?" Pearl Pureheart.

"Naked ping pong." Diamond Gemma.

"How about letting us play a little pocket pool?"

Aspen blinked. She recognized Agnes Loudermilk from the debacle down at City Hall and said, "Give the people what they want."

Poor Mrs. Ramsey. Must be frustrating knowing all the answers, when nobody bothered to ask the questions. She left the director speechless, standing on the rubber mat at the entrance while the electronic doors opened and closed.

At the nurses' station, Aspen found out the room number for Cynthia Kirk, but was told most of the residents were milling about on the sun porch.

She found Cynthia Kirk reclining in a chaise lounge. Mrs. Kirk sat next to the window, in an atmosphere heavy with memories, with her face tilted up to the blazing January sunshine. The morning sun made a latticework of light through the little square panes.

"Mrs. Kirk?" Aspen stuck out her hand. "I'm Aspen Wicklow. I'd like a moment to speak to you about your house."

Mrs. Kirk's face hardened into immobility. Blue eyes thinned into slits. "I told you people I wasn't going to sell to you. That house deserves a family in it. Not to be torn down so you can put a drilling rig out there. My husband and I raised our boys in that house, and the last thing he told me before he died was not to sell it unless it was going to a family."

Aspen stammered an apology. "I don't know what you mean." She took deep breaths until she got a dizzying rush.

"You're from that oil company. I told that land man the same thing. No sale."

"Land man?"

"Don't act like you don't know what I'm talking about. They think they can send a spindly girl to talk me into selling out cheap, and I won't. You money-grubbing so-and-sos stay off of my land or I'll get me an attorney. I won't be swindled . . ."

One of the nurses padded over, her rubber-soled shoes squeegee-ing across the tile floor. "You have to go." To Mrs. Kirk, she said, "Miss Cynthia, it'll be all right. She was just leaving."

Aspen blinked in dismay. "But I didn't do anything."

As the nurse took the elderly woman by the elbow and escorted her from the sunroom, she said, "This isn't a good day for Miss Cynthia. She usually does better in the afternoon."

Aspen could see the wisdom in not creating a scene.

She returned to Tranquility Villas at one o'clock, this time with a chocolate sampler box. Sure enough, Miss Cynthia did a lot better after the noon meal, once the chocolate took effect and her medication had a chance to kick in.

"I'd like to talk to you about Kirk House." She steeled herself for a lambasting.

Mrs. Kirk looked up in happy remembrance. "My late husband and I built that house. Had that pink granite trucked in from Enchanted Rock, down near Fredericksburg." For a moment, blue eyes retreated to a distant memory. "We raised our two boys there."

"It's a beautiful home."

"Are you familiar with what happened?"

"Yes, ma'am. I'm terribly sorry."

Using the "Loose lips sink ships" theory, Mrs. Kirk described how the architects of the home invasion — brothers who weren't actually part of their social circle, but had ties to a few wealthy members within it — went unchecked until authorities connected the dots. Those social butterflies who, say, bragged about an upcoming vacation to the French Riviera, or taking an Alaskan cruise, returned to find their homes had been burglarized.

Pulling herself back into the present, Mrs. Kirk said, "The realtor showed it a bunch of times. Said he had people interested in buying it. But they always pulled out of the deal at the last minute because of what happened."

"Miss Cynthia, I'd like to ask a few questions, if you don't mind. About the house."

"What about it."

"There have been rumors about screams coming from the house —"

Mrs. Kirk immediately stiffened. "You ask me, the land man's behind this. If there is something going on out there, he's the one with a motive."

She'd said that before, Aspen recalled. "Land man?"

"The oil company's land man who wants me to sell them the property. I won't do it. I made a promise to my husband. We raised our two boys there . . ."

Mrs. Kirk was still talking, but Aspen had

stopped listening. Distracted by the lady's words, she took a moment to digest the information.

"You ask me, the land man's behind this."

CHAPTER THIRTY-ONE

One of the happiest days of Granger's life occurred two days after Buster Root escaped, when the dispatcher telephoned him in the early-morning hours to say that Buster had been picked up in Roswell, Georgia, near Atlanta.

Granger booked a flight out of DFW around eleven that same morning, and was standing in line at one of the airport rent-a-car locations three hours later. He drove to the Fulton County jail with a copy of Buster's signed waiver of extradition and a copy of the Johnson County warrant that got Buster entered into the database in the first place.

He called Lucinda and had her book two return tickets on a Delta Airlines flight that departed for DFW at seven o'clock in the evening, Georgia time. They'd land at five o'clock Texas time.

An hour before takeoff on the return flight

home, Granger arrived with Buster at Hartsfield-Jackson Atlanta International Airport. Granger wore a tropical weight sportscoat over his trademark leather vest, white pinpoint Oxford shirt, khaki slacks and ostrich boots; Buster wore his trademark leg irons, belly chain and handcuffs. They cleared security by going through airport police, away from other customers.

Since Delta wouldn't allow the prisoner to fly leg ironed on one of their planes, Granger took off the restraints prior to boarding. Delta's policy also provided that a prisoner flying with handcuffs had to wear a jacket to conceal the restraints so as not to alarm other patrons. To comply, Granger brought along a plain, black windbreaker similar to one he owned, minus the word SHERIFF stenciled on the back in yellow Day-Glo letters.

"Last chance to use the can." Granger spoke in the somber voice of an officiate. "Pee now, or forever hold your piss." Hard experience supported the warning. He knew airplane lavatories were too small to accommodate more than one person unless that second person was a toddler. He wasn't about to unlock Buster's handcuffs, not even long enough for the man to take care of business. And he sure as hell wasn't going to leave the bracelets on and hold the inmate's whanker.

"I have the bladder of a camel, Spike. I'm not five."

"I'm not kidding." He didn't need to be telepathic to know he and Buster shared the same thought: that Buster might try to pull something on the plane.

"Sorry, Spike. I couldn't squeeze out a drop if you held a gun to my head."

Accompanied by the airport police, they were allowed to board the plane first, separate from the other passengers. When they reached the end of the jetway, Granger met the captain and provided the administrative paperwork necessary to get Buster on board. With Buster's hands secured in front of him, Granger herded the prisoner to their assigned seats near the tail section.

"What I need," Buster said pensively, "is a couple of midgets." He shifted his attention from the window to Granger. "Know any midgets?"

The sheriff scowled. "Midgets," he said with disdain, "what do you need midgets for?"

"My *Saw-a-girl-in-half* trick." Granger did a heavy eye roll, but Buster went on excitedly. "See, I saw this trick where a woman gets pulled in half. Well, she doesn't actually get pulled apart; it's just an illusion. See, Spike," he said, as if explaining to a slow learner, "a lot of these disappearing acts are smoke and mirrors. People don't really have the power to disappear — *Poof!* — into thin air. It just looks that way. A lot of times, once the curtain or shield or whatever goes up around the magician, he's not even there. You just thought he was there because he made you think he was there. Understand?"

"No," Granger groused, "I don't understand and I don't want to understand."

Buster relaxed against the seat back. "Everything would be fine if I just had a couple of midgets."

Granger chewed on that little nugget a while, until he felt the big L-1011 Tristar move slowly backward and gradually became aware of the engines spooling. As they taxied onto the runway, he spoke over the captain's welcome announcement. "What do you want with midgets?"

Buster made a loose fist and chucked Granger's arm. "That's the spirit, Spike." He twisted in his seat. "Okay, see, I think I've figured out that magician's pull-apart-woman trick. He gets this lady in the audience — she's a ringer, by the way; you know what a ringer is, don't you?"

Granger didn't answer, only shot him a look of disgust.

"Okay, so she's a ringer and she lies down on this park bench and one lady takes her hands and one lady takes her feet and when he says, "Pull," they pull. And presto. She comes in half." Buster's voice climbed with excitement. "Part of her is going this way, and part of her is sitting still, wiggling her toes. People are screaming . . ."

"Sounds stupid."

"It's not," Buster said with a vehement head shake. "It's like the best trick ever. And I think I've got it figured out, only I need a couple of midgets."

Several minutes went by. Silence stretched between them.

Then Granger said, "If you were to do this magic trick, how would you use the midgets?"

Buster brightened. "I'd get one of them to stand on the other one's shoulders. I'd have the top midget dressed like the top half of a person, and the bottom midget dressed like the bottom half of a person. Then the midget would get in the box and I'd saw it in half so you could only see the top midget's head and the bottom midget's feet. Then everybody'd scream . . ."

"That's stupid," Granger repeated, but he

continued to digest the possibility while Buster pouted in the window seat.

After several minutes went by, Granger said, "It'd be more effective if you had a guillotine."

"What?"

"A guillotine. Then you could put the midget where everybody could see him, and let the blade crash down. Then when everybody screams, you could pull the top midget off the bottom midget and have the midget screaming, too. Get the crowd going, you know?"

He couldn't believe he was saying this.

"But we'd have to drop the curtain right after," Buster said, "because we want them to think I chopped the man in half. Then the midgets can go back stage and you can *pretend-arrest* me."

"You're already under arrest."

"I know," Buster said as if this were merely an unpleasant technicality. "But that's when you could put the handcuffs on me and I could escape. I can tell you how to do that trick, too, if you want."

"You're not escaping at the magic show."

"I know, but I'll *pretend-escape* and everybody'll think I escaped, only I'll come back and take a bow . . . maybe I'll walk back into the room through the rows of people and hop up on stage right in front of them."

"Once I put handcuffs on you, they're not coming off."

Buster cast him a pitying glance. "They're not real handcuffs, Spike. They're trick handcuffs. Not like these." He gave his wrists a little snap, and the chain holding the two bracelets together clinked. "It's all an illusion, like I said. These" — his gaze dipped to his hands — "these are real."

CHAPTER THIRTY-TWO

The day started out with a sun-dappled morning, and Aspen had plenty to do. She'd been poring over Heath Strawn's notes again, trying to connect the dots. And there *was* a connection. She was so close she could taste it; she just needed to unearth a little more information. For one thing, Heath had confessed to killing a man, and his notes supported his claim. If the information could be believed, he had done so at the urging of Dolly Hastings.

But why would Heath do her bidding? What did a Dallas lawyer have on him that would make him commit such a crime?

The man he claimed to have killed was Art Singleton, co-owner and partner in a consulting firm called *Notario y Adopciónes*. Aspen found very little information on the business. The Web site was under construction. She picked up the office phone and called upstairs to Production. WBFD had a fact-checker on staff named Julie, and Aspen needed information quickly.

"Did we run a story about the murder of a man named Art Singleton?" Aspen asked. "I seem to recall a follow-up piece we were supposed to air when the hostage debacle took place."

"Sounds familiar," Julie said. "Call you back."

Soon, Aspen's line rang; Julie had come up with the scoop.

"Mr. Singleton was the guy gunned down a couple of days ago, right in front of his wife. When they came home from shopping after dark, the house lights were off. Mr. Singleton's wife, Libby, said the outside lights were still on when they left for the store.

"They were slow to get out of the car because of the packages they needed to carry inside. Baby items, I think. They were ambushed in the driveway by two people in ski masks. One had a shotgun. Mr. Singleton died at the scene."

"What happened to the wife?"

"She saw what was happening and ran like hell. They chased her down the street, and when they got close enough, they shot her, too. Almost severed her arm. She was in pretty bad shape. Doctors wouldn't let anyone disturb her — not even the cops. The other stations have people on it. I heard Mr. Welder say nobody's been able to get the exclusive. We have a tape if you want to come up here and watch it."

"Thanks. It can wait."

Aspen had no reason to think Libby Singleton would speak to her, but she wouldn't know unless she tried. Walking the long hospital corridor at Sisters of Perpetual Suffering, through air that was noxious with medicinal and disinfectant smells, Aspen formulated one of her fly-by-the-seat-of-your-pants plans. At Libby Singleton's room, several doors from the nurses' station, she read the sign posted outside the door: *Family only.*

A nurse padded up with a furrowed brow and a grimace. "May I help you?"

"I'm Libby Singleton's sister."

"You don't look like Mrs. Singleton."

"I'm adopted."

The nurse took a backward step, did a soft knuckle rap on the door and stuck her head partway inside the opening. "Mrs. Single-ton, your sister's here."

"Which one?" The patient spoke in a voice that came out raspy and unused.

"Do you want her to come back?"

Before she could respond, Aspen slipped

past her. "Hi, Libby, it's me." To the nurse, she said, "I'm Aspen."

Libby Singleton peered out from behind swollen eyelids.

Please, Aspen mouthed without sound, begging Libby's cooperation with hands clutched in prayer.

Libby glanced past Aspen's shoulder. "It's okay," she whispered.

The nurse closed the door behind her.

"You're the lady from TV. The one who cries over sad stuff. I've been watching ever since you did that story on that crazy sheriff." Chapped lips cracked into a faint smile. "You look just like on TV." A small thread of blood appeared on Libby's mouth where the dry skin broke.

Aspen grabbed a plastic cup. "You want water?"

Weak nod.

She poured in a splash from a thermal pitcher, then peeled the paper off a straw and bent it at the accordion pleats. As Libby Singleton sipped, Aspen looked her over. She saw an athletic woman of mixed race — possibly of Hispanic descent, or Dominican — with minimal body fat judging from the only visible extremity. She could just as easily have been recuperating in the maternity ward. Judging by her size, she was well

352

into the third trimester of her pregnancy.

Her lean left arm was attached to IVs and drips, and monitors that spiked detailed digital readings. The machines beeped at odd moments to signal a warning or maybe just to indicate that they needed resetting. Her right arm, cocooned in gauze packs and bandages, was attached to a machine that made soft growling noises as it moved her fingers in small revolutions.

Aspen had seen such a contraption before, attached to a field hand who'd accidentally chopped off a forefinger with a machete. Surgeons reattached it and hooked him up to the articulated unit, but the prognosis was poor and the doctors had worried about gangrene setting in. She inwardly shuddered at the memory of the poor guy sitting in her physician's office, her watching him through watery eyes, feeling sorry for herself over a bad case of flu while he waited, still shell-shocked, to be called for his follow-up appointment.

Libby sipped more water. Aspen took the cup and placed it back on an empty food tray.

"Why are you here?" Libby asked.

"I came to talk to you about a man named Heath Strawn. You know him?"

Libby's eyes floated up into her head. "He

killed my husband." Her eyelids fell to half-mast and her lashes fluttered back up.

"Why would he do something like that?"

"I saw you crying over him. But you didn't know him like I did. He was a bad man."

"Help me understand that. Why would he kill someone for no good reason?"

"She made him."

The "she" in Libby's accusation turned out to be Dolly Hastings.

"Why would she want your husband dead?"

"Not him, me. He was in the wrong place at the wrong time."

Collateral damage. "Why would she want to kill you?"

"I used to work for her. I know things that could get her the death penalty."

According to Libby, she left Dolly Hastings's office because she didn't like the way the family lawyer treated her clients — taking their money, promising them babies — so she started her own office doing the same thing. Only where Dolly Hastings set out to swindle people, Libby intended to run a bona fide adoption service.

"Are you a lawyer?"

"Paralegal. But I know as much as her, I just don't have the bar card." Deep sigh. "There are so many desperate couples out there, trying to have children. I had no idea until I started working for her. But she's a cheat. And she's unethical. If I had a dollar for every lie she told . . ."

"My station reported that two people were at the scene. Did you see the other person?"

"Dolly. I already told the police. She killed my husband." Anger flared. "How many times do I have to say it? I worked for her. I recognized her shape in the dark. I recognized her voice when she told him to shoot me."

"Who'd she tell to shoot you?"

"Her boyfriend. Mr. Strawn."

According to Libby, she'd told this to the police but they still hadn't arrested Dolly Hastings. When they showed up at the lawyer's office and tried to talk to her, she slammed the door in their faces. Libby hadn't yet been able to give a written statement, and doctors had her on heavy medication. Cops wanted her clearheaded when she told them her story.

"Why would she want to harm you?" Aspen asked.

"Like I told you. I know things. And because when I quit, I took half of her clients with me."

"I don't understand. You're not an attorney. Why would she feel like you were in competition with her?"

"Maybe because I opened up an office down the street. Maybe because the clients who jumped ship are Mexican nationals, or come from El Salvador, or Guatemala. They still have ties to the mother country — family members who're dirt poor and can't afford to raise all their children. They want to give their babies up for adoption. I could do that for them."

"But you can't practice law without a license."

"I didn't represent them in court. But I did have all the documents they needed to go into court *pro se.*"

"What's the name of your office?"

"Notario y Adopciónes." Libby translated. "A *notario* is like a notary public."

Aspen shook her head. "Except in Mexico, it's another word for lawyer, right?"

Libby gave her a dull smile. "Yeah. But they don't know the difference. They just want to get rid of their kids. They needed help and we provided a service. I didn't think we were doing anything wrong."

"Who's we?"

"Me and my husband. He was part owner in the business."

So they capitalized on the ignorance of foreigners? Aspen tensed. If she alienated this woman, Libby could activate the call button on the gizmo looped over the bed-rail and the nurse would be in here faster than mosquitoes on a white girl. She consulted her notes. "I ran across a name I was hoping you could help me with. Timmons. Do you know why Heath Strawn would go up to the roof of the Timmons Building?"

"Ironic, isn't it?" Apparently numbed by grief, Libby remained calm. "That's probably the only thing he did right."

"I don't understand."

"Rich people like the Timmonses don't want brown babies. They want white ones. And for the right amount of money, they can buy one."

"What are you saying? That the Timmons family — the people who own that building downtown — that they went to Dolly Hastings to find them a baby?"

"Exactly. Mr. Strawn found them one."

"How?"

Libby yawned. Her eyes fluttered. "I'm so tired. I'd like to sleep now."

"Just tell me. How'd he find a baby for the Timmons family?"

She yawned out her answer. "He knew this Goth girl down in Johnson County . . ." Her voice died out and a thin snore took its place.

CHAPTER THIRTY-THREE

An hour into Granger's return flight to DFW, Buster spotted a kid with a deck of cards. He volunteered to do a card trick, but Granger issued a stern warning.

"Don't be talking to people."

"I'm bored."

"Get used to it."

Another half hour passed while Buster pawed through the magazine holder and entertained himself by raising and lowering the window shade.

"Knock it off," Granger said.

Buster looked up at the overhead air vent. "Can you turn that on and point it at my face?"

"Do I look like your butler?"

"If I do it, people will see these cuffs."

Granger blew out a heavy sigh. He reached up and twisted the knob with such a vengeance that Buster's hair blasted back from his forehead like he was sitting on the wing of an F-16.

"Gotta go to the can." Buster unhooked his seat belt.

"No bathroom breaks. You know the rules."

"But I've gotta go."

Granger wanted to dough-pop him. He viewed his prisoner through slitted eyes. "Fine. Then go right here."

It was a real *Double-dog dare you* moment.

Buster's gaze dipped. He squirmed. Then he did a conspiratorial lean-in. "I don't need to pee."

"Good." Granger reached for the in-flight magazine. "Didn't think so."

But Buster wasn't having any of it.

"I don't need to pee," he said in a ventriloquist's growl. "It's worse than that. I've gotta go" — he did a little head flop — "*you* know. I've got the trots."

Granger imagined the vile smell permeating the cabin, an invisible cloud engulfing people around them, and could almost hear gagging sounds. His shoulders tensed. He couldn't help but consider that hearing people's gag reflex would automatically trigger others to grab their barf bags and fill them to capacity. No, Buster didn't give him much choice. "All right," Granger conceded. "You can go to the can, but I'm not unlocking those cuffs."

"How am I supposed to clean myself?"

"Hey, don't look at me," Granger said and set his jaw.

Pulling his jacket sleeves down enough to shroud the handcuffs, Buster ambled back to the lavatory good-naturedly. He returned almost immediately, with his eyes downcast, muttering that the two bathrooms were occupied. Then he started toward the front galley.

"Where do you think you're going?" Granger snarled.

Stricken, Buster said, "To the front, boss."

"No, you're not. You're not leaving my sight."

"C'mon, boss." He did an uncomfortable, in-place shuffle and pleaded with his eyes. "Where am I gonna go? We're in flight. For you, this is better than if we were on the ground."

Granger tracked Buster's darting gaze — up at the overhead baggage compartments, down the walls, to the overhead exit signs leading to the wings. The inmate was right. If he intended to pull a disappearing act, letting him use the bathroom on the ground would be far worse. He might bolt.

And let's face it, Granger thought, looking down at the slight paunch overhanging his own belt. *I'm not getting any younger.* The idea of lumbering after a fleet-footed felon in a crowded airport held no allure.

"Make it quick," he said, and watched the relief pour down Buster's face.

Near the bulkhead, a young mother came out of the lavatory with a toddler riding on her hip. Buster gave a polite nod and squeezed past with his eyes cast downward. Before he made it inside, a boy ejected from a seat nearby and disappeared behind the restroom door.

From his seat in the back of the plane, Granger watched, eagle-eyed, as Buster waited for the Occupied sign to slide to Vacant. The inmate shifted from one foot to the other in what seemed to be a genuine effort to contain himself. His movements had a contagious effect, like a yawn making the rounds. Suddenly, Granger felt the urge to take a leak.

For a few minutes, he sat still, barely breathing. This was crazy. Why was he worried? There was no place for Buster to go. They were stuck on this plane until it landed. With that reassuring rationale orbiting inside his head, he seized the opportunity to dart into the back of the cabin and relieve himself in the nearest can. Giving Buster a backward glance, he waited for an old blue-hair to step out. At the other end of the plane, Buster lifted his hands and gave him the thumbs-up.

Each entered their respective lavatories at the same time.

Granger finished first. He ambled back to his seat with an eye fixed on the front of the cabin, and wrenched himself back into his cramped space. The flight attendants had pulled the serving cart into the aisle up front and were serving drinks and selling snacks to the first customers. It'd be a while before Buster made it back to his seat, so Granger pulled the warrant out of his pocket and scanned the waiver.

He spent no more than a couple of minutes reading. After refolding the warrant, he slipped it into his coat pocket and waited.

And thought.

And waited.

And waited some more as the flight attendants slowly made their way up the aisle with the serving cart.

Finally, they moved adjacent to him. Poised to reach for a complimentary beverage, a pretty brunette arched an eyebrow and waited for Granger's selection.

Granger said, "Ginger ale," and she plucked one from the drawer and pulled open the pop-tab. The drink snapped open with an audible *Pfft!* Then she wrapped a napkin around the can and handed it over.

"Thank you, ma'am." Granger thought about buying a snack, but the voice of his second-grade teacher echoed in his ears: "If you don't have enough to share with the others . . ." Besides, he wasn't all that confident he'd have time to wolf it down before Buster returned and started bitching about hunger pangs.

He scanned the front of the plane for Buster. No sign of him.

In a way, he was glad Buster was taking his time. That way, Granger could finish his drink before the inmate returned. *Sorry, Buster, you lose.*

Fifteen minutes went by. Still no Buster.

Granger started getting edgy.

In another five minutes, he was fidgeting in his seat the way Buster'd done thirty minutes before. Time ticked away. He began studying the backs of passengers' heads, wondering whether Buster might've moved into an unoccupied seat at the front of the plane in an attempt to bolt as soon as the doors opened.

At the sound of a dulcet chime, the ember-red glow of a *Fasten seat belt* sign lit up.

The captain's voice came over the intercom. "Ladies and gentlemen, we'll be landing at DFW in a few minutes. Please remain seated for the duration of the flight. We know you can choose any airline and we thank you for choosing Delta. And for those of you in business class, we enjoyed giving you the business."

The loudspeaker went off, leaving only the hiss of air from the overhead vent to compete with the roar of the engines.

Granger rose from his seat in an effort to move toward the bulkhead. A flight attendant lost no time scolding him.

He moved a flap of his sportscoat aside, enough for her to see his badge. "I need to check on my prisoner."

"You'll have to wait."

But Granger was insistent. "Lady, I'm going up front whether you like it or not."

Instead of getting angry, she laughed at him. It was one of those *You're so dumb* laughs, the kind his ex-wife used to use on him before she ran off with Neil Lindstrom. "Where's he going to go? Into the ether?"

"You don't know this guy," Granger said.

As a small concession, she urged him to wait a few more minutes, and volunteered to check on Buster herself. She wended her way to the front of the plane with a trash bag in hand for her final garbage pickup.

Reluctantly, Granger sat. He took a deep

breath and held it, then let it out in a slow, relaxing exhale.

Waiting on you, Buster.

Still waiting on you.

Waiting on Buster.

CHAPTER THIRTY-FOUR

Aspen was still at the hospital when Libby Singleton woke up. For a moment, the woman didn't seem to remember her. She blinked her surroundings into focus, then appeared to recall where she was, and why she was at Sisters Hospital.

"You're still here." Her voice was unhurried and still groggy. "What time is it?"

"A little after two o'clock."

"I need pain medicine."

"Do you want me to get the nurse?"

Weak nod.

"I'll do that," Aspen said. "If it's okay with you, I'll stop by the nurse's station on the way out."

"Need it now."

"Okay. I just have a few more questions. Then I'll go." Before Libby could protest, she said, "You mentioned a Goth girl in Johnson County."

Small nod.

"Do you know her name?"

"Might be Ellie."

Aspen's heart picked up its pace. "Do you know who got that baby?"

"It was supposed to go to the Timmonses. But she changed her mind at the last minute and decided to keep it. Dolly was so mad. Said she'd make her pay."

I'll bet. "Whose baby did the Timmonses get?"

A shrug. "Don't know."

"How long ago did Dolly get them a baby?"

"Three months."

About the time authorities found Ellie Canfield eviscerated. "How did Dolly know about this girl?"

"She was one of Heath's connections. I even thought he might be the father. That Dolly paid him to do it. There are others. She's just waiting."

"I'll get your nurse." She walked over to the bed and found the call button. After she pressed it, she put it in Libby's hand. "She should be on her way."

Libby closed her eyes.

"I'd like to come back and see you, if that's okay."

Weak nod.

"You're so lucky to be here."

"I know." Libby's voice thinned. "I got away from her."

"No, I meant you're lucky to be alive."

"That's what I said. There's a saying that goes with Dolly: 'You quit, you die.' "

"But you're still here."

"Yeah, but it's only been a week. You don't have a clue about this lady. Once you cross her, she'll never stop."

The nurse came in with Libby's pain pills. Shortly after ingesting them, the young woman's attention waned.

"I'm lucky because I still have my baby. Now that Art's gone, I'm keeping it," she said through a wan smile.

"Wait — are you saying Dolly Hastings was going to adopt out your baby?"

Slight nod.

"I don't understand."

"Art and I weren't ready to be parents. And Dolly offered us a lot of money. A *whole* lot of money. We took it. But then Art said we should start our own business with the money, and we'd pay her back. Only she killed my husband and came after me."

"Do you think she still wants your unborn child?"

"Absolutely. We took her money. *We offended her.* And I think she'll kill me to get my kid. That's why I'm disappearing as soon as I get out of here."

Before she left, Aspen stopped at the nurses' station and spoke to the nurse who'd brought Libby her pain medication.

"I was wondering if you know whether the police assigned an officer to guard my sister?"

"They had one here for the first few days, but they pulled him off. Budget cuts, I suppose. They told us not to let anyone in without Mrs. Singleton's permission."

"I think you need to do better than that."

"Look around," said the nurse, a light-skinned African American of slight build, with perm-straightened hair that hung to her chin and framed her face so that she looked like a Madame Alexander doll. "Do you see enough nurses here?"

Aspen pulled out a business card and wrote her cell number on the back. "I want you to call me if she needs anything — or if anything happens. Promise me."

"Sure."

She walked out of Sisters of Perpetual Suffering with her stomach roiling. She needed to talk to Granger, but each time she speed dialed his wireless phone, she got routed to his voice mail.

She returned to the office looking for Gordon. She'd lay it out for him like a losing hand of poker; he'd call the attorneys WBFD had locked and loaded, and they could figure this out. But Gordon wasn't in.

Rochelle, bathed in the glow of the computer screen, lifted her nose as if to catch a scent. "I'm just starting the ten-page report that's due on Gordon's desk tomorrow. So far, I've written my name. What do you want?"

"Where is he? It's really important that I speak to him today."

"When he left, he said he was going to see a man about a singing dog — whatever that meant."

Fresh out of leads, Aspen called the Johnson County Sheriff's Office and asked for Lucinda. When Granger's secretary answered, she identified herself and asked to get a message to Susanna Epps. But Lucinda, who Aspen was starting to think of as Lucifer, wasn't much help. She denied knowing anyone by that name, and suggested Aspen wait until school let out and try to find her there.

Which left only one thing for her to do.

She decided to see a lawyer about a baby.

CHAPTER THIRTY-FIVE

Buster didn't return.

With a determined look on her face, the flight attendant turned around after checking the bathroom, and worked her way back to Granger. "Nobody's in either lavatory."

Granger jerked to attention. "Are you sure?"

Big head bob.

"Did you look?"

Another nod.

"You looked inside the compartments?" His voice spiraled upward. "You opened the doors and looked inside?"

"That's what I've been trying to tell you."

"Outta my way."

When she didn't move fast enough, he clasped her by the shoulders, lifted her up and set her down a foot away.

"Sir, you can't just . . ."

But Granger was already moving heavily up the aisle. While the right side of his brain

371

wondered if Buster had somehow managed to escape, the left side reasoned that there was no place for him to go in mid-flight. Granger passed the bulkhead. He reached the lavatory with clammy palms and perspiration popping up above his brows. The lock mechanism had been slid to the Occupied position.

He did a backhanded knuckle rap on the door.

Nothing.

He set his jaw, curled his fingers into a meaty fist and pounded. People seated nearby stopped what they were doing and looked up. The flight attendant he'd manhandled appeared in the periphery of his vision.

An audible whoosh filtered through the door. The sound of running water followed. The snap of a couple of paper towels being pulled from the dispenser gave Granger a modicum of relief.

The door latch slid back and the mechanism popped open.

Granger caught his breath and held it. He wanted to ball up a fist, haul back and bust his childhood friend in the chops.

But he couldn't.

A young boy in a T-shirt and baggy shorts stepped out with a scowl on his face.

Granger's jaw dropped.

The kid made eye contact with his parents and held out a hand. A pair of handcuffs dangled from his index finger.

The sheriff blinked.

Impossible.

Unless Buster Root had magically changed into a juvenile delinquent, he'd escaped.

CHAPTER THIRTY-SIX

Walking into Dolly Hastings's office was like staring into direct sunlight without sunglasses — everything seemed to be done in shades of yellow, from the ornately carved sandstone mantle around the fireplace, to the gilt rococo mirrors hanging on the walls near tons of crushed silk that billowed to the floor from curtain rods mounted close to the high ceilings. The curtains had been gathered back with silk sashes. In the middle of the room, Dolly's desk resembled the one that Blake Carrington used on the set of *Dynasty*. The upholstered chaise lounge and chairs had decorative pillows of various sizes that featured Versace's Medusa theme. The only real splotches of color other than yellow came from antique rugs on a hardwood floor constructed of blond maple, and a reproduction of an oil painting on an oak panel that hung prominently above the fireplace. Aspen recognized *The Arnolfini Por-*

trait, by Flemish painter Jan van Eyck.

The most dominating feature in the room, though, turned out to be Dolly herself.

Dolly, a petite woman with champagne-colored, cotton-candy hair piled high on her head, sat curled on the chaise with a book. Like a snake sunning itself on a flat rock, she basked in a brilliant shaft of light that slanted through the window. She must've been in her late forties or early fifties, although it was hard to tell. She'd certainly had work done; her face looked like it came from Madame Tussaud's Wax Museum, probably from too many Botox injections. Which only made her look like everything she heard came as a shock to her. Aspen estimated her age between forty and fifty-five. At this juncture, she'd need to ask Granger to run her driver's license to be sure.

Entering the lawyer's sanctuary was like walking into a blast furnace. The outside temperature couldn't have been below fifty-five degrees, but the gas fireplace had been turned on and flames were shooting up from the iron grate, licking the logs like they were Popsicles.

It didn't take long for Aspen to conclude that hell was yellow. And the devil was a tiny but formidable woman with chiseled

375

features beneath alabaster skin and fathomless brown shark eyes.

"I don't usually see people without an appointment," Dolly said, her perfect diction adding to her professional façade. "But you said it was important, so let's see what we can do, Miss . . ."

"Granger." For lack of imagination, she took her mother's name. "Jillian Granger."

Dolly beckoned her into a nearby chair, where she sank into a down cushion so soft it made her want to slip out of her Ferragamos and fold up like an origami stork.

"May I offer you a beverage?" Dolly asked.

"No, thank you."

"Then let's get to it, shall we? Exactly why did you want to see me?"

"I was told you help people get babies." Dolly fixed her with a hard stare. One wouldn't want to play poker with such a woman. "Anyway, I was told you're the best. So that's why I'm here. I have a problem, and I think you may be able to fix it."

"And your problem is?"

She launched into an elaborate story that boiled down to one thing — she wanted a baby and couldn't have one of her own. And there was something of a time crunch brought on by a dying parent — unless she had an heir, her terminally ill father wasn't going to leave her a single penny of the family fortune.

"I'm afraid I backed myself into a corner, you see," Aspen said. "I told him I was expecting a baby six months ago. I thought he'd put me in the will. But he's flying out to see me in a couple of weeks and if he knows I lied to him, that's it." By way of illustration, she sliced a finger across her throat to indicate a violent ending.

"Well, I don't like to brag, but I'm very good at what I do. The main thing is that you need to see results, and that's a thing I do very well — get results. It'd be best if you had no preference as to the gender of the baby."

"No preference." *So far, so good.*

"And race? Is that important to you?"

"Yes. My father must think the child's mine."

"Well, that may be a bit harder." Dolly flashed a porcelain smile as she made notes on a partly used legal pad. "This is going to get expensive."

"I can pay you a little up front, and the rest once I get in the will."

Dolly flipped the pages over and set the pad aside. "Well, dear, I think we're all done."

"That's it? And I get a baby?"

"Hardly." She laughed without humor. "This is a costly endeavor. If you want something bad enough, you'll pay for it. I require eighty thousand dollars up front. And you can bring in the other twenty when you and Mr. Granger pick up your little bundle of joy."

"Eighty thousand? That's a lot of money."

"Didn't you say your father was rich?"

"Yes, but that's not me."

"You obviously came to me because you've exhausted the other possibilities for getting a baby. Perhaps the regular adoption agencies found your home life unstable. Or maybe they thought your husband was too old. Maybe you figured they were taking too long. In any event, you ended up here. Bring me the money, and it's a done deal."

"I'm not sure I can get the whole eighty thousand right away."

"Well, you'll just have to work on that, now won't you?"

Chapter Thirty-Seven

By the time the flight attendant ushered Granger back to his seat, the sheriff was dripping sweat. Now the right and left sides of his brain weren't communicating at all, just functioning as a spongy buffer for the tinny, distant ringing in his ears. It seemed inconceivable that Buster Root had disappeared in mid-flight, but they'd checked the food service area, and the open space behind the cockpit where the flight attendants stowed their gear. And unless Buster could contort himself enough to fit into a carry-on, he wasn't here.

Granger inwardly panicked. He'd been forced to buckle himself into his seat for the landing. Despite the flight attendant's assurance that no one would be allowed to leave the plane until they'd located Buster Root, Granger's hands had gone clammy, and the pulse in his throat throbbed. Meantime, Granger'd be surrounded by irate passengers needing to connect with other flights in different parts of the airport. So even if they found Buster — and the flight attendant assured him they would, since, in her words, "there's nowhere for him to go unless he disappeared into thin air" — Granger'd probably end up being the most hated man on the airplane.

He looked out the window as the tarmac rose up to meet them. The screech of tires against the pavement told him they'd touched down. He watched the wing flaps tilt in the downward position as the plane rumbled down the runway with its engines reversed. The airplane began to slow. Almost frantic, Granger looked around for a flight attendant. The captain should've already been notified of the problem, but if he hadn't, people would start scrambling off as soon as the doors came unlatched.

Including Buster.

As the plane taxied up to the jetway, ramp vehicles rolled by in the distance. The cabin intercom crackled to life.

The captain made an announcement. "Ladies and gentlemen, please remain seated. There's an irregularity with our aircraft that we need to resolve before de-planing."

A collective groan filled the cabin. A man

near the forward galley stepped out of his seat into the aisle and made a move for the overhead storage compartment. A flight attendant half his size immediately shut him down.

As if the captain had read the minds of the people on board, the loudspeaker crackled back on, and he made a follow-up announcement.

"Folks, we've been advised that the airport will be shut down until this irregularity has been taken care of. Since DFW's closed to arrivals, if you're worried about missing your connection, just remember that all of your outbound flights are currently inbound just like we are, being delayed just as we are. They aren't manufacturing any airplanes at the airport, so you'll make your connections. Again, we ask that you remain in your seats in order to speed up this process."

Granger closed his eyes. When he opened them and looked out the window, ramp vehicles were wheeling past. He unbuckled his seat belt and moved to the rear galley, where he encountered the attractive brunette flight attendant. She beckoned him into a curtained-off area no bigger than an entry closet.

"All right," she said with a world-weary

sigh, "here's how it works. You and I are going to head up front and take a look at each of these passengers, just like a train conductor punching tickets. You should be able to spot him, even if he's in disguise, don't you think?"

Newly energized, Granger nodded.

"What you're not going to do," she said firmly, "is upset these passengers by displaying your badge."

"So I guess that means you don't want me to pull my gun, either?" he deadpanned.

"Not funny, Sheriff." Her eyes coolly narrowed. "If you think you see him but you're not sure, I'll check his boarding pass. One more thing — you may be the law on the ground, but on this bird, I outrank you. So I'm doing the talking, not you. Got it? Let's go."

What he *got* was a bad case of lockjaw. He didn't know whether to slap her or kiss her. Instead, he followed her to the bulkhead like a puppy.

An audible clunk came from the belly of the plane. Granger instantly considered the cargo area, grabbed the flight attendant by the elbow and pulled her close.

"Can you get into the baggage section from here?" he whispered.

"I suppose."

Granger's heartbeat revved. "How?" By now, Buster might already be halfway to the exit tollbooths. "How do you get there from here?"

She pulled him into the entryway and lowered her voice. "If he ducked into the front galley and took the elevator down, he could access the cargo area — if he knew what he was doing."

Granger's eyes closed for a split second. Then they snapped open. Remembering all the books on airplane construction that had been sent over to the jail from the public library at Buster's request, Granger experienced a frightening epiphany. At the time, Granger thought he might be planning to embark on a legitimate occupation such as airline mechanic — God forbid — but now . . . now he dreaded completing his own thoughts.

"What's that noise?" Granger inclined his head toward the nearest exit. "Is that the sound of baggage being unloaded?"

"That was the cargo area being unlocked," she said with a nod. Granger's shoulders sagged. The pretty brunette took pity on him. "Don't worry. The authorities are watching and they'll search that area. If your guy's hiding in the belly of this bird, there's no way he can leave without somebody spotting him."

The tension in Granger's neck let up a bit. He did a quick eye-scan over the passengers.

She let out a devilish giggle. "He'd have to be a pretty good magician to pull this off."

"He is a magician," Granger said dully.

"Yeah," the girl conceded, "but aren't magicians really just a bunch of illusionists? I mean" — she snuffled with laughter — "people don't just disappear into thin air." She snapped her fingers to punctuate the observation.

Granger gave the passengers another once-over. If Buster wanted to create the illusion that he'd escaped, and was really sitting in the cabin with the rest of the travelers, he wasn't doing a very good job. Even if he'd tried to disguise his looks by chopping off a lock of hair and supergluing it to his upper lip to make an impromptu mustache before leaving the lavatory, it didn't work because he wasn't here.

"He's an amateur escapologist."

"Well, he'd have to be frickin' Houdini to get past all these people on the ground," the flight attendant said. "This place is crawling with cops."

Granger wanted to believe her, but doubt

384

nagged him.

She locked him in her china-blue gaze. "Unless . . ."

"Unless what?" Granger set his jaw. He was pretty sure he wasn't going to like this next part.

"Unless he's small enough or wiry enough to zip himself into somebody's luggage."

The horrible knot in Granger's stomach tightened. He envisioned the cargo floor littered with Hawaiian shirts, khaki Bermudas, beach books, a pistol with a silencer and a big tube of sunscreen owned by Big Gianni Rubout of the Goumba crime family . . . while one of those huge Tongan baggage handlers heaved Buster-in-a-bag onto the truck with all the other luggage. He even imagined the suitcase sliding down the ramp to the baggage claim area, revolving on the conveyor belt as onlookers watched a finger poke out, followed by a hand that contorted enough for nimble fingers to unzip the bag.

As Granger watched the scenario play out in his mind: Buster stepping out of the suitcase, dusting himself off in front of amazed onlookers, hopping off the conveyor belt, jogging past gawking bystanders, shrugging out of his black windbreaker and discarding it into the nearest waste bin,

Buster hightailing it to freedom — Granger gradually became aware that the cabin had gone temporarily out of focus and the brunette's words sounded sluggish, like a 45-LP being played at thirty-three and a third. He swallowed the baseball-sized lump forming in his throat, shook out the cobwebs and picked up somewhere in the middle of her sentence.

". . . so I don't think there's any way he could get past Homeland Security, airport police, or the sky marshals."

Granger blew out a defeated sigh. "He's already gone."

"How do you know?"

He made a fist and thumped it against his chest. "I can feel it."

CHAPTER THIRTY-EIGHT

The first thing Aspen wanted to do when she got home was hop into the shower, scrub her skin until it stung, and watch as the evil circled the drain.

Apparently, Rochelle and Dainty had other ideas because the red Nissan *Z* and Dainty's silver Porsche were parked in her driveway when she arrived at the house.

Aspen sighed. She didn't want "girls' night out" — not tonight anyway, and not with these girls. She could see why Gordon thought the three of them fraternizing might not be such a hot idea. That went without saying.

When she walked through the front door, she had a bird's-eye view of Dainty sitting at the dining table, hunkered over a laptop computer. Rochelle stood beside her, doing a subtle lean to make out the information streaming across the screen. They made a dubious pair: Dainty with her light-blonde hair made into a halo by the glare of the afternoon sun slanting through the kitchen window; Rochelle more in the shadows with her dark-brown hair no longer scraped back from her face, but cascading loosely past her elegant neck to her shoulders.

Angel and devil working in tandem. And Aspen didn't have to wonder who played the role of the devil.

She gave a sniff of irritation, and Rochelle looked up.

"Hello, Rochelle . . ." Her eyes slewed over to Dainty. ". . . Rochelle Light."

Without stopping her task, Dainty called out an over-the-shoulder "Hi."

For all they cared, Aspen could've been background music. She slid out of her jacket and tossed it on her sofa, along with her purse and the now-ragged copies of Heath Strawn's notes.

"Rochelle," she singsonged, "may I see you for a moment?"

Gordon's assistant tapped Dainty's shoulder as if to say, *I'll handle this,* and met Aspen in the living room.

"You look tired," said Rochelle. "You should have a glass of wine with us."

"I'm not going out again tonight," Aspen said.

"That's okay, we're drinking here."

388

"Rochelle — how do you keep getting into my house?" Then she remembered. "It's that lock-picking book I saw you with, isn't it?"

The woman's eyebrows shot up into inverted V's. Then she gave a little smirk and nodded, making Aspen realize that the book had nothing to do with how they got in, but Rochelle was going along with the idea because she knew Aspen wouldn't like the real reason.

"You could get shot breaking into houses. I have a gun now, you know?"

"You *used* to have a gun. But the cops seized it as evidence."

"How do you know this stuff?"

"I know everything." Rochelle let out one of her Uzi-with-a-silencer chuckles.

"What's going on? Why are you here? Moreover, why is *she* here?" Aspen thumbed at the table.

"*Hello* — I can hear you," Dainty said, waving a hand, her eyes still locked on the computer screen. "I'm sitting right here."

"We have a surprise for you," Rochelle said.

"I already told you I don't like surprises."

Rochelle beckoned her into the kitchen. "Come on in, and I'll pour you a drink."

"That bad?"

Rochelle merely gave her a Sphinx-like smile.

A minute later, Aspen sat at the dining table near Dainty, who was sipping a bottle of mineral water that she'd obviously brought in, and waited for Rochelle to top off her wine glass. Rochelle, clearly the ringleader, poured herself another slug and pulled up a chair on the other side of Dainty.

"What's this all about?" Aspen said feeling marginally improved now that she had alcohol speeding through her system.

Rochelle's eyes slewed over to Dainty. "Go."

"Remember the other night when we went out to Kirk House?"

As if she could forget those piping screams clawing their way out of their throats.

"Remember when I told you I started the Debutante Detective Agency?"

"I thought you were kidding."

Big head shake. "So after Rochelle filled in the blanks about your boyfriend —"

"Rochelle?" Aspen's voice took an upward corkscrew, causing the secretary to pat the air in a downward motion.

"I hired her," Rochelle said. "Turns out she does pretty good work."

"Thank you," Dainty said, practically preening over the compliment, "but it's better than pretty good. It's excellent. I do fantastic work. Apparently I have an aptitude for spying."

"You spied on me?" Aspen mentally reviewed her list of crimes and came up blank.

"Not you. Him."

"You spied on Spike?" Her voice caught in her throat. She wasn't at all certain she wanted to hear what came next.

"She got it all on video," Rochelle said. "Show her."

Dainty angled the computer so Aspen could see the screen. Rochelle got up, walked over, and stood slightly behind them.

"Day one," Rochelle said, speaking in a monotone like the voice-over announcer at a high-stakes golf tournament. "Here we are at a high-school gymnasium in Johnson County, where our girl Gidget catches up with Granger scoping out the facility. Apparently, he's planning to raise funds for his campaign by putting on a magic show. Our operative" — she darted a glance at Dainty — "managed to sneak inside and shoot this amazing footage in low-light conditions, where three generations — our Gidget and the two suspects — have rendezvoused backstage: Generation X, Generation Y, and Generation 'Why not?' "

She chucked Dainty's arm and had a

howlingly good time at her own joke. Then she resumed. "Now what we see here is a blonde woman —"

Aspen leaned in for a better look. "It's her." Wine sloshed over the rim of the glass and landed on the tablecloth. It was the same woman she'd walked in on. The one giving Granger a lap dance the day she popped in, unannounced, at the SO.

"Now it doesn't look like anything serious," Rochelle soothed. "You can see they're just talking — oh, no; *uh-oh!* — looks like she's naked under that coat."

Hand to lips, Aspen gasped.

"But, hey" — Rochelle oozed sarcasm — "you can't condemn him because the woman spent so much on a fox fur that she didn't have any money left to buy clothes, right?

"Then again . . ." The devil played devil's advocate. "He's not exactly covering his eyes, is he?"

Aspen's chin quivered.

"On an interesting note, however, he does seem surprised to see her. So that could be a good sign. It's not like he invited her, right? In fact, he looks angry." She turned to Dainty. "What was he saying to her?"

"Oh. Em. Gee. I thought he'd blow a gasket. There were a couple of seconds there, when I thought I might be shooting a murder in progress."

"What'd he say?" For Aspen, the air thickened. Her heart thudded like horseshoes on a dirt track.

"Just that he'd arrest her if she didn't get dressed and get out. And how would her husband like it? He was pretty upset with her. Whatever."

"That's it?" Aspen waited for more.

"Well, she said, 'Spikey-Wikey-likey' and then sucked her finger. It was all pretty sordid, the stuff she was telling him. But, look . . . see how his fists are clenched? His body language indicates he didn't want her there."

Aspen watched, spellbound, as the blonde left the stage area and walked to where a deputy and his prisoner were standing. "She kissed him. You think that's her husband?"

"Not her husband. But you could tell they knew each other. Your boyfriend almost went mad cow on her again. I didn't figure it out until later."

"Figure out what?"

"Just keep watching."

Rochelle said, "Now here we are on day two of surveillance. The Debutante Detective Agency followed Granger to a house." Rochelle wagged a forefinger near the screen. "You can see from the video that the woman opening the door is the same woman at the magic show. See how she grabs your boyfriend's hand and yanks him inside? That's as close as we could get that day, but you can imagine . . . when he came out a while later, his shirt was half unbuttoned. I don't guess we need to go there, now do we?"

Rochelle's words carried a bit of hang time.

"Who is she?" Aspen's voice cracked. She wanted to drink until she completely anesthetized the part of her brain that created mental pictures.

"In due time, my pet." Rochelle redirected Aspen's attention to the video. "Granger stayed inside all of ten minutes that day. But you shouldn't worry, dear. Maybe they were just having a bite to eat, right? Or he spilled something on his shirt and she laundered it. That's probably it," she added unconvincingly.

Aspen ground her molars. If there'd been nothing to report, she wouldn't be sitting here swilling down wine and watching a clandestine video of her love interest with another woman. A pretty one. Correction: damned beautiful, more like.

"Okay, here we are on day three. The

Debutante Detective Agency picked up the woman coming out of a trashy lingerie store. Then we followed her to a building . . . it looks like a political campaign office . . ."

Aspen could barely make out the banner hanging over the entrance: *Neil Lindstrom for Sheriff.*

The woman disappeared inside; she returned to her car with one of Lindstrom's yard signs and stashed it in the trunk of her Jaguar. Seconds later, the camera zoomed in on the license plate.

It took a moment for things to soak in. Then they started to gel. "So, she's a Lindstrom supporter. Why would she go see Spike? Unless . . ."

"There's more."

Now what?

Video footage showed the blonde woman seated in a crescent-shaped booth across from a tall, lean man. There was nothing particularly noteworthy about his appearance, other than his height.

"Italian restaurant," Dainty interjected.

The man slid a small flat box like those that came from jewelry stores and held bracelets. The woman opened it up and delight spread over her face. She inched across the curved seat until she sat beside

395

him. She took what appeared to be a diamond tennis bracelet from the box and allowed the man to hook it around her wrist. They shared a kiss, and then the camera zoomed in on a bit of hanky-panky going on under the table.

"I don't understand." Aspen again, thoroughly confused, and sounding out incomplete thoughts to the picture on the computer screen. "If she's with . . . but why would she go after . . . the day I caught them . . . she drives a Jag." Aspen looked up at Rochelle. "The day I went to his office. The day I saw her. I thought somebody in a Jaguar was following me."

"Watch." Rochelle redirected her.

The blonde abruptly pulled her hand away as another couple approached the table. The man stood, backslapping another man with his back to the camera, and air-kissing the woman with a *mwah, mwah.* Then the visiting couple left the table, and the blonde picked up where she'd left off.

The rest of the restaurant footage was uneventful, except for the part where the blonde used her cloth napkin to wipe off her hand after she'd finished thanking the man for the bracelet.

Then a new piece of footage popped up on the screen, of Aspen and Granger getting into the patrol car. As the cruiser sped off, the camera panned to the Jaguar, parked across the street. The blonde got out holding what looked like a flyer. She approached Granger's pickup, stood near the tailgate, and scanned the area. Then she wiped one corner of the truck's bumper and slapped on a bumper sticker. When she turned around, the camera zoomed in on her face. Dainty turned up the sound on the computer.

"Excusez moi," Dainty's voice said, off-screen. "I wonder if you could help me? Is this the sheriff's office?"

"Yes." Said warily.

"I'm new around here and I was wondering if this is where you go to report somebody following you?" Said innocently.

"You could do that," said the racehorse blonde.

"Oh. Because I wasn't sure if I should be at the police department, or here."

"Yes, well, I wouldn't know. But I'm sure if you check inside, someone can help you."

"I'm new in town and I don't know anybody. It's kind of scary."

"I wouldn't know. I've lived here all my life."

"That's amazing," Dainty gushed. "I'm Gidget, by the way. Prescott."

"Dallas Ostrander."

The camera shook, temporarily blurring the picture. "Oh. Em. Gee. Is that a real diamond? It must be six carats."

"You have a good eye."

"Love the bracelet, by the way."

"Thanks. My husband gave it to me for our anniversary. Look, I have to go."

"Wait. What's the sheriff like?"

"He's a dick. But don't worry, my husband's running against him, so we should have us a new sheriff here in another month."

"Who's your husband? Maybe I'll vote for him."

"Let me give you a bumper sticker and a yard sign. They're in my car across the street."

Dainty paused the footage.

Aspen, having another synaptic misfire, said, "I'm lost."

Then Dainty disengaged the computer's pause feature. The camera zoomed in on Granger's bumper, which now bore a *Neil Lindstrom for Sheriff* sticker.

Aspen barked out a laugh. "Is she nuts?"

"Looks to me like she's trying to sabotage your man," Rochelle said.

Aspen mulled over this new development. "I need to talk to Spike." She took a deep breath and slowly let it out. Wine with the girls had been so overwhelming. "Is that it?"

"Not quite," Dainty said with a grin. "Hold onto your hat."

CHAPTER THIRTY-NINE

Buster's escape through the cargo area had merely been an illusion.

Granger *got* that.

He even *got* that once Buster entered the lavatory and picked the locks on the handcuffs, he'd ducked into the front galley and went down the elevator into the lower galley.

And he *got* the fact that the lower galley connected to the E & E compartment, and the baggage area.

What he *didn't* get, was that even before authorities began their search of the baggage bin, Buster'd already let himself out of the electronics equipment room and apparently jumped, unnoticed, onto a ramp vehicle. From there, authorities surmised that he'd either driven or been driven to an employee area, where he exited the airport through an underground passage and made his getaway.

Granger gleaned this information by sitting out on the back porch with his dogs, Jake and Ray, drinking coffee and reading the morning paper beneath the porch light, waiting for the sun to set. The article appeared next to a column that proclaimed, "Granger leading in polls" with a photo of himself sporting a huge grin.

Fat chance.

Tomorrow's news would read a lot differently.

He reviewed the events of the last few days and wondered what would make a man want a job that caused him to be surrounded by people like Buster Root, Crazy Sheila, and an ex-wife who periodically showed up to jerk him around.

But he knew.

The motivation to hang onto his position came from all the other people: like Harvey Thomas over at the high school, and Sue over on the square. Even Carliss over at the post office. Especially poor, sweet Carliss. And a whole county of other good folks that needed protecting.

And then there was Aspen.

She'd promised not to blow his investigation wide open until the indictments came down on the Goths. And the deputies who made the call out at Crazy Sheila's house were two of his best men, and they weren't going to say anything. He had his finest investigator putting together a report on Blaze Clarke. Preliminary reports from the medical examiner's office indicated that Clarke had suffered a heart attack, which dovetailed nicely with what Crazy Sheila said happened.

As for his and Aspen's personal relationship, that remained to be seen. They'd made great progress, considering all that had happened. And they still needed to get together to pool their notes.

To figure out what the hell the connection was between Kirk House and Ellie Canfield and that stupid urban legend.

His booted feet dropped from the edge of the crate he'd set up outside — it alternated between a footstool and a place to put his coffee — and hit the deck with a clunk. He'd turned off his cell phone while he'd been in flight, and with all the hoopla surrounding Buster's escape, had forgotten to turn it back on. He probably had calls out the wazzoo, but the main thing was hearing from Crazy Sheila.

He finished the last of his coffee, set his cup on the crate and patted both dogs on the head, then wandered inside the house to find his phone.

CHAPTER FORTY

"There's more," Dainty said, checking her fancy gold Piaget watch.

Reflexively, Aspen glanced at the kitchen clock, a blood-red reproduction Kit-Kat clock with tiny rhinestone accents around its eyes that moved in sync and a tail with a pendulum swing.

Six o'clock.

Noting the time triggered hunger pangs. The only food she had to offer her company was bologna in the refrigerator and week-old bread that should've been thrown out. But Rochelle and Dainty didn't seem the least bit famished, so she returned her attention to Dainty.

"I wasn't only hired to follow Granger. That was Rochelle's doing. But Gordon also hired me."

"To spy on me?"

"Just watch."

Video rolled. They were looking at a

house, a small wooden jewel box painted yellow with black shutters and black wrought-iron supports. The camera cut to the backyard, to a coyote. A man in pajama bottoms and a *wife beater* T-shirt rushed out the back door and fired off a shot. The coyote dropped to the ground, dead.

"I don't understand."

The man cast furtive glances all around, then went back inside and returned with a large garbage bag. He double-bagged the predator and carried it to the back of his pickup. The camera zoomed in for a close-up of the license tag.

Aspen stared.

Then the camera panned to the man's face.

It was the policeman from the *Asleep at the Wheel* piece. The one who'd bumped up the misdemeanor disorderly conduct charge for discharging a firearm to the felony deadly conduct charge now pending against her.

"This is just too weird." Aspen recognized the significance of such footage. "What are the odds of a coyote being in this guy's yard?"

"Astronomical, I'd say," Rochelle called over her shoulder from her place at the sink. "But it does happen. Lucky Dainty was there to catch it." This time, instead of refilling her glass, she brought the wine bottle to the table, holding onto the neck as though it were a Molotov cocktail.

"That's not the best part, though," Dainty said, through sips of mineral water.

The weightless tingle surging through her body made Aspen feel as if she could float up out of her chair.

The last piece of footage cut to Mrs. Pendleton's home, one street over.

Rochelle, dressed in a severe black suit and holding a clipboard, had her hair strained back from her face. She was in Mrs. Pendleton's backyard, talking to the homeowner. Dainty turned up the sound.

"Like I said, I need to visit with you about some anomalies in your insurance claim. This is . . . Gidget . . . my assistant —"

"Bonjour."

"— and she'll be assisting me until we close this matter."

"It is what it is. My neighbor shot out my window," snapped Mrs. Pendleton, looking as frumpy as the housecoat she had on, with pink foam curlers still in her hair.

"But you see, that's the anomaly. If she shot out your window, wouldn't the glass be on the inside of your house?"

"What?" A spooked expression settled on

Mrs. Pendleton's face.

"Yes, Mrs. Pendleton, the glass would be on the inside. But it's not. It's on the outside. Look."

The camera panned to the ground, where huge pieces of glass had fallen away next to the house.

"I don't understand." Mrs. Pendleton. "What are you trying to say?"

"There's a huge penalty for insurance fraud, Mrs. Pendleton. You could spend time in the slammer. And if it's federal time, it's day for day. No early-out for good behavior."

"What?"

"I'm saying because we're a national insurance company, this could be a federal case. And if we file on you for fraud, you could spend the rest of your life in the pen."

"What?"

"You know . . . the hoosegow. The slammer. Leavenworth."

Mrs. Pendleton clutched her robe.

Rochelle said, "Of course, there's still time. We could invoke the clause."

"What clause?"

"The clause in your policy that states if you commit fraud and tell us about it before the claim's paid, then you've committed no offense."

"But I just got the check in last night's mail."

"Did you already cash it?"

"No."

"Well, there you go. If you were to make a full confession to me, and then tear up the check in my presence, that would invoke the clause. Kind of like saying you're sorry you made up that stuff about the neighbor so you could get your kitchen redone. And then Gidget and I would overlook it."

"I *am* sorry. I heard the shot," said Mrs. Pendleton, working her jaw as she looked around for witnesses, "and then I don't know what came over me. I grabbed the hammer and knocked out the plate glass window . . ."

In a lightheaded rush from her seat at the dining table, Aspen gasped.

Rochelle redirected her attention to the laptop.

Aspen listened.

"But then you told the police that your neighbor did it," Rochelle said in a hectoring voice. "They filed charges on her because of you."

"Well, she shouldn't have shot off that gun."

"But she didn't deserve to be filed on for deadly conduct. That's where you came in.

You filed a false report to a police officer."

"You won't say anything about that, will you? I mean, you're just here to handle the insurance claim. The one I don't want to file anymore."

"And why don't you want to file the claim?"

"Because I'm invoking the clause so I won't go to prison for making it up about that girl shooting out my window."

"Because the girl didn't shoot out your window?" Rochelle again, driving her point home.

"No. I hit it with a hammer."

"To get the insurance to pay to have your kitchen redone." Rochelle nodded.

"Right."

"Don't you think you ought to write something down for the District Attorney about the false-report charges?"

"What charges?"

"So the neighbor girl won't go to jail."

"I wouldn't know what to say." Dentures clicked as she mulled this over.

"I'm pretty sure they have a clause, too. If you were to write it down on a piece of paper and sign your name, we could witness your signature. I could deliver it to the District Attorney and they could drop the charges."

Mrs. Pendleton nodded. "Yes. Get them to invoke their clause."

"That's a swell idea."

Dainty's hidden camera captured it all. The written statement, the check being torn up before their eyes, the entire thing. The video ran out and Dainty opened the computer's CD tray and removed a disk. After sliding it into a protective sleeve, she placed it on the table. "This copy's for you. The District Attorney has one, too. No need to thank me — just recommend the Debutante Detective Agency to your friends."

For several seconds, Aspen did nothing but breathe and blink. Then she turned to Rochelle. "Why would you do this?"

"Even though the people at WBFD may not always get along, we're still a team. But us?" She included the three of them with a finger motion, "Well, we're family."

By the time Rochelle and Dainty left, Aspen knew there was no way she could sleep.

If Spike wouldn't return her phone calls, she'd just have to show up at his office.

CHAPTER FORTY-ONE

The sky looked like somebody had melted a rainbow and smeared it across the horizon. With the scenery flying by, Aspen drove the back roads to Johnson County, taking the same shortcut she'd used to get to Kirk House. When she neared Tiny's Drive-In, she recognized Paper Cut's ratty tin can vehicle parked out in front. It seemed to be the only car there, except for the faint outline of a dark pickup truck parked at the back of the store.

The painted lines for the parking spaces had long since worn away, so she wheeled the Accord off the highway and created a parking spot next to the junker. She'd barely made it out of the Honda when Paper Cut glided out of the store with her face as white as liquid paper, wearing her Goth garb and carrying an icy drink the color of old blood, with a straw poking out of its dome lid.

Paper Cut said, "Hey," and for the next

several minutes, they exchanged idle chit-chat. "So . . . ," the Goth glanced around as if to see whether they were being watched, ". . . what are you doing out here?"

"I need to talk to Spike."

Paper Cut winced. "Get in my car."

"What?"

"You heard me."

Aspen did as she was told. As soon as the passenger door clunked shut, Paper Cut lit into her.

"Do not say that name like I even know who that is. You don't understand what's going on here."

"Why don't you tell me?"

"I can't. So stop asking." She huffed out a resigned sigh and started the rattle trap's engine. "You want to talk? We're going for a ride."

"Where to?"

"Kirk House."

Aspen had thought the next time she went out to Kirk House, it'd be with Granger, or maybe Reggie. But either way, she knew she'd have to make one more trip, if for no other reason than to check out Mrs. Kirk's eerie comment about the oil company's land man.

"Do you have your gun with you?"

Paper Cut cast her a sidelong look. "That

411

goes without saying."

"Okay." Aspen settled back into the seat, breathing easier. She decided if she had to go to Kirk House, it might as well be with a gun-toting gal on the right side of the law. "This will give me another chance to look around."

"I brought a few lanterns," Paper Cut said. She thumbed at the backseat, where Aspen could see three battery-operated lamps. "In case you don't know, he's got it bad for you."

"Who? The guy whose name I'm not supposed to mention around you?"

Paper Cut laughed. "Yeah. That guy. He's crazy about you."

"I figured out who the blonde is."

"That's been over a long time. She hurt him really bad, running off with Lindstrom. For a long time afterward, he walked around like a zombie. Then you showed up and changed all that."

Tears blistered behind Aspen's eyeballs.

"He's a real catch. Hell, I'd chase him myself if I didn't have so many other damned problems."

Paper Cut slowed at the gates of Kirk House. She put the car into park and unlocked her door.

"Where are you going?"

"To unlock the gate."

"You have a key to the gate?"

"Honey, I'm the only one with a key to that gate. Except for Mrs. Kirk. She has the other one. What better way to have a close patrol on your house than to give a key to the cop who's going to hang out there?"

After opening the gate, the Goth returned to the car and drove past the granite pillars. When she started to get out again, Aspen grabbed her sleeve.

"What are you doing?"

"Locking the gate."

"You're locking us in? I don't want to be locked in."

"Listen, I'd a lot rather be locked inside here than to have somebody sneaking up on me."

"Please don't lock it. I feel safer with it open."

Paper Cut gave a derisive grunt, but she left the gate open and drove down to the tree line. Rabbits darted across their path, spooked by the lights.

At the house, they each took a lantern. The third, Paper Cut set inside one of the window openings.

"You never said why you were coming out here," Aspen ventured.

"Looking for something."

She got that. But looking for what?

"Well, as long as I'm here," Aspen said. "I want to have a look around outside. You mind?"

But Paper Cut wasn't listening. She'd moved to the far end of the house where a set of stairs had once been. There, she began to conduct a search. Aspen left her alone and walked out onto what had once been the back porch steps.

Without warning, an unearthly scream of the damned pierced the night.

Aspen vaulted the steps and ran toward Paper Cut. "Ohmygod, we're about to die," she screamed.

But Paper Cut held her hand out for quiet, listening as though she could pick up airwaves. "Shhh." She bent over and pulled her gun from the leg holster.

Aspen moved behind her.

"Did you hear that?" the Goth whispered. "Sounds like scratching."

The only thing Aspen could hear was the whooshing sound of blood between her ears.

"Hello," Paper Cut called out to the room at large.

They both stood statue-still and listened. Nothing but the sound of the breeze, whispering through the window openings. Despite the cold air, Aspen felt her shirt tacking itself to her back.

Then another scream sounded like the Earth opening up.

Aspen grabbed Paper Cut by the arm, but the Goth shook her off and walked toward the back steps. Aspen followed. "What are you doing?"

"Shhh."

A minute went by. Then Paper Cut yelled, "Is anyone there?" Then she began to whisper, "One . . . two . . . three . . ."

When she reached thirty, another blood-curdling scream shuddered up to the heavens. Instead of showing alarm, Paper Cut grinned. Her black-lipped smile was more like a baring of teeth. "Ingenious. Freaking ingenious."

"What?"

"I think I just figured out where the screams are coming from."

"Yeah, Kirk House," Aspen said sarcastically.

"No, dummy. It's a recording. Probably outfitted with a time-delay mechanism. And they're not just audible at midnight. Somebody wants to scare people away from here."

Tension drained from Aspen's body.

"You're right. I'm going to find it. After I get outside the house, I want you to say something so I can try to pinpoint the location."

She'd gone twenty feet, crunching dead grass beneath her feet, before turning around. She waved the lantern as a sign.

Paper Cut hollered back, "Hello."

One Mississippi, two Mississippi . . . thirty Mississippi.

As if on cue, a scream erupted, filling the night.

Aspen trotted in the direction of the sound. Thirty feet from the house, she found it — a recording device with a voice-activated time-delay switch, just as Paper Cut suspected.

"Here it is," she yelled, giddy with enthusiasm. But Paper Cut, backlit by the window, looked out toward the roadway. Then Aspen shifted her gaze and saw what had captured the Goth's attention. Car lights from a heavy, low-slung vehicle bounced over the ruts.

Aspen's heart stampeded.

She grabbed the recorder from its camouflaged housing and hurried toward the house. When she reached the porch, Paper Cut moaned out a scary "Oh, no" and switched off her lantern. "Cut that light off. *Now.* Hurry."

"Who is it?"

"Big trouble. Stay out of sight, and shut the fuck up. No matter what happens — no matter what you may hear — don't come out until I say so."

Then Paper Cut faded back into the darkest part of the house.

CHAPTER FORTY-TWO

Aspen had already plunged down the steps and retreated to the rear wall. She pressed her back to the hard granite and listened to her heart pound. If it got any louder, whoever was coming up the front steps could pinpoint her location just by listening for the drumming sounds coming from inside her chest.

She thought of how Paper Cut wanted to lock the front gate, and how she'd pleaded with her not to.

She lingered over her mistake.

Overhead, the moon shone like a huge pearl. Just beyond the house, swaying branches danced on a slant of light. Shadows from the few remaining leaves made lacy patterns on the stones.

A drop of sweat descended down Aspen's back and into her panties. She stood perfectly still and unblinking, waiting to find that these scary moments had all been a mistake, and for Paper Cut's friendly voice to return and greet the visitor.

She peeked over the window enough to see that Paper Cut had moved without her hearing.

The tip-tapping sound of heels against the concrete created an echo more frightening than anything Aspen could've imagined. Then a voice that could've frozen salt water sent a lance of fear straight to her heart.

"Come on out, Susanna. I know you're here. Let's you and I have a little chat, shall we?"

Aspen recognized the voice. It was a heady realization.

Dolly Hastings.

She wanted to cry. Thanks to her stupid mistake — whining to leave the gate open — they were both going to die.

"I can see you by the stairs. It's no good, you know? There's nowhere to run. Now, come on out. I just want to talk to you about the baby."

Baby?

Aspen's flesh crept.

Paper Cut spoke in a soft, childlike voice. "Go away."

Dolly answered in a similarly hypnotic tone. "Now, we both know I can't do that. Come on out. No need to be afraid. I just want to go over the ground rules with you."

Seconds passed.

Aspen realized she'd been holding her breath. Her lungs burned with oxygen deprivation. Tears ran down her cheeks in rivulets, like rain on a windowpane.

"That's a good girl. Now, let's have a friendly little talk."

"It isn't friendly if you're holding a gun on me."

From her place on the outside of the house, Aspen's ears pricked up. She stared at the recorder and made a split-second decision. When she pressed the play-record button, a tiny red light came on. Then she placed her thumb over the light and waited.

"I just needed to get your attention, that's all," Dolly said.

"What do you want from me?"

"I think you know."

"Look, I don't even know you," Paper Cut whimpered.

"Sure, you do. I'm Heath's friend. You know Heath, don't you, dear?"

"No."

"Sure you do." Her voice went stern. "Plex Rominus. The man you've been screwing. He told me about the baby." Dolly's voice turned deadly. "I want it."

"What're you saying — that I'm just supposed to give it to you? It's not even due for another eight months."

"And when it gets here, you're giving it to me. Where I can place it in a good home. With parents who will love it."

"With people who'll pay," the Goth challenged. "Well, I don't want your money. This baby's all I have left of Plex. You're not getting it."

"Oh, but I am. What Dolly wants, Dolly gets. We just need to finalize our terms of agreement."

"We have no terms," Paper Cut scoffed.

"My terms were with Heath. He promised me your baby, and I paid him for it. That baby's mine. I'm willing to offer you a nice chunk of change right now. And when the time comes, you give me your child. I brought the papers. All you have to do is sign them."

"I'm not signing."

"Yes, you will."

"What makes you so sure of that?"

"Because if you don't, I'll kill you."

"Ha," Paper Cut said, "you don't have the nerve."

"I've done it before."

"You're just saying that to scare me."

"I hope you are scared, little girl. You wouldn't want to end up like Ellie Canfield, now, would you?"

"You murdered Ellie?" Paper Cut's voice spiraled up in a high-pitched whine.

Aspen grimaced. Fear snared her in its grip.

"We had to. She reneged on our deal. Heath tried to talk her out of it, but she was just so stubborn. Just another stubborn little girl, just like you."

"Plex Rominus wouldn't kill anyone."

"You're right. He didn't have it in him, so I did it. He was just there to cut out the baby. Then he got rid of her. You wouldn't want to end up like that, would you, Susanna?" The cavity-inducing sweetness went suddenly lethal. "Sign the fucking papers."

"It won't stick. I'll go to court and fight you. I'll come after you with everything I have."

"No, you won't. Haven't you heard? I'm untouchable. Now, sign it."

A muted click filled the night air. It sounded like the snap of a broken tree branch, but Aspen knew better. The recorder she held in her hand had shutoff.

Now she was certain Dolly Hastings couldn't leave witnesses.

CHAPTER FORTY-THREE

"What was that?" Dolly demanded.

Please don't kill us, Aspen thought.

"Armadillos. They're everywhere." Paper Cut, trying to save them.

"Don't move. Don't so much as twitch."

Aspen heard the scraping sound of tentative footfalls from Dolly Hastings, backing up for a peek out through the porch opening. She pressed herself harder against the outside wall, as if doing so would render her invisible.

"How much money?" The Goth's strident voice halted the footsteps. "How much are you willing to pay me if I agree to give you my kid?"

Thoughts of survival fragmented inside Aspen's head. The thread of hope that she'd been clinging to turned to white noise. The temperature seemed to drop in inverse proportion to her climbing fear. Her knees quivered.

Then Paper Cut relented. "Give me the pen."

The attorney's heels clip-clopped against the concrete.

A split second later, a gunshot exploded, ricocheting off the walls in a reverberating echo. As the spent round slapped into the wall behind Aspen, muffled cries erupted inside the shell of a house.

Paper Cut screamed, "Help."

Aspen took the steps in twos. She found Dolly straddling the Goth, banging her head into the concrete floor. Each horrible thud sounded like eggs breaking.

Aspen rushed up from behind, aiming for the back of the lawyer's head and wielding the lantern with all her might. At the last second, Dolly must've noticed the looming shadow closing in, because her face caught the full weight of the lantern as she glanced over her shoulder.

Aspen had provided the break Paper Cut needed.

Dolly fell off to the side, and Paper Cut rolled away. She glanced around, frantic. As she reclaimed her gun from a few yards off, she yelled, "Outta the way." The shot hit the lawyer square in the chest.

Dolly Hastings lay still on the floor.

"Is she dead?" Aspen whispered.

As if the third act of a bad play had abruptly ended, the gauzy clouds veiling the moonlight parted like curtains. Aspen saw a sheen of blood on Dolly's chest.

"I sincerely hope not," Paper Cut said. Only this time, it was Sheila talking — cool, calm, and very much in control. "Do me a favor: There's a handy-talkie in my car under the seat. Turn it on. There's a red panic button. Set it off. Then bring it to me."

"Where's her gun? I don't see a gun."

"I don't know. My head's killing me. You're wasting time." Without taking her eyes off Dolly Hastings, Granger's deputy did a one-armed, low crawl, inching closer to the wall, moving sideways like a crab. When she reached the pink granite, she propped her back up against it.

Aspen didn't want to leave her. Those nasty cantaloupe splats against the floor could've given the deputy a concussion.

"Go on. And hurry." With a dismissive wave of her revolver, Sheila urged her toward the car. "I'll be fine."

Aspen ran for the vehicle. She found the police handheld exactly where the deputy said it would be, and made the mad dash back to the house. She returned to a surprise — and not the good kind.

Crazy Sheila had gone limp, her body slumped off to one side. Her pistol rested in her lap.

With blood pooling next to her, Dolly Hastings had rolled onto her side with reptilian agility. She must've been lying on top of her handgun — an evil-looking revolver that glinted in the moonlight like a deadly chunk of ice. Now, she'd trained it on the deputy. It took the strength of both hands to pull back the hammer, but when she did, each ratcheting click echoed through Kirk House like the snap of a broken bone.

Aspen didn't think. She barreled toward the lawyer like she was kicking the winning field goal.

This time, when Dolly went down, she stayed down.

A brisk wind scattered dead leaves across the floor. With the weapon kicked safely to one side, Aspen hurried over to Sheila and dropped to her knees.

"I saw that," Sheila mumbled. "You're a very violent person."

"I have a police record," Aspen said with a nod.

"I'm not surprised. It's always the quiet ones. Hand me the radio and help me sit up."

She handed it over and assisted Crazy Sheila to an upright position, then watched as the undercover deputy took control again.

"William four-two-one. Need an ambulance at Kirk House. Shots fired."

"Ten-four," came the dispatcher's calm, capable voice. "Are you down, William four-two-one?"

"Negative. But send Unit one hundred. I have a Dallas attorney under arrest. With a bullet hole to the chest."

CHAPTER FORTY-FOUR

Breaking news for WBFD-TV's ten-o'clock broadcast didn't cover the shooting of Dolly Hastings in Johnson County, since nobody but Aspen knew about it. And she was tied up giving a statement to Granger's investigator.

The report Steve Lennox put out had to do with Libby Singleton, the woman in Dallas who'd been shot the previous week. Reports were still sketchy, but it appeared that a woman dressed as a nurse had slipped into her hospital room and administered medication meant for another patient.

In other news, a Fort Worth police officer had been suspended with pay pending allegations that he'd conspired with an elderly woman to file charges against news anchor Aspen Wicklow. A hearing-review was set for later in the month to determine whether the officer would be terminated.

And last but not least, an escaped felon

from Johnson County was found sleeping in the bed of the sheriff's pickup when the sheriff left work earlier that evening. The Johnson County sheriff declined to say whether additional charges would be pressed against Alvin Wayne "Buster" Root.

Aspen was coming out of the interrogation room when Granger sauntered down the hall.

"Where's your car?" he said.

"Back at Tiny's Drive-In."

"I can take her," offered the investigator.

"That's all right," Granger said in his *Awshucks* baritone. "You've done enough. Go home and get some rest."

Aspen scowled. "You make it sound like a job even the janitor doesn't want."

He steered her by the elbow out to the patrol car and locked her safely into the passenger compartment. On the ride to the convenience store, he took a detour. He veered off the main highway, onto a county road where the streetlamps played out. In the distance, the faint glow of two incandescent bulbs flickered in the night.

"What do you think you're doing?" she said. "I'm still mad at you."

"We need to drop by the house. I have something for you."

"What is it?"

"A surprise."

"I hate surprises."

"You'll like this one."

"Where have I heard that before?"

The cruiser bumped over a cattle guard, and he continued up the long, unpaved road. When he reached the sprawling ranch house with the glider on the front porch, his two old bloodhounds weren't resting on their tattered blankets. Not that it mattered. He suspected he knew exactly where they were.

Aspen chuckled.

"What's so funny?"

"There's a *Neil Lindstrom for Sheriff* sticker on your bumper."

"Son. Of. A. Bitch."

"You didn't notice?"

But Granger was grinding his molars and thinking, *Dallas Ostrander, damn her hide.* When he pulled to a stop, he left Aspen in the car. Outraged, he stalked to the back of the truck. In seconds, he'd stripped off the offending sticker and crushed it. Then he went back to the squad car, opened her door and left it ajar.

"You coming in?"

Standing beside the car, she said, "I don't think that's such a hot idea."

He pulled her off to one side and slammed

the door shut. "What the hell were you doing out there? You could've been killed tonight."

"I'm still here."

"Don't ever do anything like that again. Understand?" When his concern didn't seem to faze her, he grabbed her by the shoulders and shook her. "What's wrong with you? Don't you get it? I don't know what I'd do if something happened to you." His throat closed around the words, and he bit his lip. That part hurt to admit.

"It's okay. Everything's fine. And if it's not fine, it's going to be."

Years of conditioning had toughened him up. But it only took this redhead to wear down his resistance. "What do I have to do to convince you?"

She crossed her arms in a standoff. "I don't understand why your ex was there in the first place."

"That's how Dallas operates. She'll be dormant for a while and then show up out of nowhere, for no good reason, just to get my goat. I have no idea why she was there. If I had to guess, I'd say she knew you were coming. I know that sounds crazy — I mean, how could she know?"

"Even if she did have the heads-up that I was on my way over, why would she care?"

431

Now it was her turn to look flustered.

"They're in a fight to the death for my job. Maybe she thought if you and I were on the outs, I'd slack off on the election. How should I know? It's hard to think like a crazy person."

"Do you still love her?"

"No. And I haven't given you a reason not to trust me. But you take whatever time you need to think this through. I'll be here."

He left her beside the car with a "Be right back," and returned a few minutes later with a red-and-white corgi mix he'd picked up from the corgi rescue. The little dog looked like it had on eyeliner.

"Her name's Deep Fry."

"What? No. I'm not taking that home with me. No, no, no. I've had enough problems with you and your so-called dog rescues."

"Look at her face. She likes you."

"She doesn't even know me."

He waited until she made eye contact with the animal and then thrust it at her. Aspen held the dog with reluctance, but at least she did it.

He viewed this as a small step, but it was a step in the right direction.

Then Aspen did something he'd never before seen her do — crushed the dog against her like a plush toy and cooed,

"Aww, come on, gimme some sugar."

When he dropped Aspen off at her car with Deep Fry secured in a crate that he'd loaded into the backseat, she stood by her driver's door seemingly lost in thought.

He said, "Call to let me know you made it home."

She nodded. Then she fixed him in her emerald gaze, and asked the strangest question.

"Do you think you could ever live in a place like Kirk House?"

CHAPTER FORTY-FIVE

After leaving Tiny's Drive-In with the new dog in the backseat, Aspen didn't go straight home. She'd been thinking about what Rochelle had said at the house earlier that evening, about them being family. And she wanted Rochelle to know that she appreciated what she and Dainty had done. Plus, it'd give her a chance to update Rochelle on Granger. Even though things were far from perfect, it looked like her relationship with Granger might be back on track.

She pulled into the driveway of Rochelle's rose brick townhouse, located in a garden home community, and cut the engine. Before getting out of the car, she checked the rearview mirror. Other than a Mini Cooper parked at the curb across the street, the rest of the vehicles in the neighborhood occupied spaces in people's driveways. She remote-locked the car with the dog inside and the windows cracked a few inches for ventilation, and walked up to the front porch, past Grecian urns that bracketed the front doorway.

The undraped windows that made for a light, sumptuous feel in the daytime looked dark and foreboding, except for shafts of light from the outside fixtures that bounced off the highly polished French and Italian provincial furniture. She waited at Rochelle's door beneath the copper overhang, feeling uneasy and vulnerable in the pale glow of the gas lights. When the secretary didn't answer after numerous jabs at the doorbell, she gave Rochelle one last chance to show herself.

She lifted the brass door knocker and banged it hard against its backing.

The faint glow of an incandescent light flickered on in the hallway. Aspen craned her neck for a look, and saw nothing.

Then the lock snicked back and the door flung open.

What the hell?

She took a backward step in disbelief.

Instead of Rochelle, her gaze dipped to a squatty little person in red satin boxer shorts, hopping on one foot as he jammed the other into the tiny leg of a blue velour jogging suit.

Ulysses S. Bumgardner.

435

Dead silence stretched between them as she digested this strange new twist. So much for the protective order Rochelle supposedly swore out on him. He'd probably killed her menopausal friend.

Distress puckered her lips.

The theme from *Figaro* leaked out from the far side of the house.

"Oh," he said dully, tightening the drawstring of his pants. "You're the TV girl. Step on in and I'll go get her."

Okay, so Bumgardner hadn't murdered Rochelle.

The dwarf angled off toward the hall leading to Rochelle's bedroom. A few minutes after the buzz of their conversation died down, Rochelle glided into the room dressed like a French maid, carrying a feather duster.

"What?" Rochelle said, indignant. "I have needs."

"You let that man in your house after he tried to kill us?"

"Overblown."

"Hey — don't try to rewrite history. I was there. I had a gun held to my head, remember?"

"He's really very sweet once you get to know him," Rochelle said. "Besides, he's out on bond. Now what do you want?"

"You're absolutely amazing." Aspen gawked at the secretary, and not in a good way.

"Look, don't blame me. I can't help it," moaned Rochelle, as if she'd been caught with a dirty little secret. "He's got this strange power over me . . ."

"I seriously doubt that."

"He does. He's absolutely phenomenal in bed. It's so fantastic I can't even describe some of the things he does . . ."

Aspen's hand went up like a traffic cop's. Some things, like the making of bologna, were better left alone.

"And I'm . . . well . . . needing a romp in the sack."

"I can remember a time when you hid from him."

"Yeah, well, that was before I went to bed with him sober. He's really quite compact. And he has amazing stamina."

"For the love of God, stop talking. I just dropped by to tell you thanks for all you did for me with the Debutante Detective Agency, and to let you know Spike and I are back together. Sort of."

But Rochelle couldn't have cared less. She was still extolling the virtues of her new man-toy. "Believe me, if I had a long dress, I'd sneak him into work."

"You're sick."

"I know. But you won't say anything, right?"

"That depends." Green eyes narrowed. The dirt was stacking up on Rochelle. First, Stinger. Now, Ulysses S. Bumgardner. That worked out to be a lot of ammo. "Where's that mug shot?"

"You wouldn't."

"Damned right, I would. Hand it over."

Rochelle left in a huff, but returned with the photo. "There. Are we even?"

"For now. But I wouldn't ever cross me, if I were you."

"We'll chat later. Oh — by the way, some black lady came to the station looking for you earlier. Said her name was Jamilla, come to see her homey from cell block F 'on account of that promise you made to put her on television.' " Rochelle corkscrewed a brow. "I left the message slip in your box, homey."

"Oh, Fifi," Bumgardner's thin, helium voice sang out from the back room, "haven't you forgotten something? You've still got work to do. Looks like you forgot to polish my obelisk . . ."

"Gotta go," Rochelle said. "Those little blue pills only last four hours, and they're about to time out."

CHAPTER FORTY-SIX

Over the weekend, Granger created new paperwork for Susanna Epps, and dropped it into the mailbox addressed to Principal Thomas. The cover letter from Susanna's mother stated that Susanna was moving out of town and would be attending a new school the following week.

Only Granger knew that Crazy Sheila would be attending a blood-spatter conference out of state. It'd actually been planned for months, but uncanny timing dictated that she should go ahead and attend. He needed to figure out what he was going to do with a pregnant deputy now that she'd gotten knocked up. And even though she told him she'd had a wild night with Blaze Clarke a month or so ago, he still wondered. Especially looking at her now, in the sequined costume from Miss Mary's Dance 'n Prance, as she flirted with his constituents at the door to the high-school gymnasium.

He glanced around and caught Aspen's eye. She looked smokin' hot in a turquoise suit, standing next to Crazy Sheila handing out campaign literature.

Seating was first come, first served. After the bleachers filled up, metal folding chairs were quickly assembled to accommodate the overflow.

Backstage, even though Buster wore leg-irons, he looked quite snappy in the tuxedo Granger'd purchased with his own money from a consignment shop owned by the Junior League. Unable to do more than take little geisha steps, the inmate inspected the boxes he and the deputies had built for the disappearing act, including the box Crazy Sheila would lie down in when Buster bisected her. A straitjacket hung on a seamstress's mannequin next to two fifty-gallon drums, one with lockable hinges on the lid and an identical container with the bottom cut out. The escapologist should have no problem kicking out the lid and "disappearing" once the drums were switched.

In accordance with Granger's instructions, Buster would remain unshackled while performing. Between acts, he'd stay trussed up like a Christmas turkey. Deputies positioned at every exit may have looked

like they were handing out campaign bro-
chures, but they'd been stationed there by
Granger in a show of force to discourage
Buster from making a break for it. Now that
things were back on track — and everybody
knew he'd solved the killing of Ellie Canfield, and was therefore a shoe-in this election — the last thing he needed was an
actual escape.

The din of voices rumbled through the
gym, locals having a good time, old friends
getting reacquainted, inquisitive strangers
making new contacts.

Once the show started, Granger made it a
point to stay backstage, close enough to
Buster to breathe hot air down his neck.
He'd brought in an ice chest filled with
carbonated drinks, bottled water and juice,
and a second one filled with beer, for when
the show ended. When he reached down to
pull out a drink, he heard someone come
up behind him.

Aspen.

"Hello, darlin'."

"Hello yourself. Mind if I have one of
those?"

He passed her a bottled water and got one
for himself. When he turned around again,
she'd opened her jacket.

"It's hot back here."

"Maybe you'd rather go back out front."

"I don't think so." Hungry eyes pinned him. For a moment, he just stared.

She opened her shirt down to the third button. Poured water into her cupped hand and splashed it over her neck and chest.

Chills crawled over Granger's torso. If anyone came back here —

Perspiration stippled his forehead.

Then she walked toward him, unhooking the front clasp of her bra.

He blinked in disbelief. His groin stirred. Then common sense took over.

"Aspen . . . we're gonna get caught."

"You think?" she said, as if she cared.

Then she took his hand and placed it on one breast.

"I'm an only child, Spike Granger. I don't share well with others. Am I making myself clear?"

"Crystal."

"Now, I'm going back out there and let you do your thing. But, mark my words, I don't ever want to catch you pulling any dumb stunts like that again."

"Never. Ever." He knew what she meant.

She re-buttoned her blouse and was gone by the time his head quit spinning. He peeked through the curtain and saw that most of the auditorium had filled up, and the waiting line to get inside went clear out the door.

Granger went over to Buster. He pulled out a key to the leg irons and held it. "You ready?"

"Yeah, but when we do the handcuff trick, after whoever you pick from the audience checks to make sure they're secure, you need to slip me a key so that I can get out of them and put the trick handcuffs on. If you don't think you can slip me one without people detecting it, then give me one now and I'll hide it in my mouth."

Granger's eyes narrowed. "I'm not about to give you a key. And the only handcuffs that are going to be slapped on you are the government issue Smith & Wesson cuffs that you'll be wearing back to the station when this fund-raiser's over."

As Granger made final preparations, Buster went back to inspecting his props. Several minutes passed before Granger realized the inmate wasn't around.

He motioned the nearest deputy over. "Where's Buster?"

"He went behind the second curtain to get a bottle of water."

"Who's with him?"

"Nobody." Seeing Granger's face contort, the deputy said, "He can't go anywhere,

Sheriff. We've got two men posted at the back doors."

"Yeah, but I don't want him getting hold of something he can parlay into a lock pick," Granger said brusquely, and strode toward the curtain with the deputy on his heels.

They located the inmate pawing through the cooler. He pulled out a soda and snapped the tab.

Granger said, "If he tries to run, shoot him."

Then he stepped out from behind the curtain, before an enthusiastic crowd, and launched into his welcome speech.

When the magic show was over and everyone took their bows, Granger slapped a set of Smith & Wesson cuffs on Buster. He invited a child from the audience, a boy about nine years old, to step up onstage and do the honors, checking for security.

"Are they on?" Granger asked as Buster stood by good-naturedly.

The boy nodded, his cheeks flushing a bright shade of pink.

"Are you sure? Make sure they're good and tight."

The boy checked again and gave another nod.

Granger reached inside his pocket and

pulled out a paper stick-on badge that read *Sheriff's Pal,* peeled back the wax paper protector and stuck it on the boy's shirt. He sent the young man back to his parents, beaming.

Then Granger thanked everyone for coming, asked them to give Buster a special applause, and wished them all a safe evening.

After giving Aspen a socially acceptable good-bye peck — there'd be time for the good stuff later — Granger left out the back of the auditorium with Buster in handcuffs, still wearing the secondhand tux. He seated the inmate in his patrol car for the ride back to the county lockup.

As they pulled out of the high-school parking lot, Granger made small talk.

"Where'd you learn the rabbit in the hat trick?"

"That?" Buster scoffed. "That was easy. Now, pulling the bird out of the scarf is hard."

They continued to relive moments from the magic show, until Granger slowed to let traffic pass.

"I really want to thank you for helping me," he said to Buster. "My coffers were all dried up and what we took in tonight will pay for campaign signs."

Buster shrugged, as if to say *Aw, shucks.*

"No, really." Granger looked him squarely in the eye. "I appreciate what you did for me tonight. And thanks for not trying to make a break for it."

When Granger glanced back at the road, the traffic light had turned red. He slowed to a stop and thought of the event's success.

"Pleasure's all mine, Spike." Buster took a deep breath and let it out slowly. "Hope you win. I really do."

"Too bad you can't vote for me, you being a felon and all."

"Oh, I can still vote," Buster said matter-of-factly. "I'm not a *convicted* felon."

"Not yet," Granger said.

"Yeah . . . that's why I'm really sorry —"

Granger's neck prickled. Instinct kicked in.

"— to do this, ol' buddy, but —"

In the time it took the sheriff to reach for his gun, Buster was out the door, running like the wind, with the words "see ya" echoing through the night.

Granger steered with his gun butt balanced on the wheel. He grabbed the mike as Buster disappeared between two buildings.

"All units — Buster Root just escaped," Granger said, and gave his location. "All

446

units — use caution, use caution."

He wracked the gearshift into park and notified the dispatcher to put out a BOLO on Alvin Wayne "Buster" Root. And he wanted the Cleburne Police Department called, directly, as well as the police departments in the surrounding towns so they could watch any connecting arteries. If he could keep Buster from reaching Interstate 35 and hitching a ride to God-knows-where, he might be able to get him back in jail before voters knew he was gone.

Then he set out on foot.

Buster turned down an alley with Granger hot on his heels. For a minute or so, he kept up with the fleeing felon. But with the extra weight of his double-rig and heavy boots, Granger was no match for his prisoner. Before Buster could round the next corner, the sheriff drew down on him.

"Stop or I'll shoot," he cried out.

Buster kept running.

In the shadows cast from the light of the mercury vapor lamp, Granger sighted him in. He'd made the SO's policy himself — no warning shots.

Shoot to kill.

He took the FBI Weaver stance and sighted Buster down the gun barrel.

And just as he squeezed the trigger, he lifted the barrel and shot out the streetlight.

CHAPTER FORTY-SEVEN

On a cold Sunday morning, Aspen pulled up to Kirk House. A man from Lucky Realty was hammering a Contract Pending sign into the ground along the easement. Her heart picked up its pace. Only yesterday, she'd dropped by Tranquility Villas to see Mrs. Kirk about buying the property. She'd even brought a contract along on the scant hope Mrs. Kirk would sell it to her.

The conversation that took place in the sunroom still orbited in her head.

"I know I don't have a track record for getting a loan, Mrs. Kirk, but I have this great job and if we could work out a deal — maybe give me an option to buy? — I'll make payments until I can get a loan and pay you off in full."

"I'm not sure." The old lady's eyes went suddenly shrewd. *"Wait just a second — you said your name's Wicklow? Are you related to that Wexford Wicklow character that lives here?"*

449

And just like that, up popped Aspen's father again, erupting out of this ongoing nightmare at Tranquility Villas, and into real life. She had no idea how to answer Mrs. Kirk, so she did the next best thing — tried to make it seem like the name didn't ring a bell by doing a math equation in her head to make herself look confused.

"Honey, that man keeps us in stitches. The women just love him."

"About the property, Mrs. Kirk, I know your husband wanted it to be sold to someone with a family. But I've come to love the house, and with your input, I think I can eventually put it back the way it was."

"Best I can do is turn this over to my realtor."

Which apparently the old lady'd done, because Lucky Realty had moved fast to post that Contract Pending sign.

By the time Aspen cut the Honda's engine and got out of the car, the middle-aged man had propped himself up against his car in a way that prevented his facial features from being clear enough to discern. With the wind whipping her hair, she walked over with her hand outstretched.

"Aspen Wicklow. Nice to see you. So, Mrs. Kirk accepted my contract?"

His brow wrinkled in confusion. Keen

blue eyes narrowed. "Don't think so."

"But I just talked to her yesterday. She promised to give it to her realtor to look over."

"Well, I'm the realtor, but she didn't give me a contract for you."

Aspen's gaze dipped to the sign. "But it says —"

"Already got a contract on it."

Her heart sank. "From who?"

"Can't say."

"I don't understand." Her breaths went shallow. "We struck a deal. We worked out the terms."

"Can't help that."

"Can we do a back-up contract?" Panic tinged her voice.

"Not much point, really. Got a reliable buyer. Escrow money's down. Deal's probably going through when the bank opens tomorrow. Cash buyer."

The slim weathered man with his economy of words had started to get on her nerves. Cash buyer? No way could she compete with some rich guy. Tears welled.

"You don't understand," she said, voice quivering, "I have to have this house. I can't explain it."

He drew in a heady breath. "Maybe you should talk to the fellow who's buying it.

Strike a deal with him." The pity in his eyes told a different story.

And that's how she walked down the long gravel drive, rehearsing a speech while pebbles crunched underfoot.

When she reached the front steps, she called out a cheery hello.

A bulky figure with the upturned pile collar of his jacket shielding his face stepped into view. She sucked air.

Granger.

For several seconds, they stared at each other.

They spoke at the same time, asking each other the same question. "What are you doing here?" Then Granger sliced a hand through the air in an *After you,* motion.

"I want to buy Kirk House."

"The way I hear it, this place is as good as sold."

She bit her bottom lip, and glanced around. Had Granger come out in response to a call? Where'd he park the patrol car?

"Are you crying?"

"Not hardly," she said with a sniffle.

"Yes, you are. You're crying."

She shook her head. Without warning, feelings of promise and anxiety that she'd stuffed on the drive out pushed their way to the surface. Words poured out in a hyperventilating rush.

"It was a dumb idea, I know. A stupid fantasy I had about fixing the place up the way it used to be in its heyday." She flicked off a tear and composed herself. "Guess I should've known with all the publicity somebody'd drive out and decide they couldn't live without it."

"Somebody did."

She let out a resigned sigh. And to think how she'd thrown herself at him at the magic show. Time to preserve what shred of dignity she had left, and go.

With shoulders stiffening, she lifted her chin. "Well . . . it's good seeing you. Oh, by the way, Deep Fry chewed up one of my new shoes."

Granger chuckled. "She'll turn out to be a good dog. There's not a mean bone in her body. You'll see." And then the awkward, "Good seeing you, too."

"I'd better get going." She turned her back to him and started for the steps.

"Aspen, wait. Don't you want to know who bought the place?"

She turned to look at him. Realization dawned. Speechless, with the air unexpectedly energized between them, she studied his face. He hadn't made the drive to Kirk House in his patrol car. He'd come with the man from Lucky Realty.

"It's me," he said softly.

"You bought my house?" Her voice cork-screwed upward. Now she really wanted to cry knowing he'd undercut her. "I don't understand. You knew I loved it."

"Yes, I do remember you saying that. I listen to everything you tell me."

"That's just mean. Why would you do such a thing? And wipe that smirk off your face. Now you're just being cruel."

"Not really. I knew with all the publicity somebody'd drive out and decide they couldn't live without it," he said using her words against her.

"Well," she conceded, "I'm sure it'll be nice once you get it fixed up." She wanted to say more, but the screaming inside her head hadn't stopped.

Then he spoke magic words guaranteed to uplift her downcast mood.

"Didn't do it for me. I did it for us." Granger dropped to one knee. He looked up expectantly and locked her in his nickel-plated gaze. "Ever since we first met, you've been next on my list of future ex-wives."

Hand to mouth, Aspen stood rooted in place and slipping into shock.

"I don't have a ring with me, because . . . well . . . I don't know your size. But if you'd do me the honor and marry me, I'll get you whatever you want. Including this house."

He opened his arms.

And Aspen broke free, running for Granger's protective embrace with her hands outstretched and her fiery curls flying.

ABOUT THE AUTHOR

Laurie Moore was born and reared in the Great State of Texas, where she developed a flair for foreign languages. A sixth-generation Texan, she's traveled to forty-nine US states, most of the Canadian provinces, Mexico and Spain. She received her Bachelor of Arts degree in Spanish, English, Elementary and Secondary Education from the University of Texas at Austin and entered into a career in law enforcement in 1979. After six years on police patrol and a year of criminal investigation she made sergeant and worked as a District Attorney investigator for several DAs in central Texas over the next seven years. In 1992, she moved to Fort Worth and received her Juris Doctor from Texas Wesleyan University School of Law in 1995. She is currently in private practice in "Cowtown" and lives with a jealous Siamese cat and a rude Welsh corgi. She is still a licensed, commissioned peace officer and recently celebrated her thirty-second year in law enforcement. Laurie is the author of *Constable's Run, Constable's Apprehension, Constable's Wedding, The Lady Godiva Murder, The Wild Orchid Society, Jury Rigged,* and *Woman Strangled — News at Ten.* Writing is her passion. Contact Laurie through her Web site at www.LaurieMooreMysteries.com.

The employees of Thorndike Press hope you have enjoyed this Large Print book. All our Thorndike, Wheeler, and Kennebec Large Print titles are designed for easy reading, and all our books are made to last. Other Thorndike Press Large Print books are available at your library, through selected bookstores, or directly from us.

For information about titles, please call:
  (800) 223-1244

or visit our Web site at:
  http://gale.cengage.com/thorndike

To share your comments, please write:
  Publisher
  Thorndike Press
  10 Water St., Suite 310
  Waterville, ME 04901